SOLSTICE

A Lake Prophet Mystery

The Lake Prophet Mysteries
Book 1

ELI EASTON

RJ SCOTT

Love Lane Books

Copyright

Solstice - A Lake Prophet Mystery

The Lake Prophet Mysteries, 1

Copyright ©2023 Eli Easton, Copyright ©2023 RJ Scott

Cover design by Anna Tif Sikorska

Edited by Sue Laybourn

Solstice

From the dramatic peaks of the Olympic mountain range to the small town of Prophet, murder is only a footstep away.

Gabriel is a former undercover cop haunted by the things he's seen and done. He returns to his small hometown of Prophet, taking on the role of sheriff, hoping to mend his fractured relationship with his estranged brother and rebuild his life. But when a chilling murder occurs at Sentinel Rocks, a sacred Makah site on Lake Prophet, Gabriel's dreams of peace and reconciliation are shattered.

Gabriel navigates a web of intrigue, with a long list of suspects; from local tribal elders to fervent Solstice worshippers and even those hunting the elusive Bigfoot. When the brutal murder leaves Duke, a loyal Labrador retriever, as the sole witness, Gabriel stumbles upon an unexpected ally—a local animal behaviorist named Tiber.

Tiber, a newcomer to Prophet, seeks refuge in this remote haven, attempting to escape his own inner demons. Armed with his extraordinary ability to communicate with animals, he offers his expertise through video consultations, helping pet owners with their beloved companions. While he attributes his skill to his academic background, his intuition and flashes of insight owe as much to his Navajo heritage as to science.

With the relentless rain washing away sins and good intentions alike, Gabriel and Tiber must begin to confront their own vulnerabilities and unravel the truth.

To Lola. who taught me how to talk to animals
~Eli Easton

Always for my family
~RJ Scott

A LAKE PROPHET MYSTERY

SOLSTICE

ELI EASTON
RJ SCOTT

Chapter One

Gabriel

THIS WAS *SUPPOSED* to be a 597.

I'd come home three months ago to this quiet corner of Washington's Olympic peninsula to reconnect with my family, lick my wounds. Heal.

I thought I'd left the dead behind, but somehow, for the first time in ten or more years in the small town of Prophet, death had turned up to mess with my head.

"Fuck," Devin murmured next to me, bending at the waist to catch his breath, or stop himself from losing his breakfast. Either way, the scene shook him as it did me.

Today had started so normally. I'd woken to rain beating against my window and flooding my porch from a broken gutter, the noisy end to a restless nightmare-filled sleep. I'd collected my usual black coffee from

Grounds for Joy, ate the warm homemade muffin that Hen, the office administrator, Dispatch extraordinaire, and town gossip, had left on my desk. While eating said muffin, I'd had a discussion about our new filing system with my rookie, Devin, and then settled back for a morning of checking licenses.

No blood. No murder. No death.

Just coffee, chatting, and muffins.

When the 597 at Sentinel Rock came in, it hadn't worried me in the slightest—maybe a dog had gotten entangled in undergrowth, or stuck somewhere it shouldn't have been, or maybe it was a wild animal in distress—those scenarios I could deal with.

Only, when I rounded the faded National Park information board, Devin right behind me, we saw a scene we wouldn't forget in a hurry.

Not an animal at all.

My chest constricted, panic buzzed, my memories created a cityscape in this remote place, where I'd last seen something like this. Where were the sirens? Where was the staring crowd? How come this horror was next to sleepy Prophet in the cold light of day, with a man lying there, utterly alone?

A corpse.

A chill ran down my spine. I'd seen bodies in LA with horrific injuries that haunted me to this day, but there was something so wrong about this man laid bare to the elements, the mist of rain swirling around him, his skin gray as drops of water collected and ran down his muscled stomach. This was a man who looked after himself, built, strong, maybe a hiker, or one of the open water swimmers who loved coming to the lake?

His upper torso was exposed to the elements but navy jogging bottoms, covered the lower, and he wore running shoes and socks. He was on his back between the two upright stones, his arms and legs spread, and his sightless eyes faced us with his head turned our way. There was extensive bruising on his face, darker on one side, running from his cheek up into his hair, but it was so bad that from ten feet away it was impossible to ID him for sure even if the guy was someone I knew.

"Fuck," Devin muttered and took an instinctive step forward, but I held out a hand to stop him moving.

"What about a pulse?" my rookie asked hurriedly. "Shouldn't we check for that? Procedure for finding an unconscious person?"

"Normally, but it's clear there's no pulse." The victim was unmoving and there was an *X* scored into the man's chest, digging deep into his breastbone, and tearing his flesh apart. I could see the purple stain of lividity at the underside of one arm. He was very dead.

I stumbled back a step in shock. The mark was deliberate, considered. *Please don't let this be a serial killer with a propensity to carving Xs into their victim's chests.*

"…Sheriff?" Devin asked. "What now?"

I shook off the images on fast forward through my thoughts, and I connected to Hen. "Dispatch?"

"Go ahead Sheriff."

"Dispatch, this is *not* a 597. I repeat, this is *not* a 597." I collected my thoughts. "We have a 10-54, I repeat a 10-54." A body. A victim. Death. I paused for a moment, my stomach roiling, my mind flashing with images I didn't want to revisit. *Focus.* Apart from the body, the scene wasn't giving us any clues. I sank to a crouch that to Devin might look as if I was examining the murder scene closer. He didn't have to know that I was fighting ghosts as the rain plastered my hair to my forehead.

Drugs maybe? A willing sacrifice?

Breathe. Fuck.

Clear. Analytical. Focus.

"Sheriff?" Devin prompted, likely expecting me to give him a rundown on what I thought had happened here, or at least some pointers on what to do next.

I felt sick. The rain was heavier, not so much a mist but a sudden cloudburst. I pulled up the hood of my Sheriff's department slicker. *Come on, Gabriel, get your act together.*

Devin shuffled at my side, restless and uncertain, and I knew I had to take control instead of standing there as if I didn't know what to do.

I settled the shock inside me, then pressed the button on my radio. "Sheriff to Dispatch."

"Go ahead, Sheriff." Hen's tone was curious, and I expected her to ask what we'd found, but for once, she waited.

"We need all access blocked to Sentinel Rocks, liaise with park rangers, put someone on the logging gate entrance, call in ISB, ensure they connect with the coroner…"

Hen took all the information, her *"copy"* was muted, and when it was just me, Devin, and a corpse again, I gestured for him to move back a decent distance, then what else were we going to do except wait?

Sentinel Rocks was inside the Olympic National Park, which bordered Prophet, so it was national park jurisdiction—the ISB Special Agents handled investigative and law enforcement activities for parks and regional offices across the National Park system and they'd need to send someone to deal with a dead person. It wasn't the sheriff's jurisdiction and a big part of me was relieved. Of course, the smaller part, the trained cop part, wanted to find who'd done this.

"We're gonna lose this to the ISB." Devin sounded bereft that some other investigation agency would come in and steal the scene. It just showed how new he was to all of this, that it excited him to have a real-life murder on his doorstep.

"Yeah, we will."

A commotion yanked my focus from the deceased to

the tangle of wilderness only a few steps away, and there was rustling and barking. That was all we needed; hikers with their dogs disturbing the scene. The barking continued, frantic, followed by mournful howls, and then silence, but not for long. The dog responsible appeared at the edge of the trees, a Labrador with creamy yellow fur, no collar, kind of scruffy, dirty, wet, and then it vanished.

"Hikers need to keep their dogs on the leash," I muttered and side-eyed Devin, who wasn't even listening to me. Shit. I recognized that vacant stare. "Devin?" I bumped his elbow, and he startled and then winced at me before staring back at the body, excited, wide-eyed but totally freaked out. "First time?"

"Huh?" he said, as if he didn't understand.

"First time with a victim?"

"Yeah."

"What do you see?" May as well make this a teachable exercise and get my head straight before this had to be handed to the ISB. I had a corpse so close to Prophet that it unnerved me, particularly because there was a feel to the scene I didn't like. This wasn't someone hiking who'd gotten lost and died of exposure, or some idiot who'd gone swimming and never came back. This was wrong. Whoever had killed him had placed him just so. It was evil, and it sent shivers down my spine. *I'm losing my shit.*

The dog started barking again, interspersed with

whines. I shot an irritable glance that way in case hikers were in the bushes staring at this. Or murderers if they were still here. I rested a hand on my weapon and loosened the clasp… just in case.

"Um…" Devin went to a crouch the same as I had, peering at the body. "Male, Caucasian, I'd say six feet. It's not workable to approximate age given the extensive bruising, but he doesn't seem *old*-old." He stared up at me just as the barking ceased, and we were once again alone with just the sound of the water lapping at the shore of the lake behind us. "No sign of a murder weapon, but given the *X* in his chest, I would assume this wasn't a death by natural causes. There's no wild animal that could make such a deliberate mark. Do we think…" He rose to his feet and brushed off his pants to give himself time to think. "Is this a murder?"

The dog started up again, this time coming out of cover and standing, tail high, barking and yelping and staring straight at us. "Jesus," I snapped. I couldn't leave the newbie here alone with the body, but I really wanted to go over and find out who its owners were.

"You want me to grab the dog?" Devin asked helpfully.

Fuck yes. "Please."

Only as soon as Devin stepped forward, the dog moved back. One step at a time. Then it vanished into the bushes, the barking getting fainter, and that was it. The dog was gone.

"Well, I tried," Devin muttered, and after a pause, he came to stand next to me.

The dog appeared from another gap in the undergrowth. The barking restarted, and Devin darted over to catch the noisy animal, but it evaded him and disappeared.

"Guys!"

I glanced up to see Rowan, one of the park rangers, sprinting down the path toward us, sliding to a halt a good distance away and on the opposite side of the body to us. He was tall, good-looking, and sue me if I hadn't thought of asking him for a drink, just as friends, because outside of my brother he was one of the few men in town around my age, and at least Rowan talked to me. Nothing to do with the fact he had a rainbow sticker in his non-work car—go me, Mr. Observant.

"What the fuck?" Rowan asked and stared down at the body. He glanced at me, then Devin, then back at me. "What. The. Actual. Fuck?"

"Murder," Devin said.

"Okay," Rowan said, his eyes wide. "So, umm... shit... I have a message for you, sheriff. Abby said to tell you she's up at the barrier, and we have a call out to the new guy but he's not due to start until tomorrow and... shit... Abby sent me here to... I don't know what? Assist you?" He put his hands on his knees and bent at the waist, settling his breathing. "Jesus, that's messed up. Is it a ritual sacrifice—I swear that shit is insane? Is it murder wrapped up to look like a ritual sacrifice? Suicide? What about the blood? Did the rain wash it away? Has he been there all night? Fuck." He muttered the questions one after another, growing paler with each one.

"Not our scene, and it's too early to say," I reassured him.

The three of us stood in silence. I didn't know how long the body had been here, but yes, it had rained last night, and yes, that would have washed away blood, and no, I didn't know why someone had taken something very sharp and carved an X into the victim's chest, nor whether it was pre or postmortem.

Rowan sighed heavily. "Abby said she was going to call this into ISB."

"Yep, but it's our scene until they arrive, so consider yourself on official duty," I said, and he nodded as if that made sense.

Our resident demon dog started up his ruckus, and Rowan jumped a mile as the noise shattered the peace.

"Get that damn dog and find its owners!" I snapped.

Devin sprinted, with Rowan close behind, falling all over each other to catch our canine companion. It would have been funny if this wasn't a serious-as-death situation. The dog vanished again, but then Rowan stopped dead in his tracks right where the dog had disappeared as if he'd seen something, frozen in place. Then, in a scramble of motion, he spun and ran back to my side, cursing when I reached out to stop him barreling into a crime scene.

"Jesus!" he yelled close to my ear.

"What?"

"I think… that dog… I think this might be…" He bent at the waist, inhaling sharply and I patted his back, not so much to reassure but for him to cut to the chase. "Oh god, his face… I can't… that's Mike. He's… he's…"

"What?" I prompted.

"He's the new guy, Mike Bressett, just transferred in from Montana. He's one of us." Rowan stared at me. "He's a park ranger." Rowan pointed to where the barking came from. "And that's his dog!"

Chapter Two

Tiber

BIG BROWN EYES stared back at me from my computer screen. They were set in a face with a shiny black nose and gray fur resembling an Ewok's. The dog, Merci, looked away, but not before I saw that he was basically a happy little guy. Nothing too traumatic there. That was a relief. New clients were always worrying.

Denise, his owner, droned on over the laptop's speaker. She was in her forties and wore a pink jogging suit that matched her one-inch pink nails. She and Merci were seated on a big white ottoman in a white room with windows overlooking the ocean.

She'd never have to worry over vet bills, that was for sure.

"... twice last week!" Denise complained. "On brand

new pumps, too. I have a cleaning place I take them to, but you can't get pee out of silk moiré. This is getting to be a serious problem! I just don't understand where it's coming from. Merci has always been such a good boy. He hasn't had an accident in the house for years, and never before on my shoes."

Her words were scolding, but her obsessive petting of Merci's ruff told me more than her words. The way Merci leaned against her told me more still. She might be annoying to me, but Merci adored Denise Lafferty. And vice versa.

Which crossed several possibilities off the list.

"My friend, Lonny said you can read pets' minds. Can you really do that?" Denise asked hopefully.

"I'm an animal behaviorist, Ms. Lafferty."

"I know. But she said you knew what Snowball was thinking. And I figured maybe because you're Native American... Or—is that the right term? First peoples? First nation? Merci and I don't want to offend."

I sighed inwardly. "Native American is fine." I re-tucked my long black hair behind one ear. If a behaviorist had been reading *me*, that would be a tell. I always felt a bit like an imposter when clients assumed I was some kind of Native American shaman. I was only a quarter native, despite appearances suggesting otherwise. And I drew from my education—which I'd worked damned hard for—and not from anything supernatural.

Well. Mostly.

"Let's get back to Merci, and see what I can pick up, okay? You say this behavior started a month ago. What changed around then?"

"Nothing." Denise sniffed. "I haven't changed his diet. He gets a delivery service. He loves it. And he loves his dog walker. He's been going out with Jojo and that neighborhood pack forever. Though I guess I could ask Jojo if there's been a new dog introduced. Do you think Merci could be afraid of something on his walks?"

Merci's ears perked up at the word walk, and his tail wagged.

"When the dog walker arrives, how does Merci react?" I asked.

Denise smiled. "Oh, he loves his outings. Don't you, baby woosey-woo?" She nuzzled Merci's nose, and he licked her enthusiastically. "He gets so excited when Jojo comes to the door."

Merci stood on the ottoman and stared towards what I assumed was the door, tail going nuts.

"No, Jojo's not here right now, baby."

"It's not the dog walks."

"Then what?" Denise sniffed. "Can you ask him?"

I am asking him, I thought. But I kept that to myself.

"Something's changed," I said. "A new job, maybe? Have you changed the hours you're home?"

"No. I don't work, thank *God*. I go out with my girlfriends a few times a week, but I've always done that." She hesitated, blinking. "I guess I have been away more often since I started seeing Jared. Just out to dinner, mostly. Or sailing. But if I'm going to be gone for over six hours, I get Jojo to come hang out with Merci."

Ah. There it was. Merci shifted his body away from Denise and his ears went back. He focused on the wall and panted.

What had she just said?

I leaned forward. "Tell me about Jared." I asked, and the little dog's ears twitched in irritation.

She smiled, still stroking Merci's back. "Oh, he's wonderful. I met him at an art gallery. He's very handsome. And generous. He's a boat person, you know? He sailed around the world. He's living on a small yacht down in the harbor right now."

Merci laid down on the ottoman and put his head on his paws.

Denise went on. "We've taken Merci out with us on the boat a few times but, honestly, he doesn't like it. I think the water makes him nervous."

It's not the water.

"I took the baby to doggy swim classes a few years ago, and he liked that fine. Maybe it's the size of the ocean or the motion of the boat?"

I wasn't a fan of people infantilizing their dogs, though it beat the alternative—ignoring or abusing them. But Denise was just noise at this point.

I shifted closer to my laptop's camera so my face would fill the screen on their end. "Merci. *Merci.*"

The dog raised its head and looked at me. His tail did a little jiggle.

"Merci, what do you think of Jared, hum? *Jared.* Is Jared at the door?"

A tremor went through the little guy. An image flashed through my mind of a man kicking the dog. Merci leaped off the ottoman and scurried away, nails clicking on the floor.

I sighed. Shit.

"Merci!" Denise called out, starting to get up.

"He's okay. Just let him be for a minute."

She sat down, a little frown on her brow. "Maybe he has to go out."

"He doesn't have to go out."

She blinked at the camera seeming unsure, but she didn't argue.

I took a deep breath. "So. About this new boyfriend. I think he's been abusive to Merci."

Denise's jaw dropped open? "What? He hasn't. No." Her tone was defensive. "Jared doesn't even pay attention to Merci."

When you're in the room.

Her face lightened. "Maybe Merci is jealous of Jared. Is that it?"

"No, that's not it."

She was dubious now. "You can't possibly know that."

"Ms. Lafferty, you're paying me two-hundred dollars an hour to know that." I was losing my temper, and that wouldn't do. The little image showing my face scowled back at me from the computer screen, my thick, black eyebrows like thunderbolts. I attempted to smooth them out and soften my voice. "Look, Merci is afraid of Jared. Really afraid. When Jared comes to the door, Merci runs and hides, doesn't he?"

Denise wrung her hands, her pink nails flashing. "Well. Yes. But he doesn't like to see us kiss."

A flash of anger sparked in my chest. Merci had been telling Denise loud and clear, but she was too busy making out with her boyfriend to notice. Typical. That little dog was her comfort and joy when she was alone. She treated him like her baby, and she'd gained Merci's complete loyalty and affection. But as soon as a man showed up....

I said none of that.

"The level of fear Merci has about Jared means something happened between them. Maybe more than once. Sometimes when people don't like dogs, especially small dogs, they can be casually abusive. Shoving them away with a kick, for instance."

"Jared wouldn't do that!" Denise insisted hotly. "You don't know anything about him."

"True. But I'm not reading Jared. I'm reading your dog."

Her lips pressed tight, but then eyes lit up with an idea. "But if Merci really hated Jared that much, wouldn't he pee in *Jared*'s shoes? He only pees in mine."

"No, because he'd be afraid of retaliation. You're his person, Denise. You're the one he trusts with his safety, his well-being, his very life."

Her hostility melted into an expression of love. She sniffed. "That's true."

"He's trying to send you a message, to let you know something is wrong in his world. I'm guessing the peeing incidents only occur when Jared's been around? Maybe right after he's left?"

She thought for a moment, then nodded reluctantly.

"Do me a favor. Take Merci to the vet and have him checked over for any bruises or sore spots. Today, if you can." I remembered the flash I'd had. "Especially around his ribs on the right side."

She was shocked. "Hang on." She got off the ottoman and marched from the camera's view. A moment later, she returned with Merci clutched to her breast. She sat down with him on her lap and talked baby talk to him as she felt over him with those pink-nailed fingers.

When she reached his ribs, he gave a sharp yip and trembled.

She gasped. "I'm sorry, baby! Does that hurt? I'm so sorry!" Denise kissed his head and stroked his back. A tear ran down her cheeks and she stared at the camera, her expression furious. "I swear, if that asswipe kicked my dog, I'll have his nuts for breakfast! Do you think he's okay? Is Merci okay?"

Something inside me unclenched, and I breathed a sigh of relief. So, if it came down to it, Denise would side with Merci. Thank God.

"He'll be fine. He's not in constant pain, or it would be obvious. But it wouldn't hurt to have those ribs X-rayed and to have him checked over for any other sore spots."

"I'll take him now." She stood, still holding Merci.

"Wait." I glanced at the clock. She'd paid for an hour, and it had only been thirty minutes. "Look, you have two options. Don't let Jared around Merci. Or, if you need more proof about what he's doing, you can pick up a nanny cam on Amazon for under a hundred bucks. I'll send you a link. That way, you can find out for sure."

She nodded. "Good idea. Thank you, Tiber. Really. My friend Lonny was right. You truly are a godsend. I'm going to the vet now."

She closed the laptop lid with a bang.

. . .

MUCH AS MERCI HAD DONE, I gave an all-over shiver. I rubbed my face. Ugh. Interactions with pet owners always took it out of me. Especially new clients when I had no idea what to expect.

It was an irrational anxiety. People who cared enough about their pets to pay my consulting fees were normally decent people who were good to their animals. But still—dealing with people was hard. Any people. I double-checked my schedule. I was done with Zoom for the day, thank God. I gave another full-body shudder before getting up and opening my office door.

Leo, Gracie, and Ferdinand were waiting on the other side. They quivered with excitement when they saw me and Ferdinand's tail made a drumbeat on the floor.

"Aw, guys." I couldn't resist kissing each one on the head.

Leo was a scruffy mutt who weighed fifteen pounds but ruled the roost. I'd found him as a puppy when I was seventeen. Gracie was a geriatric wolfhound rescued from a puppy mill and then a family with a half-dozen kids and too much chaos. She was afraid of everything. The old girl needed peace and quiet, and I was determined to see she got it.

Ferdinand, the basset hound, had been abandoned by his family when they moved out of state, left to wander his neighborhood forlornly and scavenge garbage. When

I'd heard his story at the local shelter, and looked into those soulful eyes, I'd brought him home.

They all had my heart.

"Tiber's done for the day," I told them. "How bad is it raining? Want to go for a walk?"

Ferdinand licked his lips.

"Food first. Got it."

They padded after me as I went into my bedroom and took off the blue oxford button-down I wore for Zoom calls, slipping on a comfy T-shirt. I ditched the tight jeans for a soft, roomy pair.

Leo barked at me as I put on my shoes.

"Oh, yeah?" I said. "She's just a kitten, Leo. Have some patience."

Fudge, the kitten in question, was clinging to the drapes when we went into the living room. She gave me a pitiful mew, and I gently held her up, disengaged her claws, and set her on the floor. "Come get lunch," I said.

Mealtimes were always a scene. I had to keep Leo out of Gracie's food and Patch, a calico who'd spent a lot of his years as a feral cat, needed to be coaxed to eat as if every bite was a huge personal favor he bestowed upon me. Male calicos were rare—only 1 in 3000. So Patch truly was a unicorn, not unlike myself. I hunted down Renfield, a white rabbit with a penchant for burrowing into any available fabric—blankets, clothes bins, even the linen closet when he could get into it.

Finally, when the troops had all ingested something,

I made myself a peanut butter sandwich and stared out of the window while I chewed.

A sunny day was a special treat in Prophet. Today was fair with in-and-out clouds. It wasn't even drizzling at the moment. Ah, high summer! I'd thought I'd take the trail to the lake. From my house, it was a mile's walk, and it was little more than a game trail, so I had it all to myself. Which meant the gang could go off-leash. I smiled. There were still several hours of daylight left and nothing pressing on my plate.

Something black flew into view and perched on the fence post closest to the window. It was a crow. It stared at me, its wings fluffed up, its eyes beady and knowing.

A chill went through me. Sometimes a crow is just a crow. But I hadn't seen one in my yard like this before, and the way it flew in to stare at me through the window was odd.

Some cultures believe crows are messengers. Couriers between the living and the dead. When I'd turned twelve, my grandmother had insisted I partake in a traditional sweat lodge ceremony, and the crow had come to me in a vision. The rez's shaman had proclaimed him my totem animal. What that meant, if anything, was a mystery to me. But ever since then, I'd felt a kinship with the bird.

"You'd better not be bringing me any bad news," I told the crow.

The crow didn't answer.

Chapter Three

Gabriel

MIKE BRESSETT. Park Ranger. Deceased.

"Thoughts?"

There was still no sign of an ISB Special Agent, and the Clallum County coroner—Amelia—had beaten them to it, muttering something about budget cuts. As the county coroner she would attend the scene whoever was in charge, so I let her and her two techs get on with their job, only I put a call into Hen to find out the problem with ISB. I would have expected at least a courtesy call from them. Until they arrived and officially took over, this was my scene.

Amelia glanced up at me from her crouch and smirked. "He's dead," she said. We entered a staring contest—this wasn't some weekly CSI show where the coroner got to be flippant, and I hoped my glare was enough to make her see that. I needed information, and I needed it now because this was the vital time where cases were made. "Tough crowd," she murmured, and stood. "Okay, just the facts then," she deadpanned.

Even I caught the *Dragnet* reference, as had one of the crime scene guys with her, because he snorted a laugh. I sent him the same stare I'd given his boss, and he wouldn't meet my gaze. Just because we were in Prophet WA in the middle of nowhere, there wasn't any need for levity or gallows humor right now. The victim deserved respect, as did the office of sheriff.

"That's all we need," I summarized.

She raised an eyebrow. "Okay, sheriff," she began, in a tone that let me know I was being an ass.

Wouldn't be the first time.

"I wish I could tell you the cause was obvious," she said. "We have a single blow to the left temple, and that is my focus here. A blow like this, hard enough to cause significant bruising, would have caused internal damage. Also, there are a few contusions on his neck and limbs, and of course, someone carved into his chest deeply enough that it could have caused him to bleed out if he wasn't already dead."

"So you're suggesting the cut on the chest happened postmortem?"

"No! Not at all. It's open to whether the head injury was the cause or something else. The rain at scene hasn't preserved blood pooling around the body, and until we get him back to the lab, it's impossible to assess if the carving was ante or postmortem."

"Time of death?"

"Impossible to say but if I was to guess, then sometime within the past twenty-four hours?"

Damn it. "That's as close as you can get?"

She side-eyed me. "We don't hand out dates and times at a scene just because of a random piece of evidence on a corpse I haven't even checked yet," she muttered.

"But, if you can—"

"Sheriff Thompson, for God's sake, have you ever attended a scene before? You realize this isn't a cozy cop procedural where I hand you unsubstantiated facts as if they're candy?"

"Of course I have, I was in LA…" She didn't need to know all that. "I apologize." I was standing here asking her to give me her professional opinion when I knew better than to ask for detail. No wonder she was staring at me with a frosty expression. "It's been a day. I'm expecting ISB, and it's crickets."

"You'll be lucky to get an ISB Special Agent out here that quickly. There's a scene over in Idaho that's taking resources, and they're understaffed. I imagine they'll hand it to you like they did the drowning over in Forks to Sheriff Collinson last fall."

She inclined her head, and I returned the gesture,

thinking that maybe we'd found some common ground. We'd all had our budgets cut, which was why in the sheriff's office it was me, Devin, and Hen. We couldn't even stretch to cleaners, but I had superiority over Devin, so no bathroom duty for me.

Amelia gathered up her two techs, and the first stages of moving the victim—Mike—began. I still needed to work the scene for now, whatever ISB said when they got here, so I catalogued the wider area, or at least I started to. We'd be here a long time, with all this mud, and so many footprints. Were they made *after* Mike was dead? Was Mike moved here after the people left prints? When did it rain? Had wildlife disturbed the body? Whoever had left these prints had been sure to trample all over the damn place.

"Were they having a damn party?" I said to no one in particular.

"Sir?" Devin asked, but I waved him away.

Amelia shut the doors of the coroner's van then returned to stand next to me as I stared down at the churned mud with so many footprints. I wish something here made sense—a weapon, or *something*. Anything. I knew I had to be patient and wait for the fragments we had so far to begin to create a picture of what had happened here.

"I'll have some preliminary findings for you later today," she said. "But the full autopsy, waiting on bloods and other tests will take time. I assume you know that there will be a wait?" She was teasing.

I think.

"Of course."

"Then the scene is yours for however long you wait for an ISB Special Agent, sheriff," she said, "Oh, one more thing. You might want to search for ritual killings bearing the same cuts."

My world fell. No.

"You think?"

She glanced at me, and then at the body. "You don't?"

"I'll get on that," I conceded, and then watched as they removed our victim to Amelia's van with great care. I fought the compulsion to run after her and demand she get answers for me straight away and instead focused on what remained. Evidence.

What fucking evidence?

There was nothing. No obvious blade, or object that hit the victim, or visible clues. What I wouldn't give for wild animal marks, but the way the body was laid out, the carved symbol and the drama of the position... none of that had been done by an animal, unless said animal was very lucky and had swiped a perfect cross into a man's chest. All we had was rain-washed stones, muddy earth with hundreds of prints spread around, and a dog we couldn't catch. The location itself was evidence—the land here was in dispute so was this some kind of message from the Makah to retrieve land that had been stolen from them?

Or was it personal? Rowan said he knew little to nothing about his new colleague, Mike, just that he'd moved over from Montana and was due to start work only a few days from now. Rowan hadn't known where he was living, but there again, if it was in Prophet and he didn't have a rental, or hadn't bought a place, then it was likely he'd be at the Lake Prophet Hotel, a two-star B&B catering to tourists who trekked out this far to find us. Maybe Abby would know more. After all, she was the local lead ranger and had recruited Mike.

"Abby asked you to stop and fill her in," Devin said, and exchanged glances with a very pale Rowan.

I nodded—as head ranger she could have insight into Mike, but also, he was due to work for her, and I should keep her up to date as much as I could.

Thankfully, the town was small enough for people to know Mike in a basic way, enough for us to track movements, maybe. Unless, of course, he was staying elsewhere and had just chosen to hike out here on his mini-vacation before taking on his new role.

So many variables.

The forensic technicians with the coroner were taking photos of everything, working the scene, but I could see from their expressions they weren't finding much in the way of anything at all.

I was used to a scene that told us nothing, but in a

very different way. Down in LA we could find a weapon, or prints, but the world of crime was vast, and sometimes there was too much evidence with most of it contradicting itself in twists and turns of who owned what gun and who passed said gun onto the next criminal. Add in the drugs and the crazies and sometimes a scene was nothing more than overwhelming chaos.

"Devin?"

"Sir?" He glanced at me and stepped closer, avoiding the flapping end of tape stirring in the wind that came with the start of more rain. And rivulets of water washed soil from the site as the rain grew heavier, and with it, any evidence that may have once been there.

Was there any point in standing here staring at a deteriorating scene?

Someone needs to catch the dog.

One of us, Devin, or I, should go up into town, start talking to people, lay the groundwork for the investigation and I was torn. If I left Devin here, all wet behind the ears, would he let someone contaminate everything and destroy that perfect piece of evidence we'd yet to find? Would he sit there without realizing that the integrity of the scene had to be preserved, and that if I left, then he'd be in charge of all the people working in the location? How would we control the crowds? I glanced around me. There were no crowds.

Of course, there wasn't—this wasn't the streets, this wasn't a city, this was a remote corner of a national park in the forest in the middle of freaking nowhere, and the integrity of the scene wasn't in danger. Right?

I have to trust you sometime, kid. My old training partner's voice was a whisper in my ear— Lincoln McGinnis had been my introduction to undercover work in LA, and my rude awakening after spending so long in my bedroom dreaming of being a big city cop. In hindsight, I'm sure I'd been channeling Batman, but no one would ever know that but me and my twelve-year-old self. I'd found the city a chaotic, soul-destroying place—add in the horrific undercover work and I ran from the city way sooner than even I expected.

Devin, however, had dreamed of small town cop work, and had come straight from his degree in criminology. I had to trust my gut that he was good and that the scene would be secure.

I gestured for him to follow me a few steps away and it spoke volumes that, despite following me; he didn't once take his eyes off the standing stones.

"Procedure at the scene of a murder?" I prompted.

He blinked, then appeared to pull himself together, stared back at the scene and straightened his spine. "Scene dimensions, focal point, security, tape perimeter." He swallowed and glanced back at me to check I was listening. "Plan, communicate, type of crime, document scene, primary and secondary survey, record and preserve evidence. Supervise on scene technicians." He paused between each one—this wasn't some list he'd learned by rote. He'd considered each one with care as he worked the scene and connected each part to what he saw in front of him.

"Okay then. Stay with the techs. I'll leave the ranger here—Rowan—but this is your scene, and your responsibility, until the agents from ISB arrive, okay?"

More swallowing, but there was determination in the kid's expression. "Sir."

"You control who attends the scene, you log every freaking movement, no exception. If a bird sneezes, I want to know about it." He relaxed a little at my joke. "I'm going into town to track down anything regarding the victim."

"Yes, sir." I walked away, but he called me back. "Sir, what about the dog?"

The disapproving canine had disappeared into the undergrowth again, but every so often there was barking and it would appear for a moment. So far the dog had proved to be a master at evading capture, but I'd already spoken to Animal Control, and they weren't much help. They were based in Forks and beyond the river with the crapped out bridge. They suggested we catch him ourselves, or call wild animal control, but when they saw a photo of the dog and realized it was a Labrador, they gave us a list of tactics that all involved food. As yet, our watchful guardian had taken none of the offerings to move close enough for us to capture him, but if we kept at it, maybe it would relent.

"Your priority is the scene, Officer Randall. We'll get Ranger Rowan here to monitor the dog. The dog can't be a distraction from your work at the scene. Understood?"

"Got it, sir."

"Contact me the moment that the techs apprise you of anything, or if ISB turns up, or if there is *any* situation you feel is out of your control." I kept my voice steady, not so much warning him as directing what he should do. "I want you to know that there is *no issue* for which you can't call me for backup if anything looks, I dunno, hinky."

He half-smiled then. "'Hinky'."

"Yep. Official sheriff term." I touched his shoulder to take his eyes off the scene for a moment. "Okay?"

"Sir," he acknowledged and immediately his gaze focused back on what was happening. Rowan was a little harder to pin down, but he did agreed to stay to assist Devin. He'd told me he knew little about his soon-to-be colleague and that was all I was getting from him as a source. Maybe his boss knew more; I'd had a few meetings with Abby, head ranger in Prophet for well over ten years. She'd seen weird stuff in her time that caused trouble, from Big Foot hunters towing trailers into Makah sacred grounds, to new age travelers parking their vans and searching for enlightenment while naked, right down to the simple things like hikers who didn't follow the rules.

I added Abby to my mental list of people to talk to, and I knew she'd be up by the gate and I'd have to pass her, so that pushed her to the top. As I climbed into my Sheriff's Department SUV, the rain was as heavy as it had been last night, the spot where I left my vehicle was even more of a mess of mud, and every chance we had of gathering any evidence here was also sliding away one trickling stream of water at a time.

I reached the gate, and the old logging road was becoming impassable for anything but a 4x4.

Abby was here—Chief Ranger at the local station— and she was in a confrontation with a tall guy. The man was wearing fatigues, a backpack in one of his hands, the other holding a rock as he gesticulated down the track. He balanced precariously on a crutch, and I could see a walking boot on his left foot, covered in mud. He leaned toward her and even though she stood her ground; he looked angry and had a damn rock in his hand. I killed the engine and sprinted the short distance to reach her, mud sucking at my boots.

"I have one!" the man shouted in her face, as I stepped up and put a hand between them.

"Please step back, sir." I stayed respectful and assessed the situation as best I could.

The man's eyes were wild, the hand holding the rock in constant motion, but next to me, Abby didn't appear worried, and if pushed I bet she'd tell me she'd dealt with rock-wielding angry men before, and that I should stay out of this. Her hood had fallen back, exposing her head to the elements and her close-cropped bright red hair—the one flash of brightness in the stormy day—was already soaked.

"Gabriel," she murmured, and wiped across her face.

"Everything okay here?"

"Yep."

"I have to get down there," the man announced, and leaned on his crutch before he turned his attention to me, his gaze focusing on my chest and then up to my face. "Sheriff, I have proof."

"So much of it," Abby deadpanned, which gave me the feeling maybe this mad-eyed man had nothing at all? Was he high? His pupils seemed okay in his wide eyes, but that meant nothing at all with the new drugs that hit the street every damn week.

"Drop the rock, sir," I demanded.

"It's evidence!"

"Why don't we take this to my office—"

"No!" the man yelled in my face, which was one way to earn a quick trip to the station in handcuffs.

"Sir, please calm down and give me the rock."

My first instinct was to get him away and to attempt rational communication because he was losing his shit, and I was right in the middle of him and Abby.

He thrust the rock at my chest, heavy and flat, and I caught it to stop the damn thing smashing into me, as he limped back.

"Look!" he exclaimed. "Proof!"

I glanced down at the rock, which on closer inspection was a plaster cast of something that wasn't readily identifiable.

"Ask him what it is," Abby prompted.

"Sir—"

He didn't wait for me to ask. "See the dermal ridges? The whorls on the feet that are just like fingerprints? This footprint isn't from a man or a known beast. Do you know what you're holding?"

I turned the cast over in my hand, a jagged edge catching my finger and a pinprick of blood welled, but I couldn't work out what I had here, and what it had to do with proof and the case of the body at the stones.

"A footprint!" the man exclaimed and jabbed at me. "I found this last night, took the print, and made a duplicate, so don't think that you can take this and pretend I didn't see things."

Did I have a potential witness? "What did you see?"

"Nothing, he saw *nothing*," Abby said. "He's just your typical Bigfoot hunter—"

"Sasquatch, wendigo, skookum, anything but Bigfoot," he snapped. "It's an insult when their feet are perfectly in proportion with the body, so why people call him or her Bigfoot, is a mystery to me. What you have there, sheriff, is evidence of a forgotten twig of the hominid evolutionary tree and you're stopping me from getting down there to see what else you found. Why are you blocking me from entering a public space?"

I exchanged glances with Abby, who rolled her eyes. Bigfoot. I sighed inwardly. The Olympic National Park had some of the most remote areas in the United States and was a hotbed for so-called Bigfoot sightings. Prophet had a seasonal influx of tourists looking for the mythical creature, and the grocery store stocked an entire line of Bigfoot memorabilia, which was harmless, but I knew the park rangers had to deal with a lot of problems around obsessed people searching for a Sasquatch the same as Roswell did with UFOs. The town embraced the baffling, and the wild, and it was an economy that sat alongside our tourist income, and it hurt no one. Usually.

He grew even more animated. "Was it a Sasquatch attack? They move in a militaristic operation, you know, always staying out of sight, but I've always believed they would attack if discovered. Not that it stopped me. I know I'm right, and I'll be the first person to document their existence." He paused, and I was relieved that he was stopping, but no, he had a lot more to say. "I'm not like the others who believe Bigfoot is an alien, or telekinetic, a shapeshifter, or even exists in a parallel dimension. I'm not like them, okay! I just want to know, were there more footprints down there? A dead body? Something else?"

My gaze narrowed on him. Referring to *"something else"* was way too wide, and the fact he included the words *dead* and *body* got my back up.

I passed back the mold and held a hand out to stop him from crowding me in his excitement and exasperation, as he almost fell over his crutch, which was sinking in the mud.

"Start from the beginning."

He huffed with added drama. "Oh my God, why do we have to do this? It's wasting time. My name is Hillesden, Grover Hillesden." He inserted a dramatic pause, as if the name itself was important, then offered me his hand, the crutch close to slipping. We shook with respect, but I had a ton of questions.

"Mr. Hillesden, we should take this back to the office and—"

"No. Because while we do that, the government will remove any and all evidence of my find and that is something else you'll take away from me." He pointed to his jacket, and the body cam unit on his left side. "You can't take my rights as an American citizen—"

"Okay, Mr. Hillesden, you have two choices. You follow me to my office to make a statement, or I take you back myself. Which will it be?"

"I know my rights!" he yelled and turned so fast he was a blur. He fell over his crutch and stumbled.

He slid on his ass, and went headfirst into the nearest tree, his footprint cast flying from his hand, his crutch landing a few feet away, his open backpack slamming into the ground beside him, notebooks and a second plaster cast dropping out. I was at his side in an instant, but the damn fool had knocked himself unconscious. I felt for a pulse, thankful he'd fallen into a recovery position without me having to move him.

"Fuck," I muttered, then connected to Hen. "Dispatch, we have a medical situation at Logger's Gate. Can you get Doc Winston down here?"

"Copy."

That meant I had to wait, and irritation at that made being damp from the rain worse. I picked up the notebooks and the casts and shoved them into the backpack, only they wouldn't fit, and I cursed and shoved and then gave up.

"Let me," Abby murmured, and peered into the pack, suddenly going still. "Gabriel?" she said, and her tone was calm, but from her expression she was far from feeling that way.

"What?" She tilted the bag to me, and I leaned over to look inside, the glint of metal at the bottom. "A gun and a hunting knife."

"Dispatch to Sheriff. Doc Winston is fifteen out," Hen advised, interrupting my processing of what was in the backpack.

"Copy," I answered by rote, and then spoke to Abby. "These are important. I'll bag and hold onto them."

We were out of the rain here, sheltered but every so often a leaf would grow too heavy and release collected water to splash down on us. We bagged the firearm, which turned out to be an unloaded flare gun, and the serrated knife, and took photos.

"What do you know about this Bigfoot guy?" I asked as we waited for the doctor.

"Not much. He's been hanging around town, found him berating One-Eyed Jack in the store about his Bigfoot merchandise, calling him a sellout. Let's just say that I *assisted* Mr. Hillesden from the shop, and he gave me this long spiel about missing links, or 'organisms not recognized by science'. He's a cryptozoologist, which I guess is a step up from the typical hiker up here thinking they'll get a peek at Bigfoot. He's harmless, maybe a little obsessed, broke his ankle last time he was up here four or five weeks ago, hence the crutch, but I've seen people like him before up here." She gestured at the flare gun and knife in the evidence bag. "Is the knife important? I mean, how did Mike die?"

I shrugged because I had no fucking clue how he'd died. "I don't know."

My gut told me the gun and knife weren't evidence of anything, but I would send the knife to get it checked out. Grover Hillesden might seem like nothing more than a man obsessed, but the fact he'd been around here last night to get what he said was a footprint, and the knife in his pack that may or may not have carved an X in our victim's chest, added up to something else altogether.

"Can I ask, off the record, what happened to Mike down there, sheriff?" she asked quietly, and it occurred to me I hadn't even extended my condolences to her about a man she'd likely helped to hire. "All Rowan said was that he was dead."

"Yeah, Rowan ID'd him, but how he died, and what he was doing by the stones, I don't know. We'll have to wait for the coroner's report."

She went quiet for a moment. "He was due to start work in a few days; he was a good guy, and we shared our love for running. Hell, he ran marathons. He'd already been doing some off-the-record work for us all off his own back, working with the campers, helping unofficially. He even cleared up a dispute last week. Jeez… he was an experienced ranger out of Montana. I don't understand how this happened."

I hooked onto the one part that interested me. "What kind of dispute?"

"Nothing he said worried him, just the usual stuff. I can forward you his notes. It wasn't official or anything, so it couldn't have been too awful."

"I'd be grateful for any insight I can pass to the ISB."

"I'll dig it out when I get back to the office."

"Do you know what made him leave Montana to come here?"

"A bad breakup, or at least that is what he implied, but digging into his personal life wasn't part of the interview."

"Sure," I agreed. "Can you tell me anything else about him?"

"He was a good fit for what we needed, had worked closely with the Siksikaitsitapi in his previous role, which was something he was keen on doing here with the Makah. I didn't know him well, but he was passionate in his causes, outspoken in all the best ways and confident. He would have been an asset to us; I'm sure of it."

"Had you seen him since he arrived in town?"

"Briefly, maybe a week ago, for coffee. He has a room in the hotel, but I know he was looking to rent a place out of town, said he liked to live remote."

"Nothing in your coffee meet-up with him gave you pause for thought?"

"No. I mean, I don't get it. He's a big guy, and I don't know what you found down there, but it would have to be someone strong to hurt him. Was he shot? Is that what this is?"

"We don't know," I repeated, and I had more questions, but then we were interrupted by Doc Winston's 4x4 at the gate, and the general mess of getting a now semi-conscious, irritable cryptozoologist into Doc's car to head to the clinic in Prophet. I had no choice but to follow Doc and talk to Mr. Bigfoot hunter directly. Not to mention I needed to get someone to catch the dog, talk to the hotel owner, Daisy Simmonds, and write reports.

"We want to stop people from getting down there from this road, at least until the scene is cleared." I knew catching the dog was a priority, even if it meant coming down here with a pound of steak, but for now all I could do was fix who went down this way, even if I didn't have the personnel to stop anyone going to the site using the park trails or rowing across the lake. Talk about the impossible.

"I'm on it," she confirmed.

"Abby, if you need me to relieve you—"

"It was one of my men. I'm okay here." One of her men? I respected that.

"Last thing, Rowan is down there with Devin, but there's a dog that we think belongs to Mike. He's loose and we can't catch him."

"Yellow Lab?"

"Yeah." Her surprised tone filled me with a hope because she knew the dog at least by sight. "Any chance you could help catch him at some point?"

She snorted a laugh. "All I know is he's slippery. No way will he trust you, or me, to leave Mike's side. He's obsessed with Mike…" Her breath hitched and she frowned. "*Was* obsessed. The poor thing must be grieving. You'll need to call animal control."

"They're a day out. I could do with something today."

"You'll need a freaking dog whisperer," she deadpanned, and then her eyes widened. "Tiber, something or other, he's the one you want. Supposedly he's a regular Dr. Doolittle, Ana swears he talked to her cat. Tiber… I want to say Rusty, or Russell…" She tapped her lip, then clicked her fingers. "No, Russo. That's it. You get Tiber Russo down there, and he'll get you the dog."

Chapter Four

Tiber

THERE WAS a knock on the door, firm and sharp.

Barks rose hysterically. I had so few visitors, the dogs weren't used to it. You'd have thought Death was on the front stoop, eight feet tall with a scythe.

Fuck. Any delivery person should be able to read the sign that said, *LEAVE DELIVERIES ON MAT. DO NOT KNOCK.* Idiots.

Gracie cowered behind the sofa as I went to the door. Ferdinand and Leo were already there, Leo snarling and braced like he was gonna rip someone's face off.

"It's okay. Chill. I'll take care of it," I told him, and any other animal within earshot. "You two go lay down. No, go lay down." I pointed toward the living room.

With a betrayed glare, Leo trotted off, followed by Ferdinand.

Now. Who the fuck would come to my house? I peeked through a long, thin curtained window that looked onto the stoop.

It was a cop. A guy in a uniform. A hot guy in a cop's uniform. He stood casually, looking towards an SUV parked on the road with *SHERIFF* written on the side.

My gaze lingered. Brown hair, well cut. Strong jaw. A good face. Not weak. Not cruel. But the uniform.... I wasn't a fan.

I let the curtain fall, straightening up. "Who is it?"

"Mr. Russo? I'm Sheriff Thompson. Can I have a moment of your time, please?" The voice that came through the door was professional, calm.

"Do you have identification?"

There was a pause. "Sure."

I tapped on the window. "Hold it up here."

I moved the curtain and took a good, long check of his ID. Not that I really thought the person on the other side of the door was a serial killer pretending to be a cop. But it never hurt to be sure.

The badge was for the Prophet Sheriff's office, and the photo was of the guy. The name read *Sheriff Gabriel Thompson*.

This was the sheriff, huh? I'd heard a new one had recently been hired. He was handsome. Taller than me, with dark hair, hazel eyes that were more green right now, and a scruff of beard, he was doing a good job of being broody and exhausted. Not that it mattered how he looked. I'd stopped caring about attraction to anyone a long time ago.

For real.

"Okay. I'm coming out."

"You don't have to—"

I turned the knob and slipped outside, closing the door behind me. Within seconds, Leo was on the other side, barking. My protector.

"It's easier this way," I said. "I have a lot of animals."

The day wasn't as warm as it'd seemed from the window and my feet were bare, the stoop wet. I put one foot on top of the other to warm them and hugged myself. The cop's gaze dropped to my feet and lingered there a beat too long before staring back up at my face.

Huh. Now that little tell socked me in the gut.

"What do you want?" I said, more harshly than I'd intended.

The sheriff frowned. "Mr. Russo? Are you the, er, animal guy?"

"Animal behaviorist. Yes. But I only work remotely unless it's a very special case. You can find my website at—"

"This is a special case."

His face was serious, even grim. It cut off the

flippant response that came to mind. My pulse picked up. This was something bad. Was it something bad? Jesus. I hated bad things.

"I was hoping—" The sheriff began. But he jumped, staring down in alarm. "Shit." He took a hasty step back.

I fought an urge to laugh. "It's only Frank."

I squatted down. The tortoise's appearance had broken the dread I felt, and I was grateful. "What is it, Frank? Want your lunch?"

His big, scaled foot scratched at the cement of the stoop once, twice.

"He wants to be put in his pond. I'll be back." I heaved Frank up. He was over two feet long and heavy. It took both arms to lift him. I carried him around the side of the house, ignoring the cop. He could just wait. Frank looked ahead content, and happy to be given a ride.

It was tricky to open the gate while holding Frank, but I managed and took him to his pond. I put him at the head of the ramp. "I've got a nice bowl of veggies for you when you want it. Just come to the back door."

Frank had an expression of bliss as he pushed himself down the ramp and into the water. I dusted off my hands and went back out front. Frank had obviously dug under the fence again. I'd have to check for the spot and fix it later.

The sheriff was waiting with a skeptical expression. "You didn't really know what he wanted, right?"

I glowered. "Yes."

"Uh-huh. What kind of turtle is that, anyway? I mean... is it legal to keep something like that as a pet?"

This asshole. I planted my bare feet and crossed my arms over my chest, giving him my dirtiest look. "Frank is a sulcatas, an African *tortoise*, and, yes, they're legal. People unfortunately import them to sell as exotic pets. Frank was stuck in the tiny, sunny window of a reptile shop in California for twenty awful years until they closed. Now he has a home here for as long as he lives which, hopefully, will be a lot longer than you."

"Hey!" the sheriff said, offended.

It wasn't much of an insult since sulcatas lived over eighty years, but I wasn't gonna tell the sheriff that. "Can we get back to why it is you're here? I have a lot to do today." I knew I was being rude. But my home was my sanctuary, and I didn't like strangers invading it.

He straightened his spine, his expression neutral. "Of course, Mr. Russo. It's.... There's a dog. Over by Sentinel Rocks in the park. We tried to get him, but we couldn't."

Seriously? "Yeah, I'm not a dogcatcher. There's a county number for that."

"I know. But they can't come today, and this is urgent. This dog... he's part of an investigation. His owner appears to have been murdered. We think he was out jogging with the dog when it happened. Now the dog is hanging around the... the crime scene area. Possibly disturbing evidence. We can't just leave him out there. But he won't let anyone get close."

A bad feeling washed through me—heavy and sour.

Murder.

The dog's owner had been murdered, and maybe right in front of him.

Had it been bloody? Had it been violent and awful? Well, hell, wasn't that the definition of murder?

I got a flare of a vision in my head from the sheriff —*rain, darkness, violence, the flash of a knife*. It was like a firework bursting in my brain. Then it was, thankfully, gone. I shivered. God.

Was that from the murder or something else this man had done? Or was my imagination playing tricks on me?

Probably my imagination.

"Mr. Russo?" the sheriff prompted, worried and staring at me.

Right. The dog. The pup could be wounded. Any dog would try to fight off his owner's attacker. He needed to be brought to safety, and he needed to see a vet. I guarded my heart against new animals—because, God knew, I'd have a hundred living in my house if I didn't. But this hit me deep in the feels. Ugh. The poor dog.

"So if you think you could help?" the cop pushed.

His jaw tightened. "The sheriff's office can pay for your time, if that's what it takes."

Did he honestly think that money was what it took for me to give a shit? God. This was an animal in distress.

"Stay here, *officer*," I said flatly. "I'll get my shoes."

Chapter Five

Gabriel

I STARED at the closed door in shock.

The fuck?

Did the cute dog whisperer with the curtain of long dark hair and the pillow soft lips just shut the door in my face and tell me to wait?

I didn't have *time* to wait; I had a to-do list as long as my arm, from talking to the ISB, who still hadn't shown up, to asking questions around town. But no, I'd been told to stand outside and wait like some kind of doorstep salesperson. I raised my hand to knock, but thought better of it, because I wasn't sure why I wanted him to hurry.

Was it so I could get on with my day? Or was it

because he was gorgeous and for the first time in a long time, I'd noticed a man in that way?

"I don't have time for this." Tense with the need to do something, I checked my private emails, a ton of junk mail sat there mocking me, but there was one important message forwarded from Sam to me, and it originated from the veterinarian in Forks—Thompson Cabins had an outstanding invoice to pay on medication for one of the family horses. The message that Sam had added to it for my attention was succinct.

Your turn to pay.

I'd always loved our horses—Blue had been mine, had been since I was old enough to ride—but he'd passed when I was eighteen, and I missed him. I missed riding.

I missed a lot of things.

The family company—Thompson Cabins—stabled five horses, four for the tourist trail rides, and Eben; Sam's horse. I was more than happy to cover all costs. In fact, a third of my salary automatically deposited into the family business account and had done since I'd moved away, even when undercover. I couldn't be there in person for the people I loved, but I wanted to help as much as I could.

Not that it counted in the long run when all Sam wanted was for me to be there.

"On it," I read out as I typed a reply. Should I sign off with love, or a line asking if we could talk about if I could help with the business? I stared at the screen for so long my eyes blurred. Shaking off the melancholy, I logged into my phone banking app and sent the veterinarian more than enough to cover this bill and many more.

It didn't make me feel like a better brother, but it made me feel as if I was doing *something*.

My phone vibrated, and I answered as soon as I saw it was Hen. Given she was calling and not contacting me via radio, I assumed this wasn't an official call. Maybe she'd be able to talk me off the cliff with my reaction to the cute, sockless man with the wide dark eyes and the hair so black it shone, because today I was locked into irrational mode due to lack of coffee.

"What's up—"

"I'm sending you a link," Hen said without preamble. "Damn fool idiot has uploaded it."

By damn fool idiot, she could have meant any of the many people that fit her assessment. From One-Eyed Jack, who she said flirted with her, to Darren in the garage who refused to listen to her advice; they were all fools not worth her time. Only this sounded way more serious than just her low-level irritation with those who messed with her day. She was angry, and the last time that happened I didn't get muffins for three entire days.

"Who did what now?" I stepped away from Tiber's porch and picked my way toward my SUV, taking special care not to step on any random animals that might be loose in the yard. The place was a mess of big-leafed plants, in pots and beds, and there could be anything lurking under there.

"Our resident Bigfoot hunter has uploaded what he claims is evidence of a sighting to his social media."

I froze and ran her words back to make sure I'd heard correct. "What evidence? What sighting?" My chest tightened. I'd questioned Hillesden as a potential material witness, taken both plaster casts into custody, and he'd even handed over of his own volition the video he'd taken where he found the alleged footprint. Part of me had hoped he'd caught an image of the army or people who'd left footprints at the scene, or even that he incriminated himself. Still, it didn't even look that close to Sentinel Rocks. It was nothing more than Hillesden limping around, crunching twigs and squelching mud and gesticulating at the shadows, at the mess of nothing he swore was a print. Of course, his handing it over didn't mean he hadn't already backed it to the cloud, but that wasn't anything I could control, and there was nothing on the video that made my day any easier. I'd had no grounds to keep him, and after a few hours of questioning, he'd headed back to the hotel with a caution not to leave town. What had I missed?

"I've sent you a link," Hen said, and then ended the call.

I opened my email and clicked the link. The video began with Hillesden talking to the camera, light blue drapes behind him, and there was nothing of the mad-eyed conspiracy guy I'd met by the site. Here he could have been any businessman about to conduct a meeting, his smile welcoming, his tone smooth, and when he talked through his theories about what he'd thought he'd seen, he spoke with conviction. Jesus, by the time the video he'd taken had started, I'd almost fallen under his spell, and the shaky footage jarred me back to the here and now.

He was clever.

It was the same footage I had and it seemed to have been taken between me getting the call to the rocks and then meeting Abby at the gate.

Every so often he'd paused the recording, and used something to draw shapes to show what he'd seen. There was a rough footprint outline around the mud and he spoke about ridges and toes and then, worse, he'd outlined a blurry shape on the film and suggested we all look *real hard* and draw our own conclusions. His suggestion was that an unknown ape-like figure had murdered someone and that tomorrow he'd reveal everything. Fuck. He mentioned a freaking murder in a national park. That would make it easier for people to connect whatever he said to Prophet. The video presentation finished with a call to like and follow, and then an official-looking logo appeared that was very similar to the one used by national parks. Using that logo offered the suggestion that he was legitimate, and that this was a primary source. The one saving grace of the entire mess was that he hadn't given out a location, but he definitely teased it in what he called his explosive follow-up post about the murder and the evidence that was dropping tomorrow.

Fuck.

I blinked at my phone, and then replayed the video, turning down the rousing narration until it was a dull murmur, and instead focused on the images he'd highlighted in the strategic pauses. He was manipulating what he'd filmed to suggest other things, but it didn't matter if all of this was a lie—he already had twelve thousand views and it had only been posted an hour ago. I refreshed the screen—two hundred more, and the comments…

Who wants to go hunting!

I told you it was real!

Oh. My. God!

Where is this? It spooky and shadowed, and it's raining!

I connected with Hen, this time over the radio where everything was recorded. "Sheriff to Dispatch."

"Copy."

"We have a situation."

"Go ahead."

"It's possible we'll have an influx of…" Of what? Conspiracy types, media, college kids? "…people. We might need to request ISB to provide additional security for the crime scene and keep the rangers involved." It wasn't as if the sheriff's office, being as it was just me and Devin, could do crowd control, even with help from park rangers Abby and Rowen. What else could I do to keep the site secure against anyone motivated to visit Prophet if Hillesden revealed the name? I imagined a horde traipsing all over the scene, down to the lake, into the trees. What if they got to the dog first?

"Copy, Sheriff."

What was taking Dr. Doolittle so long? I spun back to the house and came face-to-face with Tiber, who'd ninja'd his way to stand right behind me. I stumbled, righted myself, and through all of that he considered me with the softest brown eyes I'd ever seen, framed with inky black lashes. His cheekbones were a thing of beauty, his lips pressed into a line as if he were judging me and finding me wanting, and the way he stared at me left me feeling blindsided. His long dark hair and the beautiful warmth of his skin spoke of his heritage, and I wondered if he was Makah, or if it was some other first nation tribe that had gifted him with a face that drew me in and made me think things I shouldn't.

"You okay there, sheriff?" Tiber asked, and raised an eyebrow.

I was staring, there was no defense. He tilted his head a little as if he was studying me.

"It's vital we get the dog," I blurted.

He continued to stare at me, and my face burned. He

couldn't know I was judging him by his looks, or that he was shorter than me and would fit under my arm just right, or that—

"We should go then." He gestured to the car, and I noticed his hands were empty. Shouldn't he have equipment? One of those poles with the rope? I'd seen the animal catchers in the city round up whole groups of dogs—packs—using those, and fighting to get them into trucks.

"Don't you need uhm, *tools*?" I couldn't think of the word, and his careful staring turned to a frown.

"Like?"

"One of those neck things?" I pointed to my neck, because of course I did.

His lips thinned again. "I have what I need." He reached into his pocket and showed me a leash and a small bag of something.

"That's it?"

"What else do you think I need? A cage? A tranquilizer gun? You want me to build a pit with sharp sticks?" Each word was harsher than the one before, and I could see temper flare in his eyes.

"No. Of course we don't want the dog hurt, but—"

"Then assume I know what I'm doing, sheriff." He stood his ground.

I glanced from him to the yard where the tortoise had been placed, and back to his house, wondering how to catalog all of this in my thoughts. The temper hadn't come to anything, but the emotion was there in the way he kept his gaze steady on me.

"Sure." That was about all I could say as he slipped around me and headed to the passenger side, waiting for me to unlock the car. Then he climbed up, drew the belt over his chest and then said nothing as I left his place and headed past town to Lake Prophet.

Chapter Six

Tiber

THE CAR RIDE WAS AWKWARD. To avoid looking at the cop, I studied the car.

So this was the inside of a sheriff's SUV. Huh.

The interior was dark gray. Leather upholstery. Mega sturdy dash. A wire mesh barrier was behind me, between the front seat and the rear. A large flashlight was clipped under the dash on my side. It took effort to avoid it with my long-ass legs. The police radio was built-in with a small black handset hooked to the front. There was a big switch to turn it on and off.

When we'd gotten into the car, Sheriff Thompson had used that handset to tell someone he'd picked me up and was taking me to Sentinel Rocks.

Sentinel Rocks? Was that the crime scene? That was

in the national park. A murder in a national park. Sounded funky. Not that any murder wasn't funky.

A loose dog in a national park was also bad news. They had strict leash laws, which was one reason I rarely took my pack over there. My guys had three different speeds and, while I could handle them all on leash together, it wasn't much fun for any of us.

There was nothing else to see in the car so, to avoid checking out the guy not two feet from me, a guy whose woodsy smell tickled my nose, I shifted in my seat and stared out of the window. The drizzle had started up again, and the pine trees, ferns, and lush vegetation rolling by had that heightened green of wet foliage. The sky was now overcast and a sickly bone-white. Gloomy. It fit the task at hand. I shivered.

Being involved in a murder had not been on my agenda for the day. At all. I thought of the crow that had come to my window that morning.

Thanks for the warning.

Out of my peripheral vision, I saw the sheriff turn up the heat. He cleared his throat. "So…. You said you're an animal behaviorist?"

I gave him a sideways glance and stared back out of the window. "That's what it says on my master's degree."

"Is that sort of like zoology?"

"It's a specialization that includes both psychology and zoology courses."

"Huh. I didn't know that was a thing. Or that we had an animal behaviorist in Prophet."

What was I supposed to say to that? Sorry for your ignorance? But I hadn't forgotten all my manners. "Well, I've only lived here about a year."

"Ah." He nodded. "I got your name from Abby. She's a park ranger, said you helped Ana Ainsley with her cat."

"Yes." I didn't know this Abby person, but I remembered Ana Ainsley and the black feline with golden eyes. Unfortunately, she had a stomach tumor the vet had not diagnosed. When I'd told Ana what was wrong, she'd taken the cat to a different vet who'd found the tumor. But not in time to save Sheba.

"So you think you can get this dog?" the sheriff asked.

"I have no idea until I see him. Or her."

"Oh."

The sheriff fell silent. I got glimpses of the lake through the trees on the right. It looked gray and foreboding today, rough with little whitecaps. So much for June in Prophet.

"It's a yellow lab. Male," the sheriff said. "Does that matter?"

"Yes." I hesitated. I didn't want to engage in conversation. Not with the guy so masculine and so... present, just to my left. It had been a long time since I'd been this close to another human being, let alone a man who wasn't old or whatever. But there were things it would be useful to know. "You said the dog's owner was murdered?"

"All evidence points to that." The sheriff's tone darkened. Sadness? Anger? I glanced at him. There was something else there, too. A tinge of fear or unease in his countenance. I got a flash of intuition again. Whatever this was, whatever he'd seen today? It triggered things for the sheriff that he'd buried. Bad things.

Then his expression shifted to determination, and whatever I thought I'd read there vanished. Probably, I'd imagined it. It was none of my business, anyway.

"There's a lot we need to confirm as part of our investigation," he said, "but it looks like the victim was out jogging with his dog. This dog. The yellow lab. And he was attacked. Dog stuck by him, I guess."

As dogs do.

"What's his name?" I asked.

"The vic? I'm not sure I should release that—"

"The *dog*."

He blinked. "Oh. I have no idea."

Because the dog was obviously not important. It was just *the* dog. *The* yellow lab. I pushed down my irritation. "What was the owner like? Young? Old?"

"Thirties. He is—*was*—a park ranger."

So a healthy young outdoorsman out jogging with his dog.

He likely did that often. Maybe daily. Labs were outdoor dogs too, and they needed a lot of exercise. He'd gotten that breed for a reason. Bet they spent a lot of time together. Running. Hiking. Camping They'd have been close. The throb of empathy I'd felt for the dog echoed again in my chest.

Outings with a man and his dog were supposed to be joyous. They weren't supposed to end this way.

We were on the main road that circled the lake. The sheriff turned right onto an unmarked gravel road, probably a logging road. We approached a gate, and he got out of the car to open it. I was thinking about the dog, mind distracted. But I caught myself watching the cop as he swung the gate open.

Traitorous eyes.

The sheriff had a good body. Strong. Fit.

Think about the fucking dog. I shifted my gaze to the trees.

Sheriff Thompson got back into the car and drove through the gate. He stopped to shut it behind us. Seemed overkill to me since we'd be leaving this way, I assumed. But maybe he wanted to be sure no one else came in. It made me think of secret things, of dark deeds that had to be hidden. Of murder.

Once he was back in the car, he proceeded down the gravel road.

He cleared his throat. "So. The dog might have witnessed the murder."

No shit. My stomach gave a sickening lurch.

"As my deputy pointed out, he's kind of a witness. The dog, I mean."

I said nothing.

"Too bad dogs can't talk."

His tone was complex. He was upset. Angry about the murder. But that last bit was doubtful and yet leading at the same time.

Ugh. People. Their motives were never straightforward. There was always a hidden agenda.

"Yeah. That is too bad," I said flatly.

He was fishing, and I wasn't gonna take the bait. I could tell he was the type who wouldn't believe anything I said anyway. Like, he wanted me to say *oh, I can talk to dogs!* Just so he could scoff.

Fuck you, but no.

The rest of the drive passed in silence.

The logging road climbed to a ridge above the lake. I'd hiked this part of the Olympic National Park a lot, being so close to it. And I'd taken the trail to Sentinel Rocks a half dozen times. I was naturally drawn to it since it had a history as a Native American ceremonial site. But it was a three-mile hike in from the trailhead. I'd never realized there was a forest road on the ridge that could provide a shortcut.

The sheriff turned the SUV onto a rocky track and downhill we went. I saw Sentinel Rocks out of the front window as I braced my hand on the dash. Approaching it from this direction was a new vantage point. Two tall, vertical stones stood alone in a natural clearing on the edge of the gray-blue, white capped lake. The trees formed a semi-circle around the stones, creating a natural stage. Beyond the trees, the still-white peaks of the Olympic mountain range were visible.

It was breathtaking, no doubt. But I felt a dark energy here—maybe because of what the sheriff had told me, and the yellow crime scene tape stretched around the clearing. But I didn't see a body. Thank God. They must have moved it already. A uniformed officer stood to one side, waiting for us.

As we drew closer, I saw the dog. A yellow lab lying between the two stones, perfectly still, and I could tell there was something wrong. If a posture could be desolate, his was.

Sheriff Thompson stopped the SUV, and I hopped out. He started to say something, but I ignored him. I ducked under the crime scene tape and took a careful step towards the dog. To my ears, I was silent, but the dog's head raised and he stared right at me. He got up and trotted into the trees.

"For f—er, pity's sake!" Sheriff Thompson said, and I thought he was angry with me, but apparently his ire was for the officer. "You let him lay *there*?"

"I tried to stop him," said the other cop, who looked to be in his early twenties. "But he was determined. I thought maybe I could grab him there, but he just takes off if I get anywhere near. And the evidence team was done, so I didn't think it was that vital to keep him out."

"That's where his owner was found." I said, looking at the two stones. It wasn't a question. Duke had told me loud and clear.

"Yes," the sheriff sighed.

I glanced at the two men. "Look, can you go stand by the car? Just give me some space."

The sheriff stared into my eyes, his mouth twisted with skepticism, then he glanced at the stones. He clearly didn't like it. What had he said on the stoop? Something about the dog messing with evidence. Because that was the important thing. I narrowed my eyes at him. "Do you want me to get the dog or not?"

"Fine," he blurted. "But try not to touch anything you don't need to touch."

He stalked away and the younger cop followed him, repeating his excuses about the dog.

"If you could be quiet, that'd be great!" I called after them. They shut up.

I walked to the stones.

The dog had been out here since the previous night. He'd be hungry. But he was mourning—and traumatized. Labs didn't run away from people like this, not without a hell of a reason. He probably wouldn't even eat if I put a steak in front of him. I'd brought some cooked chicken in a baggie in my pocket, but I didn't get it out. Instead I removed the leash I'd put in there too. I'd noticed the dog wore a harness. I could clip onto it if I could get close enough.

But I wasn't gonna chase the dog. Chasing a lab was like trying to grab a greased pig. Fool's errand. And I wouldn't risk traumatizing him further.

I stepped with care up to the two stones. I didn't want to look, but I did. To my relief there wasn't a huge pool of sticky blood in the grass. No blood on the stones either that I could see. The area just under the stones was more dirt than grass. There were a few small dark stains and footprints.

Oh, right. Footprints. I glanced down at my shoes. But hadn't the young officer said the evidence team had been here already? Oh well. Too late now. Anyway, that was the sheriff's problem. Mine was the dog.

I sank to my knees beside the stones and sat back on my heels. I lay the leash next to my leg, took a deep breath, and lowered my head.

Just breathe.

I placed my hands palm-up on my thighs. I kept my gaze on the ground. I thought about the lake, the lapping water. I thought about the sky.

There was one place on earth that dog wanted to be, and that was right here—the last place his owner had been. The owner's smell would be strong and that dog would lie there from now until kingdom come if he were allowed to. Poor thing.

Maybe if I was quiet enough.... If those louts over by the SUV would stay still and leave me alone for long enough....

A gust of wind sent spots of rain onto my face. My olive-green raincoat had a hood, but putting it up would only worry the dog, so I left it down. He would judge me by my face, my posture. Dogs were remarkably adept at reading people. Hell, they'd survived for centuries as our companions by reading us. Every nuance of our faces, our eyes.

They were better at reading *me* than I was at reading them.

I thought about the dog. Had to block out the fear and horror of what had happened. Right *here.* God. But no. Block that out. Let in the compassion, the sympathy. Heart heavy and full.

I didn't hear the dog approach, but I heard his quiet panting.

I raised my eyes without moving my head. A yellow lab stood two feet away staring at me. His panting was a sign of anxiety, not heat or exertion. His body was tense, poised to bolt. His eyes were terrified. He was young, maybe three, male, and in excellent condition.

He'd been loved.

He'd been shattered.

The dog stared at me, willing me oh so very, *very* hard to go away so he could be where he wanted to be— lying between the stones.

"Good boy," I said, so quiet I barely heard it myself.

Still, the dog's posture grew even more tense as he leaned back.

I lowered my eyes and said nothing more. I forced myself to relax.

I sensed rather than saw the dog trot away. But a few minutes later he was back. A little closer this time. I waited. Breathed. Tried to generate calm.

Maybe ten minutes passed. Maybe twenty. At last I heard the dog sniffing close to me. Sniffing the ground.

I raised my eyes. The dog stared at me, still tense, but close enough to touch. God, those eyes! So bleak. He stared at me as if the slightest twitch would send him bolting.

I didn't move.

I made a loud sighing sound, for his benefit, and settled deep into my repose. *I'm not worried about you*, the sigh said. *You don't need to worry about me.*

We're all just chilling here.

Another moment passed. The dog lay down between the stones. His back paws didn't touch my leg, but they were only a hair away. It amazed me how dogs can judge that sort of thing. They never ceased to astonish me.

I waited a few minutes longer. Then I picked up the leash and clipped it to his harness.

We got the dog into the backseat of the SUV. He was

unhappy to be leashed, but he didn't fight hard. Poor thing was exhausted and maybe even relieved to be told what to do again, to have someone else take charge. The world must suddenly be a very confusing place.

He stared out of the back window as the sheriff drove the SUV away from Sentinel Rocks, back up the rocky track toward the ridge road. I sat in the backseat with him, one arm spread toward the dog in case he wanted to touch me. But he was alert and ignoring me now, whining anxiously as he saw the last place he'd been with his owner recede.

There was a tag on his harness, face-up.

"Duke," I said.

"What?" Sheriff Thompson gazed at me in the rear-view mirror. He'd been quiet since I'd gotten the dog.

"His tag. It says his name is Duke Bressett. I'm assuming that Bressett was the name of the park ranger?"

The sheriff didn't answer that. He didn't have to.

Another small data point. When owners gave the dog their own last names on their tags it meant something. Not a lot, but something. Family.

The SUV climbed onto the ridge road and Duke gave an anxious pant-bark, then curled into a ball as close to the door as he could get. He tucked his nose under his legs. Tremors shook his body.

I wanted to touch him, comfort him. But Duke

didn't know me from Adam. It wasn't my place, not now.

"That was…" The sheriff hesitated. I met his gaze in the mirror. "… really good," he finished.

I said nothing.

"How did you know to do that?"

"The fairies told me," I said, just to be obstinate.

He cocked one eyebrow, a tiny hint of a smile at one side of his mouth. "Seriously. Is that something you can train others to do?"

This guy. Sure. Maybe if you'd grown up hanging out at your parents' vet clinic your entire life, then gotten an advanced degree specializing in animal behavior, and then worked with private clients for five years. Not to mention being a certified—or, rather, *certifiable*—empath. Easy-peasy.

Then again, it all seemed so obvious to me. It was more baffling why anyone couldn't do it. Did they not have fucking eyes?

But if anyone *could* do it, I'd be out of work. So there was that.

I gave the sheriff a dirty look. "No."

He bit his upper lip, probably to hold back a nasty reply. No—a smile. That was surprising. He drove on.

We reached the gate. He got out and opened it, drove us out, closed it.

"It's okay, Duke," I kept my tone soft when Duke

raised his head, anxious to see what was going on. He panted.

When the vehicle started moving again, he tucked his head back under his leg.

"So..." the sheriff began after pulling onto 110, "do you think Duke saw what happened?"

"Yes." I looked at Duke's pale yellow back and felt a throb of his anguish. "He saw it."

The cop hesitated, then expelled a frustrated breath. "Okay, so... this is a stupid question but...is there any way he can give us any information at all? About what happened? Anything?"

He sounded like he hated to even ask, but felt he had to. I wasn't in the mood to humor a skeptic. Or anyone, really.

"He could tell us a lot," I said and probably sounded sharper than I should have.

"Like what?"

"Like the killer, for one thing."

"Really?" His hazel gaze met mine in the mirror, one hundred percent doubtful.

"If we happened to run into him—or her. Absolutely."

"*Shit*," the cop breathed, sounding impressed.

"Just one problem."

The cop again met my gaze in the mirror, eyebrows raised.

"Duke is traumatized. Very. He needs to be checked

over by a vet. But my guess is he's okay physically. Emotionally, not at all. He needs time. Maybe a lot of time. He's not going to be going anywhere, or telling us much of anything, in this state."

The sheriff's face fell. "I ... I don't know who will be responsible for the dog. If the, er, vic, had relatives or whatever. We know he lived alone, but we haven't yet figured out the rest."

"If there is someone, someone else the dog is close to, that would be best."

"Right."

It was on the tip of my tongue to offer to take Duke if he had no one else. But I didn't say it. I had a full house. Besides, it *would* be better for Duke if he could be with someone he knew, someone to mourn with. If he could be at home, on familiar ground, with familiar smells.

Would it? Or would that only remind Duke that his beloved owner was gone?

I honestly didn't know. It would depend on Duke and who else might be there to comfort him. Maybe his owner had a girlfriend. A brother. Someone Duke loved too.

"I'll take the dog to the vet then. Should I drop you off first?" the sheriff asked.

"Yes. Please."

The rest of the drive home was silent. I couldn't resist laying a hand on Duke's back to offer him a little warmth. He didn't shy away or twitch in irritation, so I left it there. Maybe he was too lost in his misery to be comforted by it, but it comforted me.

When the sheriff pulled up in front of my house, he had to get out to let me out of the back. There were no handles on my side. Right. Criminals. I said goodbye to Duke, but he didn't raise his head. I shut the door.

"Well. Thank you," the sheriff said. It had started to rain again, and he stood there in it as if it were nothing. He was a Pacific Northwest native, then. "You can, uh, bill the sheriff's department for your time."

"I didn't do it for you."

I turned and stalked to my door. I didn't like the way my heart seemed to stretch behind me like a rubber band, as if it had gotten hooked on something in that car.

The dog. Definitely the dog.

Chapter Seven

Gabriel

I HAD A CAT ONCE, a tabby called Wolf. It wasn't just my cat—it belonged to me *and* my brother Sam, as much as a cat can belong to a person. Full of sass, Wolf ruled our house, lying in wait for us, stealing stuff, knocking ornaments off shelves in the dead of night, leaving half a mouse in our shoes, and worse.

We were never in doubt that he was in charge of *us*.

Until July 4th every year, when he would go into what Sam called his terror zone. Fireworks made Wolf go mad with fear, and he would disappear behind the sofa and not come out for days. Terrified and shaking, he was safe hidden by the leather sectional, and when he did finally come back out, he was right back into being a little shit.

I loved that cat.

In hindsight, I understand now that Wolf probably stayed there to process his fears away from us, to get back to where he could trust the world again, but also he never wanted to show us his scared side. He'd been such a haughty cat, and he never let us comfort him, and remained an enigma until the day he died, aged nineteen and still sassy as hell.

I wonder how Duke would process what *he'd* seen, and whether Tiber could get better results than the vet. He was shaking now as Johan, the town's vet, examined him with gentle care. Even to get close to Duke, he'd had to sit on the floor next to him, and Duke wasn't happy about the room, or me, or the vet, or indeed anything. Just like Wolf behind the sofa, he was looking for somewhere to hide, and in this sterile room, the only thing he could do was face the wall and push his muzzle to the corner. He rocked that whole if-I-can't-see-you-then-you're-not-here vibe.

"How is he?" I asked when Johan sidled away after one more reassuring stroke through Duke's silky fur.

"There's no injury that immediately presents itself, no pain when I check his limbs."

"But he's refusing the treat you offered him, and he's visibly shaking."

"Physically he appears fine, mentally not so much." Johan clambered to his feet and leaned on the metal examination table, glancing back when Duke whimpered. "He's ripped a dew claw, and there's been bleeding, but there's no telling when he did that, only that it was recent. In all other respects, he's clearly a well-loved dog."

"And can you care for him here at the vets?"

He shot me a glance. "We don't have boarding— he's better off with a family member, or someone that loved him, a roommate, or partner?"

"Okay, I'll ask Abby who Mike might have had in his life."

"We'll keep him here to monitor him for the rest of the day, but other than that... I'm sorry."

I glanced over at Duke, who was still nose-first in the corner. "Yeah, I know." It wasn't *my* responsibility to find my maybe-witness a new home, but it was my responsibility to focus on the fact that the dog was all the case had right now, and he might be our only lead. My radio crackled, and Duke went to the floor, curling into the corner as if it could swallow him. I stepped outside the room and pulled the door shut as quietly as I could. I was less used to subtlety and more to action, but even I could see that my radio was upsetting Duke.

"Go ahead Dispatch."

"I have an ISB callback for you."

"Copy. I'll be there in ten. Did they say—"

"Best you come back for that one," Hen interrupted, which didn't bode well.

"Will do."

Back in my office, I had a short conversation with ISB, who were frustrated they didn't have personnel to cover this case. There was some big stand-off with a right-wing militia group in Idaho, and they'd used all their available resources. Officer Conley, apologetic to the nth degree, wondered out loud about contacting other federal agencies, and listed them all before suggesting that I take the point on the case until they could get out to me.

Maybe a day, he said.

Two at the latest.

For a moment I panicked, which was just stupid. There was nothing happening here that I couldn't handle, and that I hadn't seen before. Okay, there'd been no sacred site in the LA crimes I'd attended unless people counted Grauman's Chinese Theatre as sacred, but it was a murder, there was a scene, and now I needed suspects.

Simple.

"They're not sending anyone out then?" Hen asked as she collated reports with vigor. I don't know what the paper had done to her, but she was putting her entire body weight into pushing the hole puncher down.

"There's an ongoing situation in Idaho, and it's taken all their homicide team resources."

She sighed and clipped the file shut before placing it in her immaculate and color coded filing system. "Okay, so what comes next?"

The familiar thrill of a puzzle that needed solving was at war with the nagging doubts of whether I was ready to handle a murder, particularly one presenting with a side order of potential ritual with the carved X. I knew what I *had* to do—create a board, start talking to people—the priority being Hillesden and his social media blast. He was already suspect number one—had he killed Mike and arranged him in the middle of the stones? Had he done that to suggest his version of Bigfoot was intelligent enough to employ symbolism in a kill? I knew there were a million things out there that I could never see, or understand, but the concept of a community of vast ape-like creatures living outside town, involved in ritualistic killing, was a step too far for me into the world of kook.

"First stop, Hillesden," I didn't have to expand for Hen to nod. "We need to shut him down."

"Take this then, and try not to hit him." She handed me a coffee in a go-cup.

"I won't hit him," I denied.

"But you want to," she poked.

"Nah, he's harmless enough."

"'Harmless', apart from encouraging hordes of people to descend on our town by making it Bigfoot central. I know he didn't mention Prophet by name, but sure as eggs are eggs that will be in the video he's promising tonight."

"I'm heading to the hotel now, and I'll get him to

shut it down. Call down to Devin and get a status update on the scene. If the analysts have cleared it, I want him back here to follow up on our victim's interactions around town, specifically the fact that Abby said her new ranger was already out there doing random things voluntarily. She mentioned trouble with campers. I should supervise, but there's only one of me, and he's got to run with this."

"He'll be okay."

"Hillesden is top of my list," I confirmed. "Did we get anything useful back on the video, like a time stamp, to give us an idea of Hillesden's location?"

"All it proves so far is that it was after the death because we were already called to the scene when it was taken."

"So, nothing to cross him off our list."

"Nothing."

I left before she could make me second guess myself. Hillesden wasn't just my first suspect, he was the *only* name on my list—the rest were nebulous suggestions of random hikers, or someone from the Makah rez, plus a few other maybes. Hillesden gave me the strongest case for what little we had to go on, and this was despite the vibe he was one cookie short of a jar.

The first law of investigation is that we don't judge someone after first meeting. Hillesden was wild-eyed, ranting about the existence of monsters in the forest that we didn't understand, but was he a murderer?

I headed out on foot over to the Prophet Hotel, more of a motel, ten small rooms, some sleeping up to six dormitory-style, in a horseshoe shape backing up against the trees, plus a small two-story building where the owner—Daisy Simmonds—lived. The whole place had seen better days, cracked glass, worn wood, and moss on the roof of all but two of the places. Still, hikers used it as an overnight stop, and I know Daisy made a good living.

"Gabriel! Wait up!" My heart sunk—the last thing I wanted to do was talk to someone, outside of pinning Hillesden down and demanding he tell me what the hell he'd been doing, least of all the one man who normally avoided me. I pasted a smile on my face as I turned to face my little brother, who had a similar forced expression on his. It was inevitable that we'd see each other—after all he had stayed in town instead of leaving like me—but I'd be lying if I said I sought him out.

We hadn't talked properly in months, certainly not in detail since I'd come back from the city. He hated the decisions I'd made to leave, the one where I stayed, and the ones where I let the family down.

The weight of secrets I couldn't share was sometimes too much to bear.

"Sam," I acknowledged, my chest tight as all the guilt I held inside tried to escape.

"Lori wants me to tell you that Ezra's back this weekend," Sam said without preamble. Sam's wife Lori was the town's nurse practitioner, and I loved that she'd thought to tell me. She was the kind of person who thought there should be a happy ending for everyone, and chose to ignore the fact that I'd destroyed my connection to my brothers.

"I'd love to see him," I said with no small amount of hope. I was lying, of course, because it would be just as hard to see Ezra as it was Sam after I'd not been here to help either of my brothers deal with the fallout of Dad passing. When it came down to it, I'd chosen work over family *for reasons*, and now I was paying the price, and messing everything up. I'd taken this job for safety and familiarity, but also family.

I'd come back broken, wracked with nightmares and guilt, licking my wounds, and maybe I'd expected to walk right back into their lives, but that wasn't what had happened. I'd tried everything to say sorry, I'd given the best explanation I could, but the darkness inside me showed in the lies I'd had to tell, and Sam had slammed that same door that Lori said was always open, right in my face.

Something had broken—his heart, mine—and all of those years as brothers were gone.

My sacrifice was worth it. I saved lives.

And as a result, I've lost everything.

"Dinner on Friday, six. I'm kinda hoping you can't

make it, but y'know how Lori is all about *family*." That barb hit home so hard I nearly staggered with the force of it.

"Sam, can I just   "

"No more lies," he snapped. "Dinner. Six."

"I'll be there," I said, even if a pity invite his wife had forced him to issue to me wasn't any real invite at all.

Sam muttered something under his breath, which sounded suspiciously like 'fuck's sake'.

I winced. "Sam—"

"Bye." He disappeared around a corner.

I felt eyes on me, and glanced around to see more than one person watching the Thompson brothers cold-as-ice meetup turning fiery. I knew what the town thought—that I'd followed the bright lights and fucked up something so bad I had to come home. Half the town didn't care, the other half wanted to know why I didn't come back, why I'd cut my family off. I stayed quiet, couldn't say a damn thing. I don't know how many times I could say sorry to Sam, and when that didn't work, I tried so damn hard to stay out of his way, but his barbed comment about not really wanting me there made the guilt all that more heavy.

Shoulders back, chin tilted, I carried on to the Prophet Hotel, wondering what gossip was going to make its way around town before sunset. I didn't imagine for one minute it was more newsworthy than a murder, but who knows—people were one hundred percent invested in the sad, sorry story of the Thompson family and how much big brother Gabriel fucked everyone over. Guilt was a familiar feeling, but that wasn't what I needed to be focused on right then, and when I stepped through the door marked *Reception* and found Daisy behind the scarred counter, I had my hat off and my game face on.

"Mrs. Simmonds."

"Sheriff Thompson! What a surprise." She shut the enormous register on her desk with speed. The same one I'd signed in when I'd first gotten to town and spent a sad sixteen days in one of her rooms before the small place I bought had been ready to move into. Familiar posters adorned the walls, advertising hiking and hunting, events such as the Christmas Lights ceremony, which on close inspection was from last year, and an advert for the hotel that called Prophet a *spiritual oasis* and featured its proximity to Sentinel Rocks, *a Native American sacred site.*

Spiritual Oasis my ass.

"I have a couple of things. First, I need to see inside Mr. Michael Bressett's room, and then secondly talk to Mr. Hillesden."

She pursed her lips. "You won't find much in Mike's room. He traveled light."

"Did you know him well?"

"No."

"But you've been inside his room?" Was that before or after Mike had died? Had she potentially contaminated the scene?

"Housekeeping," she said, as if that explained everything.

"I need a key, then I'll lock the door when I leave, meanwhile I'd like you to stay out of the room until scenes of crime can process if they need to."

"Now hang on a minute. Don't you need a warrant for that?"

"Is there something you don't want me to see?" I threw it back at her.

She opened her laptop with force. "I researched this. See, it says here that hotel occupants have an expectation of privacy during their stay in the hotel, under the terms of their contract with the hotel." She glanced up at me. "That would be me."

Great—a keyboard lawyer was just what I didn't need.

"It also says that employees and owners of the hotel don't have the right to consent to a search on a guest's behalf, though someone sharing the room with the client might. That's Supreme Court stuff right there." She pointed at the keyboard with added drama.

"That limited right persisted only as long as Mr. Bressett was in legal occupancy," I said. "Did he pay in advance?"

She sniffed. "It's sad and all, but he owed me a

week. Now he's up and died, and where does that leave me? Can I put in some kind of claim for lost earnings?"

I kept my patience, because… Well, no sheriff wants to end up in prison. "On a separate note from the dying part, Mr. Bressett violated his contractual obligations, so you're not obliged to safeguard his room. So if I could just have the key." *Before I jump over the counter and grab it for myself.* I waited for her to follow the line of reasoning. She *could* push for a search warrant, and that was the route I'd have to go, or she could just hand me the damn key.

"Okay. Okay. But can you tell me how long I've got to keep the room empty? It's killing me to lose the money?"

I held out a hand for the key. "We'll advise you in due course."

She muttered as she passed it over with an expression as if she'd sucked lemons. Then she picked up the old phone next to the register and pressed a number, grimacing at me as she waited for the call to connect. "Mr. Hillesden? Sheriff Thompson is here for you."

I waited for a stream of obscenities from our wannabe hunter, or a no, but the voice at the other end was calm and to the point.

"You can go down, room seven. He's expecting you."

"How long is Mr. Hillesden booked in for?"

She shook her head and this time she gave me one of her smiles that was more cunning than sincere. "You know I can't give out that kind of information, sheriff."

I wanted to point out that her being forthcoming would avoid me digging into what some of her guests got up to, but I didn't have time to issue the faint threat as the door swung open. An entire group entered as one, three men and four women, in long flowing clothes, the entire gaggle reeked of pot and patchouli, and the woman in charge, or at least the one who saw me and considered I needed to be acknowledged, stepped into my space.

Way too much into my personal space.

Her bracelets jangled, her hair a mix of black and purple, her gauzy skirts the same. Her pupils were wide, a cloud of weed followed her, but I stood my ground when she crowded my space and placed her hand on my chest.

"I am Madame Borschski." She simpered.

"Excuse me, I need—"

"Your aura is fascinating!" she exclaimed as she turned to the rest, who all closed up tight on me. "Look at him!" she commanded.

"It's so red!" a tall man in the back exclaimed. I glanced up at him, and he quickly averted his gaze.

"It's purple. Only a fool would think it was red," Madame Borschski corrected him.

"If you say so," the man said, although he sounded less than sure.

"Totally like mauve," some other voice joined in, and there was squabbling at the back of the group.

"I don't—"

She pressed a hand on my chest and breathed in my face. "Purple shows intuition and psychic abilities. Goodness, you have a connection to the spiritual realms." She tilted her head back, shook her long hair and wobbled. I reached for her—she was seventy if she was a day and I didn't want her collapsing at my feet. Then she stared right at me and gripped my arms.

"I've seen you on a battlefield of fire!" she exclaimed with a thick Russian accent, "I've seen you in my former life!" she added, and then shook and dropped her chin before looking up at me. Gone was the madness, and she was serene again.

"She's channeling her spirit guide," someone whispered.

"Told you I've seen her do it before," another voice added.

"It's worth every cent to be here."

"She got the aura wrong," the man who'd suggested red earlier muttered, but another man, tall, balding, and sneering, poked at him, and the man subsided.

Madame Borschski patted my arms and released me. "Friends, we must take our complimentary coffee refills and go meditate on this!" She grabbed a handful of sachets from the collection on the counter and then, in a swift move, Madame Borschski and her whispering entourage vanished through the door they'd arrived from. One of the men in the group held open the door and narrowed his eyes as if he was judging me, but I returned his gaze and he soon vanished after Madame Borschski. Unfortunately, the scent didn't leave. I turned to face Daisy.

"Who was that?"

"Rooms three, two, and nine. Old lady says she's a psychic." Daisy rolled her eyes. "Did you know she's charging two thousand bucks for each of her followers to come with her? Two. Thousand. But she dumped all but one of them in the dormitory room, it's only her and her second-in-charge who have their own rooms. Think of the profit she's making."

"Uh—"

"They're here for the spiritual woo-woo, all about the traces of something when the veil is thin, and Beelzebub walks the earth." Daisy waggled her fingers on her head, which I assumed was her way of signing horns. Who knew with her? "I don't ask questions, when they paid in advance," she said all of that in run-on sentences, and didn't give me a chance to interrupt. "They're harmless," she finished.

They'd been way too close to me, and the mumbo jumbo about auras and the recreational drugs didn't scream hiker to me. I narrowed my eyes at Daisy, who returned my gaze steadily as if butter wouldn't melt, and then when I felt as if I'd warned her just by staring, I headed out of the door, following the cloud of weed and ending up outside Hillesden's room. I knocked, but it was as if he'd been waiting for me, because my knuckles had barely found wood before the door opened and Hillesden was right there, leaning on his crutch in a loose pair of shorts and a T-shirt featuring the Loch Ness monster. He appeared less mad-eyed this morning, calmer, but there was still this edginess to him that got my back up.

"Sheriff? How can I help?"

"Can I come inside?" I asked in all politeness.

"Well, I'm a little busy—"

"This won't take long."

"I'm not..." He peered over my shoulder and then flicked at something on his chest—a body cam. "I'm recording this."

"If you're worried, we can take this chat to the station?"

"No need for that," he said hurriedly. "Please come in, sheriff."

I stepped in; the drapes were shut, but the inside was as bright as daylight, with several lamps illuminating a huge whiteboard, plus recording equipment set up like a studio.

"Sheriff Gabriel Thompson, identifying myself for your camera," I said as I held my ID steady in front of

Hillesden's chest. I'd had film taken of me before, and I'd learned the hard way to measure my words and actions when words are open to manipulation. "I'm making a polite request for you to not identify Prophet in all videos you post to your social media."

He puffed out his chest. "The truth is out there," he stated, probably hoping I'd not mainlined *The X files* as a teenager. "And I refuse to deny the public the evidence they deserve."

"Evidence of exactly what?" I aimed for polite as I edged around the whiteboard to see the things written there. In the middle was a vast family tree of sorts, not following a family name, but more a branch diagram with various words of which I knew one for sure; *Homo sapiens*. This seemed to be an evolutionary path supporting his theories around some missing link hiding out in the woods.

"You know, whatever was out in those woods ripped a man apart and carved ritualistic symbols all over him. I'm telling you, I'm on the cusp of something huge here."

I fought the desire to suggest he was on the edge of losing his shit. After all, things matter to different people in varying degrees and I should channel respect. He'd said something had ripped apart a body, and that wasn't factual. I wondered if he had seen something and was in exaggeration mode, or that he had seen something that wasn't our victim. I needed to be careful about how I treated him, torn between locking his ass away and gently encouraging answers.

"You saw the body?" I asked, as if the answer wouldn't be a pivot point in this conversation.

"Yes, of course, littered by the lake as if lightning had torn it apart. Uhm… Bigfoot prints all over everywhere. It was a family unit, I'm sure."

And there it was, the big lies spilling out that told me he hadn't seen Mike's body.

"You observed a body by the lake? Will I find evidence you were there? Footprints in blood? Fingerprints? Was it you who killed him?"

His swagger disappeared in an instant. "What? Of course you won't—"

"If I suspect you are an important part of my investigation, then I'd need to confiscate your *evidence*, put in an order to have your site and socials pulled down." He couldn't know I didn't have the power to do any of that.

He paused then, paled, seemed to consider his answer with care, and I knew I'd caught him in the lie, but stayed quiet. I'd given him rope, and now he needed to decide whether to double up and hang himself, or retreat. I watched as he turned off his body cam.

"Well, I didn't actually *see* the body," he hedged.

"But you know about the body."

"I heard stuff," he muttered.

"What stuff?" I asked with exaggerated patience.

He glanced down at his feet. "At the ranger station, when someone called it in, and also…"

"Also what?"

"I have a police scanner app, and that's not illegal, right?" *Unfortunately not.* "I didn't mean to listen, but I was right there, and I wouldn't be a good hunter if I didn't listen. Right?"

"But you posted a video that you claim is from the scene."

"Well, not exactly." He whirled in excitement to pick up yet another plaster print. "But I've heard things in town and I have this." He waved it under my nose, but I crossed my arms over my chest, watching as his gaze darted back and forth to the notes and posters he'd attached to the walls, and then I waited. When I didn't answer him, he seemed to be unsure. "My fans expect more information from me."

"My case is currently wide open if you'd like to discuss your legal options in a more formal setting, given you were at the scene."

He went from pleading to grumpy in a second. "This is what the government does!" he exclaimed. "Look at Roswell!"

"Mr. Hillesden," I began with patience, "If you post the location of your *evidence*, exposing this town and the scene to outside interference, then I will have no option left other than to charge you for tampering with an ongoing investigation."

"You can't do that! I know my rights!" Uncertainty tempered his bluster.

"I'm the sheriff, and this is my investigation, and the last thing you need is for me to escalate this to a federal level."

"Well no, of course," he agreed.

"For my records, Mr. Hillesden, could you tell me where you were last night?"

"Why?"

I stared at him. "Are you refusing to answer my question?"

"No. But wait, are you saying I'm under suspicion. Am I? I wasn't... I didn't... I was hunting for the Sasquatch."

"Where and at what time?"

He blinked at me, his cheeks flushed, and I could see the shock. He'd inserted himself into my case, and now he was moving onto my suspect list with every word that left his mouth.

"I don't know specifically."

"Generally, then."

He pursed his lips as if he was thinking hard about his answer, and then he snapped his fingers. "What if I had an original video that would pinpoint where I was that night—actual video dated and timed?"

"More video."

He shifted to his booted foot and winced. "Maybe."

I held out a hand. "Let me have that."

He muttered something but passed me a dongle. "That's my Sasquatch hunting footage. You'll see me doing some front-of-camera."

"I'll take that then."

"I have backups in the cloud, you know."

"Of course you do."

He wrinkled his nose at me before the last of his passionate defense bled away, and he slumped a little.

"So after this I can't post it all?" he asked.

I stared at him, didn't answer him, and he mumbled again, but by this time I was at the door ready to leave.

"I'm assuming we agree that there will be no more videos?" I hoped to hell he didn't call me on all my bullshit.

He narrowed his eyes at me, but the fight had left him, and he nodded.

Only outside did I relax, shoving my hat back on my head and stalking down to the room Mike Bressett had stayed in, slipping on gloves as I did.

I hoped Daisy was wrong and that the moment I opened our victim's door, there would be some overwhelming bit of evidence that led me to a killer. But she wasn't wrong—there were a couple of bags of personal belongings to one side; the bed was neat but slept in, so there went the housekeeping defense, and there were toiletries in the bathroom. I couldn't see the far side of the bed from here, but there was no scent of death in the room.

It just smelled like an old, musty roadside motel.

I observed all of this from the door, then walked into the space. Clothes were neatly folded, a charger plugged into the wall, but no sign of a phone. There'd been no phone with the body, so I added that to my list of *important things*. I opened and closed drawers, had a quick look under the bed... nothing and I'm not sure what crime scene techs could get from this room.

Unless he'd been killed here, and someone had moved him?

Nah. I'd seen enough crime scenes to know this place wasn't the scene of a major crime, and the fact Duke had been out there with him implied he'd been on a run when it happened. I took some photos anyway, just in case.

I glanced around one more time, but this was the room of someone who kept things immaculate. Hell, even his personal toiletries were all lined up in a row. I couldn't see a notebook, a laptop, receipts, notes, not even the jeans draped over the chair gave me any clues. There was a dog bed and a couple of bowls, two toys that I could see just by the bed, and a bag of kibble on the counter. The carpet was an off-cream, stained in places, but the stains were old, no signs of huge amounts of blood, or obvious splatter on the wall, no scent of cleaning products unless you counted whatever made the water pink in the toilet.

If Daisy had been housekeeping, even in the loosest sense, it hadn't compromised everything in here.

I closed the door and locked it, slapping a warning sign there that it should remain unopened. Crime Scene techs could be interested in the space if we got nothing from the site or from the coroner.

I pocketed the key and headed directly to the station. So much for evidence, or a suspect. I doubted that Mr. Hillesden could give me either, and the room wasn't giving much.

I'd almost made it back when my cell vibrated. I answered when I saw it was the veterinarian.

"Sheriff, did you find someone to take Duke?"

"Not yet, can he stay with you for tonight?"

"No can do," he said. "I'm already fostering the puppies that were dumped on my doorstep last week, plus we have a case of kennel cough, and chaos and illness are not the environment Duke needs. I suggest you take him back to Tiber. Do you want me to call him?"

God no. I wanted to do it.

Just because I didn't want to give Tiber a chance to say no.

No other reason; like maybe wanting to see him again.

"No, it's all good. I'll come and collect Duke and take him over."

"Sorry that I couldn't fix this for you."

I dropped the room key in with Hen and added a note to the file about possible storage situations—after all; Mike was moving from another state and had to have more *stuff* than what I'd seen. I was in my car in twenty with a desperately unhappy Duke in my back seat. I was secretly pleased I had the excuse to see Tiber again this soon because his cute self made me feel happy in a hundred unexpected ways.

The way he smiled with caution, the way he couldn't quite meet my gaze at times, but then stared when he thought I wasn't looking, or the way he cared so much for a tortoise as if it were his family—were just a few things. Not to mention the inky hair that fell past his shoulders long and straight and blue-black, or his unfathomable dark eyes that observed everything.

He intrigued me. I wanted to know more.

Right now though, I just hoped that his family had space for one more and he'd take Duke in.

Chapter Eight

Tiber

IT WAS after dinner when the sheriff brought Duke over. He'd texted me, so I was waiting outside on my small front lawn. Better not to subject either of them to the pack while we were doing a hand-off.

He pulled up on the side of the road in front of my house and got out. He nodded a hello and opened the back door. He had to lift Duke out and put him on his feet. Never a good sign.

But Duke walked willingly up the path. I thought maybe he recognized me. His tail was tucked between his legs, and his gaze darted left and right.

"I really appreciate this," the sheriff said, holding out Duke's leash to me.

I took it. "Yeah. No worries." I'd thought about

Duke a lot since the sheriff had dropped me off earlier in the day. I was just as glad Duke would be with someone I trusted—myself.

"Could you get me something of his owner's?" I asked. "The scent would be comforting to Duke. A used item of clothing would be best, like a T-shirt. Or possibly a blanket from the bed."

The sheriff was doubtful. "Uh… not sure. Anything Mi—er, the victim—was wearing when he was attacked is evidence. As for his residence, all property there belongs to his relatives."

My temper flared. "Sure. Let's follow protocol instead of helping a traumatized animal. I'm sure his relatives will want every last scrap that's in his clothes hamper."

The sheriff's face reddened. "I am willing to ask them, if you—"

"Forget it." I didn't have time for this, and Duke didn't need to be made more anxious by hearing us argue. I turned and led Duke into the house. I knew I'd been rude—again—but I didn't have time to feel more than a twinge of guilt because Leo and Ferdinand came running to see the new arrival.

I unclipped Duke's leash so he could respond freely to the other dogs. I wasn't worried since labs aren't aggressive and Leo and Ferdinand were both friendly with other canines. They sniffed around Duke in excitement. Duke held still, but he didn't return their interest. His head remained down and his tail tucked low. After a few moments of tolerating their inspection, he trotted the few feet of front hall into the living room, glanced around, and squeezed himself under the couch.

That was no mean feat. My couch was a mid-century repro that stood a foot off the floor on six wooden legs. It was amazing Duke could get under it, but then, Gracie had hidden there for days when she'd first gotten here, and she was bigger than the lab. All I could see of him was a thick yellow tail sticking out.

Leo started to scoot under the couch. He was not always the best at reading the room. I whistled. When he looked at me, I shook my head. "Come here."

Reluctantly, Leo moved away from the couch.

I crouched down. "All you guys, come here."

My lowered position, more than my words, made the animals come running. Well, the three dogs and Patch, the Calico, came running. God only knew where Fudge the kitten and Renfield the rabbit were. Patch rubbed himself against my leg, anxious to steal attention from the dogs, but I didn't give any of them pets. My expression told them this was serious.

"This is Duke. I need you guys to be gentle with Duke and give him space. Duke is scared. He's had a hard time. Remember when Gracie came to stay with us, and it was important not to be rough with her? Gracie, you know what I mean. I'm counting on you, especially, to be nice to Duke. Gentle, guys. Okay?"

Patch couldn't care less, Ferdinand just wanted a treat, and Leo would need a lot of reminding, but Gracie got it. She laid down a few feet from the couch, put her head on her paws, and stared at that yellow tail. If she'd appointed herself his mentor, that would be great for both of them. Time would tell.

I sighed and stood, placing one bare foot on my other bare calf in my thinking pose. What else could I do for Duke? I wanted to move him to my bedroom, where I could close the door and give him a quiet spot that wasn't so cramped. But I guessed he wouldn't come out from under the couch willingly, and dragging him out would be counterproductive.

I offered him food and water at intervals, but he didn't come out until around ten that night when the smell of chicken became too much to resist. I squatted next to the couch and waved the smell in his direction, coaxing in a quiet voice, and he slithered out on his belly. Gracie watched him intently but didn't try to get closer. I motioned Leo and Ferdinand to stay back. Duke sniffed around the plate and, with the greatest of caution he picked up one strip of chicken between his teeth. In a matter of seconds, he had gulped down every scrap.

How long had it been since he'd eaten? It wouldn't surprise me if he hadn't touched a thing since his owner had been killed. He turned to the bowl of water I put near him and lapped up the entire thing.

"Duke, do you need to go outside?" I asked with an encouraging lilt. "Outside to pee?"

Duke crawled back under the couch on his belly, his back tight against the underside. God, that must be so uncomfortable.

"Duke, want to go to bed? Bedroom? Sleep?" I hoped he'd recognize one of those words and would be interested in a little more space. But he didn't move.

He was trying to hide. The enclosed space made him feel safer. No one could get to him there, he figured. God, what had this poor dog experienced? Whatever it was, he wanted nothing more to do with a world where such things could happen. It would take time for that memory to fade. Time and a lot of love to remind him there were good things in the world, too.

I went out to the garage. I had crates in several sizes. Sometimes they were necessary for moving animals around. I dragged my largest crate into the living room. The bedroom would be a quieter place to set it up, and I could shut out the other animals. But maybe the sound of our daily life, the presence of the other animals who were not in distress, would rouse his curiosity. So I moved a chair and set the crate up under the window in the living room. I draped a blanket over the top, one from my bed so it would smell like my pack, making a dark cave.

"This is Duke's bed," I told the gang, pointing to the crate. "Duke."

Of course, I had to chase Leo out of it a few times. Then Gracie went and laid down in front of the crate to guard it, her head still facing the couch so she could keep an eye on Duke. That made me smile and gush a bit, and I had to give her some love and an extra treat. She was looking out for Duke.

Just as with a kid, information and emotions had a different meaning coming from a peer. As much love as I was willing to give Duke, should he ever let me, I knew Gracie could give him something even more important—a bridge between Duke and our pack.

Duke didn't emerge again until just before midnight. I stayed up later than usual and was watching a documentary on TV with the gang around me—Leo and Fudge snoozing in my lap, Gracie on one side of me, Ferdinand on the other, and Patch lying across the back of the couch. Duke's backside appeared in halting movements as he scooted out. He gave me a quick glance and went over to stand at the sliding door to the deck, panting.

"Good boy, Duke." I disentangled myself and got up to let him out.

Gracie hurried to follow him into the backyard, putting herself between Duke and an over-enthusiastic Leo. I turned the deck light on so I could watch them. Duke raised his leg on a beleaguered bush and then wandered around, skittish and jumping at any hint of a sound. Leo peed where Duke had, just to show he was boss, but Gracie stuck by Duke, keeping a respectful distance.

Duke sniffed the whole back yard, ever tense, and ready to bolt. Was he searching for something? Maybe his owner's scent? Or maybe he wanted to be sure there was no trace of whatever person had terrified him. At the pond, he eyed Frank warily—the large tortoise was sleeping at the top of his ramp, his head and limbs withdrawn into his shell—before moving on.

Eventually he seemed satisfied that the backyard was not a source of danger. He returned to the back door, standing just out of my reach, not looking at me. I had a small plate of chicken ready and Duke's gaze went right to it. He licked his lips, then sat, as if that would be the key to getting the chicken. Offering me behaviors was a good sign. His brain remembered old responses instead of fixating on the trauma.

"Duke has a bed," I said. "Come on I'll show you Duke's bed." I backed away with the chicken and went to the crate. I dumped the cooked chicken onto the pad near the back and moved away. Gracie went to the open door of the crate and looked at Duke. She took a few steps back and waited, tail slowly wagging. Go on. It's okay.

Fuck. I was gonna cry. It reminded me of the suffering Gracie must have endured, locked up in a too-small cage for years to breed puppies that were taken away from her.

No, don't think about that now. That was too heavy and Duke would sense it. I forced it from my head.

Duke approached the crate as if it were a trap, sniffed all around the three sides of it that weren't against the wall, spending extra time sniffing the blanket. Then, hesitantly, he went in. I heard him eat the chicken.

"Good boy. What a good boy. That's Duke's bed," I said softly.

He turned so his head was toward the door, and lay down on the pad. He got it all right.

My heart leaped in the special way it did when I helped an animal. "Good boy. Is that better? You're safe here, Duke."

He refused to look at me and started to shake, so I decided he'd had enough of me for the day. I called the gang, and we went to bed. All except Duke and Gracie. Duke stayed in the crate, and Gracie lay on her side near it but facing away. She was giving Duke space but letting him know she was there.

If only humans were as kind.

———

THE NEXT MORNING, I realized I needed more food. I managed to give everyone breakfast and then headed to town.

The Prophet Mercantile was the closest grocery store, though it wasn't much bigger than a 7-11. One side of the funky old building was stocked with fishing and camping supplies, a display of Bigfoot items, and a few items of clothing. The other side carried enough food to make sure no one in town starved. I shopped there once a week since the Safeway in Clallum Bay was a forty-minute drive, and I didn't like to leave home for that long. Besides, I liked the Mercantile owner. He was one of the few people in town I'd connected with since moving here a year ago.

One-Eyed Jack was at the register checking out a customer when I walked in. He gave me a solemn nod, "Hey bruh."

"Bruh," I said back.

He was ringing someone up, so I didn't linger. I grabbed a basket and started shopping.

One-Eyed Jack called himself that because he wore an eye patch over one eye. Maybe he thought it was funny, maybe he was a big poker fan, or maybe he just preferred to make his disfigurement a badge of honor. I never asked what had happened to that eye, and he'd never volunteered the information.

One-Eyed Jack, aka Jack Ellis, was one of the local Makah tribe. He was probably mid-forties, chubby, copper-skinned, and with his dark hair worn in a buzz cut. The shorn hair showcased the turquoise loop he wore in one ear—the opposite ear from his eye patch.

He had a wife and a few kids. His wife, also Makah, worked the deli in the back, and their little mini-me's were sometimes in the store, though I didn't see them today.

I filled my basket. As usual, eighty percent of the items were for the animals and twenty percent were for me. By the time I got to the counter, I was the only customer in sight. One-Eyed Jack took my basket with a welcoming smile. "Hey, Bruh. Good to see ya. How's it goin'? You doin' all right?"

Since the first day I'd entered the store, One-Eyed Jack had called me Bruh and looked at me a certain way —the way a Native American looked at other Native Americans. Like you were in on the true skinny. Like you knew the lay of the land.

I wasn't sure if One-Eyed Jack thought I was Makah too, or if any Native American was okay in his book, but I felt the same. That was one of the things I loved about Prophet. This far northwest tip of the United States was still heavily tribal, and I felt at home here.

That might sound weird since I'd grown up in the white suburbs of Portland, and I was half Italian. My grandparents on my dad's side had immigrated from Sicily, and they were awesome. I'd take my Grandma Russo's cooking any day of the week. But it was my Navajo heritage from my mom's side that fascinated me. She was half Navajo and half Mexican. Growing up, I'd spent a few weeks every summer with my Navajo grandmother on the rez in Arizona. She'd tried hard to instill an appreciation for our history and culture in me.

Maybe she worked so hard to make me Navajo because that was what she saw when she looked at me. Hell, One-Eyed Jack wasn't the only person in town who'd assumed I was Makah. My appearance was more native than his was.

"I'm good," I told him. "How's the fam?"

"Plenty of trouble, but the good kind. And your zoo?"

"Got a new dog I'm fostering, so I needed supplies."

One-Eyed Jack rang up my large packet of chicken —and, fuck, the sticker shock. He shook his head. "I swear, your animals eat better than I do."

"Oh? I'll tell your wife that when I see her." I glanced toward the deli.

Jack laughed. "You do and I'd have to hurt you, Bruh."

"Fine. Lips sealed." I smiled.

I felt a little giddy at the exchange. God, I was becoming too much of a hermit if a brief exchange at the grocery store felt like a moment. But there it was. Human interaction was rare in my world. And, mostly, I didn't miss it.

Jack finished ringing me up, and I paid with my card. But instead of handing my bag over, he held onto it and looked around as if he wanted to share a secret. He lowered his voice. "Hey. You hear about that murder? Some ranger dude. It's seriously fucked up, man."

"I heard." I didn't mention that was where I'd gotten the dog.

"Could be bad news for the tribe."

"Oh?"

Jack nodded solemnly. "Yeah, Bruh. You know the guy was found at Sentinel Rocks, right? That's sacred Makah land. Major juju. We've had a lawsuit goin' against the US government to get it back for, hell, years now."

I hadn't known that, but I wasn't sure I saw the connection. "So?"

"So I heard the dead guy was a park ranger. Kind of makes it look like the Makah did it. You know? Especially the Bowies, 'cause Charlie is the one behind the lawsuit. And there's Jimmy. Honestly, I can't blame him for thinking the courts will do fuck-all. As if any judge would ever side with us. But, man, I hope Jimmy had nothin' to do with it. Charlie's a good man, and that'd break his heart."

If I were a dog, my ears would have perked straight up. This was important information. Wasn't it? Sheriff Thompson's face swam into my mind.

I leaned in closer. "Jimmy? Which Jimmy do you mean?"

"Jimmy Bowie. Charlie's grandson," One-Eyed Jack said, as if I should know.

"Right. Jimmy's not a fan of park rangers, I take it?"

One-Eyed Jack looked cagey. "Ah, Bruh, you know how it is. People say a lot of things. Some guys talk a big game. Doesn't mean they'd do something like that. Still. It's bad news. Yup. Bad news all the way down." He shook his head, his eyes filled with worry.

It wasn't until I was heading for the door with my groceries that it occurred to me... I liked Jack. I even felt akin to Jack. But in that conversation, my instinct hadn't been to commiserate with him. It had been to get any info that might be useful to Sheriff Thompson.

That made me pause.

But the victim was a park ranger, a man beloved by his Labrador. He didn't deserve to be murdered, and whoever did that needed to fucking be behind bars. Full stop. So if I heard anything, of course I was gonna report it to the police.

I'm not doing it for the sheriff. I'm doing it for Duke, I told myself.

I even *mostly* believed it.

Chapter Nine

Gabriel

AFTER TWO DAYS without ISB arriving, or forensics of any sort, candy was about the only thing that would fix my frustrated inner need for something to do. Despite knowing how long autopsies took, it grated on me that there was always a long waiting game. Without forensics, I had no time of death, no cause... nothing. I needed some of the sweet stuff and it was this impulse to get candy sent me straight to the mercantile and right into Tiber as he exited.

"Sheriff," he murmured and sidestepped, but even doing that, with his hands full of paper bags, he was blocking the doorway, and it was me who needed to step back and open the door wider. When I did, he thanked me with a nod, but that same craving for candy became a hankering to talk to Tiber, and hell, I wasn't an impulsive man, but there was something about Tiber that dug inside me. Maybe he'd want to have a coffee with me, explain about his dogs, and about himself. I should ask him. He'd probably say no.

"Wait," I said as he was opening his car door and placing the bags inside.

He turned as he shut the door. "Can I help you?"

He was suspicious of me, and it hit me I didn't know why I was asking him to wait. Work. It had to be connected to work. Why else was I drawn to talking to him in the middle of the day? "Sheriff? Are you okay? You're not having a stroke or something?"

"No. Duke," I coughed up, and he raised an eyebrow at me. "How did it... how was he... has he slept?"

That was so lame. Sleep? My head was too full of the case, and I couldn't even talk properly. It was a relief to see him, a welcome break from wondering if I had a murderer in my town, but I didn't realize I *needed* to see him until he was right there in front of me. The only connection we had was Duke, but I could have asked something insightful about Tiber's other dogs, or hell, even the tortoise, but no, I went with sleep.

Tiber considered me for a long moment, tucking his long dark hair behind one ear as he narrowed his eyes at me. What did he see, besides an idiot sheriff who'd lost his social skills? I felt as if he was far too intuitive and that he saw more than I wanted him to.

"He's hurting," Tiber said, and I had to recall what I'd asked him. So much for not staring into Tiber's velvet-brown eyes and getting lost in thoughts of maybe hugging him close and burying my face in his hair.

I wanted to do that—lean on him, inhale the scent of him, and… the fuck?

"I'm sorry." I said, and as much as I wanted Duke up and at 'em and chasing down the bad guys, the hurt and sadness in Tiber's expression killed me. His animals were his entire world, and I didn't fit into that universe with my darkness and the stress and being so freaking tired. I hadn't had peace in a long time and maybe I never would.

"Not much else to report," he added when I'd zoned out again. I needed caffeine.

"But you'll let me know."

"I will."

"Okay then."

"Okay then," he responded and then that was it—he was in his car and I was staring at him as he drove away.

"Smooth," I muttered to no one at all. "So fucking smooth."

I stalked inside the store, grabbed my go-to sour fish and headed back to the office, happy to see Devin adding notes to the board. That had to mean we'd found something else, or maybe that by some miracle forensics had come in earlier than we expected.

He glanced back at me on hearing the door, and his gaze fell on my candy. "Sour fish?" he asked, and for someone like him, all gym-fit and young, that was probably shorthand for what-the-fuck-are-you-eating? I pulled out another candy, popped it into my mouth, and then shoved the rest in my pocket.

No one called me on my medicinal use of sour fish, or on the huge mug of black coffee I poured for myself.

"You're late, boss," Hen was way too bright when she came out of the small kitchen.

I smiled anyway. "Had to do stuff."

She nodded as if that made perfect sense, and then she chatted at me, and I slipped into that part of the day where she talked *at* me, and I listened. Hen didn't know it, but listening to her was my way of learning more about the town I'd left, and as if she knew I needed it, she was in fine form today.

There was nothing as valuable in small town policing as the inside story on who'd done what to whom, and there was nothing that slipped past her. But before the important work stuff, she had to get the gossip out of the way first.

"... The mail is delayed again, but I have them doing a special run. Also..." I tuned her out for a moment, waiting for her to get to the good stuff. "... so, I said to Darren that it needed a new cam belt, and I was right. Only then I saw he was blushing and when I asked him what was wrong, he blurted out that he needed one of my special cupcakes, you know the ones with the ribbons, because he's only gone and fallen for someone in town." She paused for dramatic effect, and I sipped at the hot, dark brew as she carried on talking. "…about time that boy was sweet on someone, don't you think? Just like someone else I know, Mr. Lonely Sheriff."

What? I wasn't lonely. I was focused, and healing and not looking at Tiber and thinking how nice it would be to talk to him just to have company…

So I was kind of lonely, but whatever.

"I'm not—"

"So, I wrote the cake order down, but he was all cagey who it was going to, which just makes me think the rumors about him falling for someone his aunt wouldn't approve of are true. I don't know who it could be, but you know how picky Gwen can be about her nephew."

"Sure, I—"

"In other news, the bridge on North Shore Road is still out, which means the loop drive remains impassable. Still. I mean, does the county not realize some people live up there?" she huffed. "Nope they're all about the fact it doesn't impact access to the trailheads, never about how Jeremy and Sandra now have a twenty-mile detour just to get groceries. People are getting restless, and we've had five complaints already this morning, and then—"

"Okay," I interrupted here. "Did anything from forensics come in?"

"Not yet," she gave a sniffy huff at being interrupted, but while she was in huffy mode, I slipped away and tracked down Devin, who was in the incident room staring at the large board with our notes.

"Where are we at with the second video Hillesden gave us, the one that supposedly shows where he was the night of the murder?" I asked Devin, who straightened and went from uncertain rookie to confident in an instant, flicking open his notebook.

"Okay, so, the geo-tagging and timestamp of the Hillesden video puts him five miles from Sentinel Rocks between eight p.m. and midnight. Unfortunately, that is all we got from the video itself, and of course, it doesn't disprove his involvement until we get the full autopsy results back with a better fix on time of death."

I nodded as he took a whiteboard pen and drew a timeline extending four days back from us finding the body, and also one under which was just twenty-four hours. He marked the video times on there and stepped back to check what he'd done. I'd already put my notes under Hillesden's name, and there wasn't much more I could add apart from the man being a little unhinged, but also that his entire purpose was to find validation of his wild theories.

"What does your gut tell you about Hillesden?" I asked Devin.

He frowned at the board and then back at me. Devin would need to learn to listen to his gut—in LA it had been the difference between life and death in way too many situations. I thought Devin had good instincts, that he'd be a fine cop, and I needed to be the mentor he deserved.

"Okay, well, my gut tells me Hillesden has nothing to do with the murder." He glanced at me and I nodded in encouragement. "I think what's actually happened is he's co-opted the crime scene and cross-referenced it with his theories about Bigfoot as clickbait." He glanced at me. "Clickbait is when you—"

"I know what clickbait is Devin, I'm thirty-two, not eighty."

"Sorry, sir," Devin apologized, and I rolled my eyes at him. Next he'd be explaining what the internet was. "So that was the video results," he summarized, and cleared his throat. "Abby suggested that—"

"Abby who?" I poked.

To his credit, he didn't get flustered at me reminding him of the level of information we needed to share. Of course I knew who Abby was, we all did, but the sooner he learned to be specific the better, because if ISB made it here in time to take over I'd need him to be efficient in sharing information.

"Sorry. Senior Ranger Abby Fullerton has confirmed our victim had a run-in with campers at the Green Rocks camping area, and provided us with information, but she says she found cell phone footage that she thinks we'll be interested in. She's not able to transfer it to us, and suggests we head over for…" He checked his notes. "Coffee, crullers, and crime scenes."

"Gallows humor," I remarked when his expression twisted. "We'll head over after this," I confirmed. "Carry on."

"We also have an ongoing court case with Charlie Bowie over the land where the Sentinels stand—I can't see what he'd gain on having a murder there, but I have a call out with Will Abraham from the Makah Tribal police and he's coming back from an event and will be in the office tomorrow morning. Again, we currently have little to take to him, but I suggest some local background on the lawsuit would be good while we wait for forensics."

I nodded. Hell, anything was better than sitting on our asses waiting for things to happen when we had a horrific crime and no killer in custody. We locked the board in the cupboard I'd labeled the situation room—six feet by six with two chairs and the boards; it was a private space for discussion and only myself and Devin had access. Not that we'd needed to discuss much before this event, and this was our first murder board since I'd taken over.

"Also, we had results on that search you did for ritualistic murder, which I read, but Jesus, people are twisted." He shuddered as he handed me a file. "Three matches, Denver, Miami, Phoenix, all bodies left with crosses slashed in their chest, but always oriented like the sign of the cross, with a longer length in the middle of the chest. Certainly no matches to the X we have."

"That's good news, at least. The last thing we want is someone out there on a murder spree and leaving messages."

"Can I ask a question, sir?" Devin sounded cautious.

"Sure."

"Have you ever seen a ritual murder case, or dealt with a serial killer, down in LA?"

Loaded question. "Yeah, I have, and it's not pretty."

"Sure," Devin murmured, but he asked nothing else and instead we headed out for the rangers' station and Abby.

Hen handed me another coffee as we walked past. "A word before you leave, sheriff?" she asked, which put up all kinds of red flags.

I glanced at her and she had that determined expression that meant gossip, and I couldn't help but wish I could walk out and ignore her. Still, it could be useful information at least. Devin stopped by my side, but the way she arched a brow at me suggested this was for my ears only.

What now?

"I'll see you in the car," I said to Devin. It was

telling that Hen waited until he'd left before she leaned over the desk.

"There's been some chatter about you and Tiber Russo," she went straight to the point, and then sat back as if the job was done.

"And?"

She arched her brow again, and I wondered if it could go any higher. "Just chatter."

"About the case?"

"Some."

Exasperated, I leaned over the counter. "Spit it out, Hen"

"Now, this isn't me saying this, but a friend of mine saw you outside the mercantile and suggested your body language was... y'know."

"No. I don't know." I was out there with Tiber not more than twenty minutes ago. How did our casual accidental meetup become town news so fast?

"I don't want to speak out of turn, sheriff..."

"But you will." I wasn't playing her games where she tried to be subtle and I played dumb.

Affronted, she sniffed, but got over herself fast because this was clearly too juicy to ignore. "Tiber lives a long way out because he doesn't like to interact with people much," she said, and again with a dramatic pause. "He's so good with animals, people, not so much, and he's a very sweet man who's been terribly hurt. Joanne thinks he lost someone tragically, and Cindy thinks it's a badly broken heart, but all I know is he's vulnerable. Also, people like him more than you, and he's been around town longer."

"I was born here," I reminded her.

"But you moved away and messed that up," she reminded me right back, and guilt bubbled inside me. "Anyway, should you have relations with that sweet man, then you need to know that the town might not know him well, but they're very protective of him."

"I'm not having... I refuse to... whatever."

I left before she could accuse me of deflowering the town virgin, when all I'd done is talk to the man. Okay, there was staring involved, and also lack of social skills on my side. Despite that, it had been just talking. When I got outside, I tossed the keys to Devin.

"You drive."

He was happy as a kid at Christmas when he got behind the wheel, but given it was only ten minutes to the rangers' station, he didn't get much of a drive. It made him smile though, and it gave me a chance to work through my embarrassment.

Relations.

Jeez, who even used that term anymore?

And god, what if the rumors reached Tiber, or fuck, what if he'd been able to read me like a dog and knew I felt an attraction to him?

Fuck my life. Freaking small towns.

And what did she mean about a broken heart or a

tragedy? I felt protective and fought the urge to ask Devin to turn around and go straight to Tiber's place so I could …

…do what exactly? Wrap him in a blanket and keep him safe?

Shocked, I realized this was the first hint of the old me, the protector, the same Gabriel who wanted to serve and protect, the same man who'd been destroyed by three years of hell. Was it a step in the right direction for me to feel anything for someone at all? My counselor would be so proud when I told him at our next Zoom meeting. If I managed to connect with him while this case hung over me. He'd remind me he'd been right, and that I wasn't dead inside, and that yes, I could have attraction for another man without fearing I'd lose it all.

What did he know? He wasn't me. He didn't have the same clear memories of what I'd seen and done.

"Sir?"

I snapped back to Devin, who'd caught me staring into the middle distance. We were already at the rangers' station and he'd parked.

"Let's go." I was out before striding towards the log cabin and up the steps with Devin hot on my heels. I was angry with myself because where the fuck was my brain this morning? Luckily, there was no one behind the door I pushed open with force, but it made enough noise for Abby to poke her head out of her office.

"Sheriff! Devin! Welcome—I have coffee and crullers."

Music to my ears, although I also sneaked some sour fish before anyone noticed. If anyone accused me of eating my feelings right now, then they wouldn't be wrong.

The coffee was hot, the cruller soft, the sour fish tart, and once I'd had enough of everything, I was better able to process what Hen had told me about the small town chatter, which I decided was nothing, and the weird feelings I had for Tiber. End of story.

I will not obsess about this.

"So we have something I thought you'd like to see," Abby began. "It's a big file and I tried to upload it to you, but our system couldn't handle it. Basically Mike was spending a lot of time hiking around the park—he couldn't start work officially until he'd used up all his vacation time, but he was bored." She sighed. "He ran interference with a couple of camper situations when Rowan and I were busy, and there was one that he was concerned about that occurred on Monday.

Mike's body had been found Thursday morning. The timing was interesting.

"I pulled out any paperwork I could find for you, but I warn you now, it's not much." She waved to the left of the table and I leaned over to gather what she had. License plate, a last name—Smith, but little else.

"So to summarize, Mr. Smith and his wife," she

shook her head at the name, "stayed too long at the Green Rocks camping area, and normally in situations like that, either me or Rowen would head over to the camper, have a quiet word, and in more cases than not the campers will move on. Sometimes they never even realized they were in a place with time restrictions, given how many signs we have to maintain." She gave a small huff as if that was a heavy burden to carry. "So Mike was running out that way, said he'd look in, and he came back and wrote this report, but he also copied over some cell phone footage. Hang on…"

We all peered at the screen as the circle just went round and round to show it was loading. Finally, a shaky phone recording played, and at first it was difficult to make out what we were looking at, and then it steadied, and there was narration I assumed was Mike's.

"Mr. and Mrs. *Smith*, name to be confirmed, Volkswagen Auto Sleeper Trident camper van four berths. 1990 maybe 91." The narration stopped for a moment, with simple views being collected around the van. "I knocked on the door to tell them they needed to move on, but they refused to move, so I want to document this for future reference." Devin scribbled notes, a whole page of them so far. Someone needed to give the kid a medal for speedwriting, but I paused it for him to catch up. The camera froze on Mike's hand, and I caught a flash of silver, peering closer.

"Mike told me in his interview that he toured British

Columbia in a van," Abby interrupted my thought process, and then her face fell, and I reached over and squeezed her hand. Empathy cost nothing, and she nodded even though her eyes were bright with emotion. "He was a good guy."

"And we'll get whoever did this to him. I promise you."

Okay, so in my position I shouldn't be promising anything, but I *was* going to solve this, whatever it took. Devin was caught up, so I restarted the video.

Mike zoomed in on the license plate, which matched the paperwork.

"Idaho plates. No sign of—"

"Hey! You can't film us!" A man stormed out of the van, carrying some weight on his body. He was as big as a linebacker and stalked over in a temper.

"Mr. Smith—"

"You can't film us. I know my rights!"

"I've asked you to move on from what is clearly marked as a two-night stay camping area, and you refuse to do so, and I'm within my rights to gather evidence." Mike sounded patient, caring, but firm.

"This is American land!" Mr. Smith snapped. "I'm American! We fought to take this land, and if I want to live on it…" He loomed over Mike, who to his credit didn't step away or back down.

His camera was shaky now though, as Mr. Smith lunged for it. I could see the man was armed.

Beside me Devin took a sharp breath. "Did you see the gun?" he asked, "And the second amendment T-shirt?"

"Yep."

The audio continued in which Mr. Smith explained his God-given right to park wherever he damn well wanted. It went on for a while, threats to call his friends who would help him stay—clearly not a man who backed down from a fight. He demanded that Mike delete whatever photos he took, saying he'd call the law on Mike. Then everything stopped, and then there was another voice caught on the film, or voices, a group of chattering school kids and a teacher herding them along a nearby trail, by the sound of it. The group interacted with Mike, the ranting camper went quiet, then Mike cut the video.

We replayed the audio, and Devin set about trying to fix things on Abby's computer so he could transfer it to us for forensic analysis.

I focused back on the video and paused it at the view of the silver which turned out to be an exercise watch, the kind that tracked runs and counted steps.

"Mike had a watch that tracked steps," I pointed out to Devin. "I don't recall a watch on Mike at the stones."

"No, there was nothing on his wrist, or close by. Do you want me to extend the search?"

"We should ask forensics to check on if they can tell whether he was wearing it at the time of death. There

could be obvious bruising, or... I don't know.
Meanwhile, we should see if the data downloads
anywhere."

"I'm on it."

"So, other thoughts?" I asked Devin when he'd
managed to upload the file into our secure system.

He cleared his throat. "We have a defensive second
amendment guy facing off against a park ranger. I didn't
hear any overt threats to physically harm Mike, but Mr.
Smith was sure interested in not having photos taken
and saying he'd bring in outside help to enforce his
rights. He was armed and aggressive, plus suggested
calling law enforcement, which would be us, but we had
nothing reported to us."

"What did Mike say to you after this happened,
Abby?"

"Mike came in, and he must have been unsettled
because he said he'd made a couple of calls to friends
down at Winchester Lake, Idaho, requesting them to ask
around, just to see if the plate, or Mr. Smith, were on
their radar. Turned out there was nothing they knew
offhand, but I know they put the word out on the Idaho
park's intranet."

"Why didn't Mike ask us to run the plate?"

Abby shrugged. "He wanted to, but I suggested we
wait, and go back the next day to see if they'd moved
on. We often find that these things fix themselves. I'm
not sure if he did go back or not. I didn't talk to him

again before.... Well, I guess I never did talk to him again. Maybe if I'd suggested we escalated the situation to you, then he'd still be alive..." She stopped and sipped at her now cold coffee, her expression tight.

"Because you think these people hurt him?"

"No. I mean, as far as I know, that was the only time Mike interacted with them. Like I said, he wasn't even on duty. But I should have at least followed up on it."

"You can't blame yourself," I reassured her.

She was sad. "But I will."

Devin tapped his notebook. "Do we know if this Mr. and Mrs. Smith are still up there now?"

"I hiked through Green Rocks on Wednesday morning, and they weren't there."

"We'll run the plates, see what we come up with."

We were almost out the door when Abby called after us. "One other thing, sheriff, I know it would be way down on your list of priorities, but I wanted to report a chicken thing."

"A chicken thing?" Devin and I exchanged glances.

"Yep. We found two chickens, one dead and covered in blue paint, one very much alive but a quick runner, out near the lake. We don't get a lot of chickens running wild here, so assume they belonged to someone in town? In case anyone comes in saying they've misplaced them, can you let them know Rowan and I tried to catch the live one, but it pecked its way from us in a hurry, and given that was a couple nights ago now, I assume it's a chicken dinner for a predator."

"I'll make a note." The thought of Rowan and Abby catching a chicken was funny.

At least that made me smile.

BUT, the smile was temporary because as soon as we were back in the car the radio crackled and Hen passed over the latest on our Bigfoot hunter and the fact it seemed he'd told people the story about him, footprints, and a murder at Sentinel Rocks. The story was trending in cryptozoology land—her words not mine.

"Shit," Devin snapped.

My sentiments exactly.

"Hotel then?" I said, and we headed straight there and to room 6.

"I only told my group," Hillesden defended as soon as he opened his door, knowing damn well why were there and looking all kinds of guilty. "They said they wouldn't say anything, and I trust them all."

"How many people are in your group?"

"Well, it's not the main group. That would be thousands of my fans, and I'm not stupid." He was huffy with us now, as if he wasn't the cause of maybe hundreds of people descending on Prophet.

"How many?" I asked with about as much patience as I could muster.

"Only two hundred. Probably less." He winced as he said this, taking a shaky step back on his crutch, maybe because I was towering over him and was pissed as hell.

Devin touched my elbow to remind me where we were, but I didn't need that. I couldn't arrest Hillesden for being an idiot, but I could threaten the fear into him and that was exactly what I was doing.

"No. More. Sharing. Anything. Or I will arrest you for interfering in an investigation."

He confronted me then as if he was going to argue, but soon backed down when I didn't move. "Okay," He snapped and then shut the door in my face.

Fuck. Save me from the stupid.

I've not had enough sleep to deal with this.

We headed back to the office, and parked the SUV. "What now?" Devin asked as he unbuckled his seatbelt. I stepped out, went to the driver's side, and held my hand out for the keys.

"Make a start on the license plate, find what you can on Mr. Smith and his wife, look for make and model. Contact the Idaho rangers, see if they had any luck. Send the new Hillesden video to forensics, but make sure you also run it over and over yourself, see if we pick up anything. Also, call the school, ask to speak to the teacher and kids that were on that video confrontation with camper."

"On it."

"Ask Hen to follow up with ISB for me."

"Okay."

"You got all of that. It's a long list."

Devin tapped his temple. "Steel trap," he joked.

"Okay then, I'm heading out to the Makah rez to talk to Charlie about the Sentinel Rocks lawsuit."

"Okay." Devin chewed his lip, which was a sign he had a question. "Can you just go to the rez and ask questions? Don't we need to wait to have Will Abraham there to liaise between tribal police and the sheriff's office?"

He was right of course—there was no cross-jurisdictional agreement in place between the rez and the town, a reluctance with deep historical roots that was grounded in fear of state encroachment on tribal sovereignty, and also a long-standing distrust of outside law enforcement. But I wasn't going there to arrest someone or accuse.

"I just want background on the lawsuit, is all. I'll message Will, but it's all good at this level."

Devin looked dubious. I felt dubious.

But instinct told me this is what I had to do.

So I did.

Chapter Ten

Tiber

I took the groceries home and checked on Duke, who didn't want to eat and didn't want to go out. But he met my gaze without shifting his eyes away, and I saw Gracie had moved a good six inches closer to his crate. Both good signs.

"You know I'm here for you, right?" I told Duke, squatting down to get close to eye level. "If you want some comfort, some pack time, or belly rubs, I'm here. I'm not your person, and I know you miss him. But if you need a sympathetic human, I'm here."

Duke watched me as I spoke, then closed his eyes. I reminded myself to be patient. He was less fearful today, but he was despondent to the point of immobility.

He was grieving. The only image I got from him was that of Mike, his owner—a vibe suffused with smiles and love and heartache. Duke knew Mike was never coming back. People didn't think animals understood about death, and it was true, in that they didn't spend time worrying about it. But when someone they loved, or an animal in the household, died, they knew. They *absolutely* knew, and Duke was feeling full-on grief. It broke my heart.

But I couldn't push myself on him. He'd let me know when he was ready. I wandered around for a half hour. The run-in with the sheriff at the Mercantile kept popping into my brain like the earworm of a song. He'd acted odd. I made him uncomfortable. The nasty voice in my head—which sounded like Jeff—said it was because I was a freak, a weirdo. But my gut said it was the opposite. Sheriff Thompson was gay—I'd read that right off. So was it… could it be… attraction?

No. That was unlikely. He was hot in a way that was out of my league, and most likely in a relationship.

Not that plenty of men didn't cheat.

Ugh. Fuckers.

The sheriff had looked tired, but then I bet he'd been working long hours and was off his game. He probably wouldn't even remember running into me.

Anyway, I didn't want the attention of Sheriff Thompson. Or of any guy. Or woman! Or anyone, really.

But I'd had a chance, right then, to mention what One-Eyed Jack had told me about the Makah and the Bowies, and I hadn't done it. It had gotten stuck in my throat. I hesitated to pass along gossip about the Makah without first doing a little fact-checking myself. But it didn't feel right to withhold information, either.

I decided to drive over to the Rez. It was sunny for a change, and the views of the water at Neah Bay, with its outcropping of rocks, were stunning. Also, I hadn't visited in at least six months. And if I happened to learn anything about the Bowies, or any possible involvement of the Makah in the murder, that would be a bonus. I took Leo to give him a little one-on-one time and to make sure he didn't bother Duke.

As I got to Neah Bay, I passed the *Welcome to the Makah Nation* sign. This was reservation land, but tourists were welcome. At least, their dollars were. The town was quaint, with a rustic, weather-beaten sort of charm, arranged as it was along the water with a marina, shops, a tiny cafe, and parking.

I parked at the Makah community hall. The town was so small, you could walk everywhere from there. The building's doors were open, but the big space inside was empty. There was a wall to the right that held photographs. I studied them. There were historical photos of the tribe as well as current ones. A recent framed newspaper clipping showed three Makah my age with a dead whale in shallow water. The headline bragged that the Makah had won back their whaling rights.

I had super-mixed feelings about that one. But good for them for reclaiming part of their heritage.

Also on the wall was a photo of the Makah tribal council. I checked the names. One of them was Charlie Bowie, the guy One-Eyed Jack had mentioned as the person who'd brought the lawsuit to get Sentinel Rocks back from the national park. He was an old guy, probably in his sixties or seventies, with bushy white hair and a very stern face. Even from a photograph, I could tell he had a strong spirit.

Would he kill, though? I had no idea how Duke's owner had been murdered, if it had been a deliberate act, like being shot or stabbed, or if it could have been an accident. I didn't know if it'd been drawn out or sudden. Sheriff Thompson had given me none of those gory details, and all I got from Duke was a stew of dark emotions. But I knew dogs, and the fear Duke had shown at the site, and even at my house initially, told me it hadn't been quick and easy. Whatever he'd seen, it had been brutal.

Was Charlie Bowie capable of something like that? A distinguished tribal elder? It didn't seem likely. And Duke's owner was young and I guess he was fit, not an easy guy to take down.

I left the community hall and got Leo out of the car. I'd promised him a walk, and I could use one myself.

The beach was visible from the sidewalk, and we headed in that direction. The tide was out and bits of dead shellfish, pebbles, and seaweed fronds littered the sand.

As Leo sniffed around, searching for anything edible, I noticed a couple of guys hanging out by their motorcycles in a little parking lot next to the sand. They seemed like trouble. They were around my age and struck me as locals, Makah. One of them was good-looking with long black hair he wore loose, a heavy metal T-shirt, and jeans. The other guy was mixed race with frizzy red hair and acne. His T-shirt was black with a fist and said *NATIVE POWER*.

The vibe I sensed coming off them was of two guys who had chips on their shoulders and were anything but friendly. On any other day I'd avoid them, but I had come here hoping to sniff around. No offense to the creatures who literally sniff around.

There was a rusted metal trashcan in that small parking lot, so I found an old receipt in my pocket, and walked Leo over there to throw it away. The guy with long hair watched me approach with a glower. I tossed the bit of paper and was about to compliment his bike, when Leo started barking at them. He pulled at his leash, yapping his little fool head off.

That was unusual behavior for him. I wasn't the sort of dog trainer who had to control their animals absolutely. Fuck that. I wouldn't want anyone telling me what to do twenty-four-seven. But Leo was not a puppy, and he neither pulled on the leash nor got quite so mouthy with strangers. He didn't like the look of these guys.

"What kind of fuckin' dog is that?" Long-hair sneered.

"The small kind," I said. "He's a mutt. Leo, quiet. *Hey*, look at me." I gave his leash a brief tug.

Leo glanced up at me. When he met my gaze, I knew he was listening. "*Quiet*." I touched my finger to my lips.

Leo gave a grumble, but he stopped barking. I motioned, and he came close to me and sat in front of my leg protectively, glaring a warning at the two guys. *Just try something, buddy.*

My hero. I slipped a treat from my pocket and gave it to him.

"Obedient little dude," said the one with the frizzy red hair. He nodded as if impressed. "I got a pittie that won't listen to a fucking word."

"Ain't that the truth," said Long-hair. "Dog's a menace."

"Pitbulls can be tough to train," I lied. "I'm Tiber."

"I'm Ben," said the redhead. "This is Jimmy."

Jimmy. It could be a coincidence, but given the vibe I'd gotten about Jimmy Bowie from One-Eyed Jack, I was pretty sure this guy was one and the same.

"Tiber," Jimmy repeated, frowning. "What kind of name is that?"

It was Italian. Actually, Roman, but the name cropped up a lot in my dad's family tree. My mom said she and my dad had fought about names when she was pregnant. But when I was born, she took one look at me and gave me the name Dad had picked. Because, she said, I had her blood. The least she could do was let my dad give me my name.

I wasn't about to tell Jimmy any of that.

"I dunno. It's a river somewhere, I think. My mom just liked it."

"But you're skin," Ben said. "Where you from? You're not Makah."

I shrugged. "Navajo on my mom's side."

Jimmy stood, going stiff, and his face went the kind of blank that was scary. For a moment, I thought he'd tell me to get the hell off his land, or even punch me. As if old tribal warfare was still a thing.

Ben said, "Navajo is cool."

The words broke the tension, as if they were a hint to Jimmy about how he should react. He relaxed, propping his ass back on the seat of his bike, and scoffed. "Navajos think they're hot shit."

I wondered if he was just mouthing off, or if he'd run into one he didn't like somewhere. But I knew from his body language that he wasn't going to try to start something. That was good since I hadn't had a fist fight since fifth grade, and I'd likely get my ass handed to me in pieces.

Jimmy took out a cigarette and lit it.

"I've met some Navajo who do," I agreed.

Ben took out a pack of cigarettes and offered me one. I shook my head and he lit up.

"So whaddya doin' on Makah land?" Ben asked. "Hiking or something?"

I saw the opening and took it. "I wanted to. I was gonna hit up a trail in the national park today and check out Sentinel Rocks. Only it was closed off and there were cops and stuff. Something big must have happened."

Jimmy didn't look at me, but he flinched. He exhaled a long stream of smoke and tapped the ash from his cigarette. It all seemed forced—way too casual. And I didn't miss the way Ben shot Jimmy a worried glance.

Neither of them said a word.

"Did you guys hear anything about that?" I asked. "I wondered what was going on."

"Why the fuck would we hear about that? Does this look like the national park to you? 'Cause it ain't," said Jimmy, hostile again.

"Just seemed like a big deal." I shrugged. "Figured news would spread. I don't know about Neah Bay, but on the rez in Arizona you can't take a shit without everyone knowing."

Ben huffed out a laugh. "I hear ya."

But Jimmy didn't crack a smile. "Well, we ain't heard jack."

His tone was disdainful, and Ben glanced at him, his smile fading. "Yeah, why should we know what happened, man?"

Curiouser and curiouser.

Before I could think of anything else to say, there was the sound of an engine. A sheriff's SUV pulled up in front of the community hall. I knew that car. And I knew the man who got out of it. What was a surprise was the way the sight of him socked me in the gut.

I wasn't the only one.

"Shit, man sheriff!" Jimmy hissed. Within seconds, the two of them had revved up their bikes and ridden away, swinging onto the road and going in the opposite direction from the community hall.

The sound of the bikes made Sheriff Thompson look over. He saw me and headed my way.

"Mr. Russo. What are you doing here?"

I raised my eyebrows. "Free country, last time I checked."

His jaw tightened, and he seemed a touch embarrassed. "Sure. I didn't know you had connections on the rez, is all."

"I don't. Just taking a walk."

Leo pawed at my leg and his eyes pleaded with me. He wanted to be picked up. Why? I wondered if he was feeling insecure for some reason. I picked him up.

"Who was that?" Sheriff Thompson stared after the bikers.

"Jimmy Bowie and his pal, Ben. They're suspects."

"Why do you say that?"

I had to adjust my hold on Leo, who was leaning toward the sheriff, sniffing. "Let's see. Fleeing at the sight of you was one clue. Also, they acted cagey when I asked if they knew what was going on at Sentinel Rocks this morning."

The sheriff was thoughtful. He reached out and stroked Leo's head distracted as Leo licked his hand. "Do you know him? Jimmy Bowie?"

"Met him five minutes ago, and that's all I can tell you, Sheriff Thompson."

Thompson looked as if he wanted to quiz me some more—maybe ask why I'd been talking to Jimmy at all. But, perhaps remembering the *free country* comment, he refrained. Meanwhile, he stroked Leo's head, which made me uncomfortable for several reasons.

Leo was a friendly little guy, but he wasn't normally *this* interested in strangers. What was his attraction to the sheriff? Was it a scent-thing or a vibe-thing? And then there was the unconscious way the sheriff petted my dog, without asking and without regard for the formalities or professional distance you'd expect from a cop. I wasn't sure if that made me like him more or less.

Okay, more. Liking animals was kind of rule one with me.

There was also the fact that it put his hand super close to my arms and chest, which created unwelcome warmth and the activation of certain desires I didn't need right now. And especially not in relation to the law.

I took a step back and put Leo down. I motioned to him with my hand to sit and stay.

"Is that sign language?" the sheriff asked.

"I have a hand motion for all the commands I teach my dogs."

"Oh." Sheriff Thompson took off his glasses, and the prettiness of his hazel-green eyes struck me again, although they were red-rimmed with exhaustion. "How is Duke doing, by the way?"

"Better. He's not as fearful today. But he's very depressed. He is eating though, so that's promising."

"You said he might recognize the killer if we—"

The sheriff looked past my shoulder. I turned to see what he was focused on. An older man with bushy white hair was stalking towards us, his face stony. I recognized him from his photograph. Charlie Bowie.

"Mr. Bowie," the sheriff said as the man drew close. "I was coming to see you."

"Say what you need to say then," Charlie said with a hard edge to his voice. "Got things to do."

Sheriff Thompson's back went stiff. He glanced at

me. "Perhaps you and I could have this conversation at
the community hall."

Charlie set his feet in the sand and crossed his arms
over his chest. "There doesn't need to be a conversation.
Ask what you came here to ask and be done with it. I've
got nothin' to hide."

The sheriff glanced at me again, as if he wanted me
to leave. But I wasn't going anywhere. I gave him a
serene smile.

Thompson cleared his throat. "Very well. There was
an incident near Sentinel Rocks on Wednesday night."

"Yeah, I heard. A new park ranger was found dead."

"Yes. And I just wanted to ask you about the lawsuit
the Makah brought since it involves Sentinel Rocks."
The sheriff's voice was neutral.

"So we must have killed the guy? How would that
help our case? Figures you'd go there." Charlie's tone
held all the disgust, scathing hatred, and accusations of
racism it was possible to fit into a couple of sentences.
"I was at home Wednesday night." He hesitated for a
beat. "I was with my grandson, Jimmy. We were there
all night. We had nothing to do with whatever the hell
happened over there."

"What do *you* think happened?" I asked.

Charlie gave me a hard look. I knew he'd noticed
me, maybe wondered about me, because he would. He
was a tribal elder, and he'd be curious about any young

skin on his rez. But he was too defensive and pissed at the sheriff to acknowledge me. Now I'd forced him to.

He seemed stumped for an answer, then said, "How should I know, young man?"

I shrugged. "It just seems ironic, given the legend of Sentinel Rocks. Don't you think?"

"What legend?" the sheriff asked.

Charlie watched me, not answering, so I spoke up. "According to legend, the two stones each house a spirit, shapeshifters, who guard against intruders invading Makah land. The stones can shapeshift into… what?" I asked Charlie.

"Anything," Charlie grunted. "Wolf maybe. Or bear. Or something so fearsome, it doesn't even have a name."

I nodded. "That's cool. Yeah. Anyway. The stones can shapeshift to fight off intruders. That's why they're called the sentinels."

Sheriff Thompson raised his eyebrows and I could tell from his expression that he had no idea why we were talking about legends. I wasn't sure myself, except that I'd hoped to get something other than a brick wall out of Charlie. And talking about tribal history should be his jam.

Charlie nodded. "Kid has a point. Maybe the rocks did it. I've been warning the rangers they're inviting the wrath of our ancestors. Maybe they awakened something. The kind of thing you don't want to wake up and see you."

His tone was ominous now, but I'd swear he was secretly pleased at this turn in the conversation. Happy to give the sheriff the booga-wooga runaround.

Thompson seemed as if he had no idea what to say. "I don't think... this is a very serious crime. A *real* crime."

Charlie shrugged. "Is there anything else you wanted to ask me?"

The sheriff sighed. "No. But if you hear anything that could be even tangentially related to the murder, I hope you'll call me." He took out a card, but Charlie refused to take it.

"I know where to find you, sheriff." Charlie gave me one last glance and strode away towards the community hall.

When he was out of earshot, Sheriff Thompson rubbed his face and sighed. "Well, that's a new one. The rocks did it."

"He doesn't really think that," I said. "Also: he was lying."

The sheriff's head whipped around and he stared at me, puzzled.. "About the shapeshifting rocks?"

"No. I mean, yes, but that's not what I meant. He was lying about being home with Jimmy the night of the murder."

The sheriff put his hands on his hips. "How do you know that?"

It seemed obvious to me. I shrugged. "His defensiveness. From the get-go. And the fact that he showed up after Jimmy took off. I'd be willing to bet Jimmy went straight to his grandfather and told him you were here."

"So?"

I frowned in frustration. "I could just tell when he said it. It was in his voice, his posture. If I had to guess, I'd say he's not lying about being home himself. But he said Jimmy was with him—he just offered that up without you asking, and there was a hesitation before he got it out, as if lying was uncomfortable. He's creating an alibi for his grandson. I don't think he *knows* that Jimmy murdered the ranger. He'd be more freaked out if that was the case. But I think there's part of him that worries that Jimmy might have done it. Hence the proactive alibi."

"How the fuck did you get all that from a tone of voice? Excuse my language."

I shook my head. There was no way to explain it.

Sheriff Thompson studied me. I expected him to be skeptical. Most people were. Or downright dismissive. But he was intrigued. Then his gaze dropped to my collarbone where it stuck out of my T-shirt. Then my mouth. He gave a little cough and looked away.

A lick of heat went through me. Goddamn. The

sheriff *was* attracted to me.

I wasn't sure how to feel about that. It had been a minute since any man had shown me that kind of attention—not surprising since I'd buried myself away in the middle of nowhere, according to my mother, and rarely left the house.

Part of my brain wanted to scream. How far did I fucking have to go to get away from this shit? I didn't want to get involved with another guy. *Ever.*

Part of my brain was flattered.

And the rest acknowledged that it was normal human behavior. After all the sex drive was one of the primary motivators in every species. So why should I take it personally?

I'd just ignore it.

The flush of heat I'd felt, though, informed me that my body had other ideas. Damn it. *Yeah, thanks for waking* that *up.*

"So you're not just a dog whisperer. You read people, too?" The sheriff asked.

I scoffed. "What? Uh, no. I don't even… no." *I don't even like people* didn't seem like the sort of thing I should admit out loud.

"You do, though. Read people."

"No."

We stared at each other. There was a challenge in the sheriff's eyes, but when I didn't give in, he looked away. "Okay. So. About Duke. Are you telling me that, if Duke had been here, and if he was somewhat recovered from the trauma, he could have told you if Charlie Bowie was the killer?"

"Oh definitely."

The sheriff rubbed his face again, frustrated. "Jesus Christ. Shapeshifting rocks and talking dogs. And when do you think Duke will be able to assist us? Maybe it would be good for him if you brought him over here. He might like a walk on the beach."

"I told you: he's not ready."

It came out with a little too much force, and Sheriff Thompson held up his hands. "Okay. I'm just asking. Anything you could do to speed it along."

"Anything I can do for Duke, I will do. *For Duke*," I answered testily.

Sheriff Thompson sighed a discouraged sigh. "Need a ride anywhere?"

"No, I drove. I'll be at home if you need me." I put Leo down, gave his leash a little tug, and we walked away.

If you need me. Why had I said that? I wasn't at the sheriff's beck and call. And I didn't want to give him that impression. Professional or… otherwise.

But this case had me intrigued. It had been a long time since I'd had any interest outside of my clients' pets and my own little home menagerie, and I found my mind fully engaged. I wanted to know more.

I wanted to find the killer.

Chapter Eleven

Gabriel

I'll be at home if you need me?

Did Tiber really say that?

I had no reason pertaining to the case for *needing* Tiber, other than that he had Duke, of course, but something about those words meant I felt out of sorts for the rest of the day. That Charlie Bowie's grandson might be involved, and that Charlie was possibly lying to give him an alibi, didn't sit well with me. Thanks to the lack of sleep last night—again, I tilted back in the chair in my office to think things through and fell asleep when all I'd done was sit down to check my email and think on the Jimmy situation.

And Tiber.

My thoughts were so full of Tiber and how he got all

ferocious with me while defending the dog he was protecting.

Luckily, or unluckily, depending on the point of view, I woke myself up when my chair tilted too far back and I ended up on my ass on the floor. Unlucky because fuck that hurt, but lucky because if Hen had come in, or worse, Devin, then I wouldn't have known what to say.

"You okay in here?" Hen said from the doorway. Thankfully I was up and straightening my chair and not still sprawled on the worn carpet.

"Yep. You got something for me?"

"A visitor," she murmured, and waved behind her.

I waited for more information, and there was even a spark of hope that maybe Tiber was back. "Tiber?"

"Nope. Why would Tiber be here?" She narrowed her eyes. "What did you do to him?"

"Nothing," I hurried to say. "So who is here?"

"Your nephew."

"My what now?" The only nephew I had was Aaron, and he was five and it was a school day, so what was he doing here? "With Sam or Lori?"

"Nope. Just Aaron. On his own."

Given I wasn't welcome at Sam's place, and he'd told me in no uncertain terms he didn't want his kids *confused*, I saw little of either Aaron or his twin, Sarah, apart from a couple of awkward accidental meets in the grocery store, or at the park. I headed out immediately to find my nephew sitting on a chair swinging his legs, slumped to one side, and looking a little sickly.

"Aaron?"

He glanced up at me and gave me a wobbly smile. "Hello Uncle Ganabrianel." Neither of the twins could say my name properly—but then I hadn't been around for them to learn it, and I assumed Sam didn't talk about me much.

I glanced around, expecting Sam or Lori to be lurking in a corner, but no one was there—he was all alone. I crouched in front of him, my hand on his knee, and threw a glance back at Hen. She nodded, and that was shorthand for me saying to call his mom, or dad, and her saying she'd already done that.

"Sarah's sick," he informed me with a sniff. His sister, a cute as a button kid with the longest dark hair, had a smile the same as Sam's. "So I did an adventure."

"With your mom?"

"She's sleepin' with Sarah, so I did it on my own."

Jeez. Prophet was a small town, but the thought of my nephew wandering down from their house, which was a good quarter mile up the hill from here, had my chest tightening.

"Where's your dad?" I asked, because if Lori was ill, then surely Sam would be at home?

"Workin'." He scratched at his belly. "I wanted to see your prison."

"Uhm…" I didn't have a proper relationship with

the twins, things between me and Sam getting in the way, but I was still Aaron's uncle, and that he'd come to me because he was interested in me, or my prison, was like sunshine on a cloudy day. Well, apart from the fact his appearance came with a truckload of worries. Were Lori and Sarah okay? And why did Aaron look as if he was about to keel over?

"Just keeps ringing at the house," Hen said from behind me. "I'll try Sam's cell, but he might not be in range if he's up at the cabins."

Aaron stared up at me with this one hundred percent cute expression, scratching at his belly again and wincing.

"Are you okay? Did you hurt yourself?" I lifted the hem of his shirt, his skin peppered with red marks, and it was clear why Sarah was off sick, and why Lori might be ill as well.

"Chicken pox," Hen muttered. "I've had it, you?"

I nodded as I recalled part of a summer I'd been so sick I couldn't even go swimming. I held out a hand, which Aaron took without hesitation, then helped him down off the seat, but he was shaky, and running a temperature. I picked him up and settled him on my hip.

"Let's get you back to Mom, yeah?"

"I wanna see where the bad guys go," Aaron whined, and I guessed it wouldn't hurt giving him the two-cent tour. We didn't have lockup facilities in the traditional sense, no bars and hard metal cots with thin mattresses, but we had a room that was internal and lockable, and the bed was comfortable—I knew because I stayed on it for a few weeks when I'd tired of staying at Daisy's hotel and before my small house went through escrow.

I showed it to him, plus my office, and the computer and the bathroom, but by the time I'd circled back to Hen, he was drooping in my arms, his face in my neck and his soft breath on my skin.

"I'm taking him home," I whispered.

"You want me to do it?" She sounded concerned. "What if Sam… y'know…"

"Aaron's *my* nephew," I was reminding myself more than her. "Whatever my brother thinks of me darkening his doorstep is irrelevant."

"Sam's just…" she started, but subsided just as quick. "Sure thing sheriff."

I headed out, Aaron tucked in my arms, and he mumbled about random things as I walked up to my brother's place—the old family home—a million memories flooding my thoughts as I drew nearer. Built sturdy like most of the places in town, the siding was white and parked outside was my sister-in-law's 4x4. I headed straight for the back door, the main way into the house, which took a person direct into the kitchen. The door was wide open, and there was a stool lying on its side on the tile, which I guessed Aaron had somehow found, used to reach the bolt, and gotten out.

In a town that had just seen a murder.

Aaron was sleeping now, his head hot. I took him upstairs, but didn't know which room was his.

I *should* know which bedrooms my niece and nephew used.

When I peeked inside my mom and dad's old room, Sarah and her mom were in there, and with a bed that big, I thought maybe Aaron would be best off with Lori and his sister. I tucked him in next to Sarah, then gently shook Lori awake. She peered up at me, her eyes glazed, her forehead as hot as her son's.

"Sam?" she groaned, then her eyes focused and widened. "Gabriel? Wha'appened?"

"Just checking in on you," I lied, and thank god she was too ill to argue.

"M'okay," she murmured and turned to look at the kids, pressing the back of her hand to the forehead of each, and then whispering she loved them before falling back and closing her eyes. She had the telltale spots of chickenpox as well, so I pulled her covers up, refilled glasses with water, tidied her bedside cabinet to make sure she could see the aspirin, the kid's Tylenol, and the calamine lotion, and then I didn't know what to do, so I headed downstairs. Should I call Doc Winston? What would he say? Hydrate, rest, meds for pain, don't scratch.

I placed a call anyway—Doc was out on a call, another case of chickenpox, and his secretary gave me the same advice that I already knew. Turned out most of their class had the same thing, and she said she'd had a lot of calls.

I poured myself a water, knowing I was staying put until Sam came back, and dreading it at the same time. The kitchen was the same one my dad had built when he and Mom first bought this place, a scuffed solid wood layout that would last a lifetime. I traced the marks on the large table in the middle, recalling the time I thought it was a good idea to scratch my name on one leg. I'd only been six, and I tried to blame Sam, but backed down when my mom just gave me one of her special mom-looks and then explained Sam was four and couldn't write his name, let alone mine.

Busted.

The front door flew open, my brother storming inside, his expression frantic, his eyes wide when he spotted me.

"Upstairs," I thumbed.

He took the stairs three at a time, and I could hear his footsteps as he went into his bedroom. There were some muffled noises—he'd woken Lori—and then the sound of the door closing, and finally his steps back down.

I could have left, but some part of me thought I'd

rescued my nephew and maybe I deserved at least a few minutes of Sam's time.

"What happened?" Sam snapped from the hall outside the kitchen. "Hen said that he... that..." He slumped to the nearest chair. "I was only up in the cabins. Jeez. We keep the door bolted... Lori wasn't ill this morning, and the roof is leaking and she said I should..." He wasn't the Sam I'd become used to. There were no shards of bitterness being thrust at me, there were no recriminations. He was exhausted, and he was running on adrenalin.

"He came to me," I explained, "Said he wanted to see where I work."

"I can't believe he reached the bolt, let alone slid it."

"He used a stool."

"But the bolt is hard to move..."

"Says the kid who did that when he was seven. Don't you remember? You were pissed that Mom wouldn't let you eat the cookie you'd taken. We searched everywhere for you and I'd never been so scared because it was me that told Mom you'd taken the cookie." I chuckled at the memory, but Sam didn't join in.

"Don't do that," Sam snapped.

"What?"

"Just go away, Gabriel," Sam said tiredly. He wasn't angry or loud, he just didn't want me in the house. I had so much to say, so many things to explain, but I also had things I couldn't say and it was that which was coming between us.

Why had I left town? What happened in LA? Why hadn't I come back? I wanted to tell him everything—I wanted Sam back; I wanted my family again. Who would it hurt for me to tell Sam the truth now? The last of the people I'd put away were dead, there was no specific intel about Cyrus searching for the name I'd used undercover—Zachary Owens. Zachary was dead now. In fact there was no chatter about my undercover name or Cyrus at all. I'd helped to take down his operation, bit by bit, and I'd broken him.

Almost as much as he'd broken me.

But I'd kept people safe.

I'd saved lives.

So many lives.

And in doing so, I'd lost my family.

"This is stupid," I murmured, more to myself than to Sam, and he bristled as if I'd been saying it was him who was stupid. I didn't mean that but he didn't give me a chance.

"I'm not doing this with you," Sam snapped.

"I *wanted* to come home," I said, and a familiar shame stole over me. If Sam ever found out the kinds of things I'd done, he'd never look at me the same way again.

Of course, he never regarded me with anything other

than sadness and anger, so disgust might be a welcome change.

"So you said," he replied, and then scrubbed at his eyes. "By the way, Friday dinner is off—we called Ezra, and canceled his visit. No point in his coming here if his family is ill."

But, *I* wasn't ill.

Oh.

I wasn't family. I get it. Message received, and my heart broke a little.

"Okay."

"You should go."

I opened my mouth to explain, to reason, to make amends, but as usual, nothing came out. Secrets were acid inside me, and denial was my constant companion.

"You'll call me if I can help?" I prompted as I stood.

Sam stared at me. "Thank you for bringing Aaron home. I'm grateful for you doing that for him, but we don't need your help."

I wanted to shout that I'd kept his son—my nephew —safe, and that I would do anything to keep his entire family safe, whatever he thought of me, but I didn't want another fight.

We were in a faceoff, and traditionally this was the part where I got defensive and all the broken parts of me scratched together, and where he got angry and called me on my shit.

Just the thought of all of that exhausted me.

He didn't need me around him now.

So I left.

I EXPECTED Hen to ask me what had happened, but she didn't even wait for me to take my hat off.

"Amelia the Coroner called. They have preliminary autopsy data, emphasis on preliminary. She's is in the office until five for you to call back."

I glanced at my watch and hurried into my office, dropping my hat to the desk, and connecting to the Coroner's office before I even sat down. Amelia answered on the third ring.

"Locksley."

"Hey Amelia, this is Sheriff Thompson, over in Prophet."

"Ah, sheriff, I have some preliminary intel for you."

"Great."

"Okay so, there's extensive bruising to the face, other bruises, and scratches on the limbs, possibly from a fall as they're random and randomly spaced and some are embedded with dirt, but obviously I can't say for sure. The large X crudely dug into the upper torso happened postmortem, which I expect will be a relief to everyone involved. How far postmortem is difficult to assess, but I would put it at maybe two to three hours. The actual cause of death is blunt force trauma to the left temple, a blow which was hard enough to crack the skull and cause internal hemorrhaging. Now whether it was caused by a fist, or the use of an object, I don't know, at least not yet. I would put time of death in the four-hour window of between 7p.m. and 11p.m. the night previous to when I attended the site. I'm waiting on full toxicology, but the victim was otherwise a healthy adult and, from his medical files and tissue presentation, I don't expect it to show anything untoward. There's one more thing. I found traces of glass in the subject's hair at the back of his head, quite apart from the whatever hit him in the temple, which I've sent for analysis. Results to follow shortly."

"Again, thank you." At least having a short window for time of death meant we could narrow down suspects.

"Of course. I'll send over these findings, and anything more as soon as I have them."

The call ended. I headed for the small room, grabbing Devin as I passed, and relayed the findings as he added them to the board.

He pointed at the name, Mike. "I have something extra from Abby," he said. "She told me she knew little about Mike's friends and family. His parents were both dead, but we already know that from our own research, and no siblings."

Okay. That sounded sad, to be so on his own. Not that I was much better off with one brother physically not talking to me, and the other brother on radio silence with me.

"What about the schoolteacher and the kids? The ones who witnessed the altercation with the camper?"

"Teacher said she didn't really see anything. The kids weren't much help, although one of her pupils mentioned there was a clucking blue monster living under the van, but that's irrelevant. I thought maybe a chicken?"

Ah, a blue chicken again? That must be the chicken had Abby spoken about.

"A chicken, yes," I confirmed.

"Blue though? I don't get that part, but maybe the other chickens belonged to them? The ones that Abby mentioned."

"I doubt campers would have chickens. What about the campers themselves?"

Devin checked his notes. "Abby called in to say she thinks they're now up at the Applecross camping area, that was my next port of call."

"We'll go together, first light." There was no way I was sending the rookie up to confront an angry camper on his own, and certainly not when it would be dark by the time we reached it nor because it was in such a remote location as Applecross.

I checked the timelines of the scene again.

"Damn it," I muttered when one thing became very obvious. Hillesden's video overlapped with the potential window for the murder, but he would have been a couple of miles away as the crow flies from the scene itself, and while not unbelievable that he could have gotten there and back, he was on crutches. Also, he wasn't that big, so would he really have been able to beat up a guy Mike's size?

That left who? Jimmy Bowie? Campers? Some other nameless person who was just passing through?

Bigfoot?

I huffed at my train of thought, rolled my neck, stretched my shoulders, and then shut down my laptop. I had one more thing to do before I went home—retrieve a shirt or something to take to Tiber's place for Duke.

Chapter Twelve

Tiber

"You know, Ti, if you hadn't moved to the edge of the known universe, it wouldn't be so challenging for you to make it down to Portland to visit."

Mom called me weekly, mostly to dispense life advice and make sure I wasn't dead. I couldn't help but laugh at her comment, because Prophet sort of was the edge of the known universe. But I'd never admit it. "I live in Washington state. It's hardly the icy depths of Siberia."

"It's as far northwest as you can go without a wetsuit, and it's separated from civilization by the Olympic mountain range. Even if I fly to Seattle, it's a four-hour drive!"

"I know. It's a pain to get here," I agreed.

Personally, I considered that a bonus. "But I love it. The town is so quirky, and it's close to a rez, and the Olympic National Park, and I can walk from home to a gorgeous lake. The weather is cool, my house was affordable, plus, it's quiet and—"

I was about to say *peaceful*, but an image of the crime scene at Sentinel Rocks came to mind.

Mom went on unaware. "I'm glad you're happy, Ti. As long as you're not running away from life. As long as you're at least trying to meet a nice man. Animals are wonderful companions, but you need a partner. A human one. Animals can't care for you when you're sick. They can't give you advice and be your rock when troubles come...."

She went on espousing the glories of human relationships. I tuned it out. Of course, those things were true about a perfect relationship. If such a thing even existed. But the dark side was equally compelling. Animals were never abusive. They didn't gaslight you, or lie, or cheat, or break your heart. And they were never critical. They loved unconditionally.

"Hey, Mom? I heard you, okay? I'll take it under advisement. I'm glad you're enjoying retirement, and I'll try to make it down to Portland at some point. But I haven't found a pet-sitter around here yet, so it would be easier for you to come up here. We can do some hiking."

"And cooking?"

"And cooking."

There was a pause. I could picture her resigned expression. "Okay. How does your August look?"

"Probably fine. I'll check my calendar and pick a few days I don't have client calls scheduled. I'll block it out for you and let you know."

"Okay. But before you go, there's one other thing. Now don't get upset, honey, but… Jeff stopped by the other day."

"What?" My heart lurched and my skin went cold all over. I was out on the back deck and I felt around for a chair and slumped into it. "Mom—"

"I did not. Tell him. Where you are," she said.

My head swam. Oh god. "Okay. Okay. But what the f— What was he doing there?"

"You told me not to tell him, and I didn't. So don't worry."

"Okay! But what did he want?"

I heard her sigh. "He said he has some mail for you. Said it looked important. And he has a box of your stuff."

Bullshit.

"I told him I'd pass the message along, and now I have. You can contact him or not, it's up to you. But he was really very nice about it. I think it hurts him that you won't even talk to him."

"Mom, he's playing you! That's what he does."

She was silent for a moment. "I told you: you can

contact him or not. It's up to you. He did ask about you, of course. I said you'd moved away, and he wanted to know where, but I didn't tell him. I wouldn't do that."

I hung my head, phone pressed to my ear.

Jeff had gone to my mom's house and tried to get her to tell him where I was.

I felt like I might be sick.

It'd been over a year since I'd last seen him. I'd hoped he'd forgotten. I'd hoped he'd moved on to some other unfortunate lover, that the whole ugly situation was in the rearview mirror. There was a reason why I made sure my pet consultant website gave no clue as to my location. And he'd never used the site's contact form.

"Aren't you even curious about this mail he has? He said it might be important."

I squeezed my eyes shut. Mom just didn't get it. Jeff was handsome, polite, and was studying to be a doctor. And he'd always sweet-talked her. He could sweet-talk a porcupine. She tried to be supportive, but she truly didn't understand what Jeff was.

"If it was so important, why didn't he leave the stuff with you?" I asked. "It was a ruse, Mom."

She sighed again. "Whatever you say. Just don't *stew* about it. It sounded like he's slammed with his residency anyway, so I don't think you need to worry about him looking for you."

She was right that he was probably busy with his

residency at a Portland hospital. Hell, it had taken him over a year to go by my mom's place. That was hardly a motivated stalker.

But that would be just like Jeff. Make you think you were safe and then....

It's fine! He doesn't know where I am.

"All right, niño. That's all the news I have. Gotta run. I miss you! Love you."

"Love you too, Mom."

After hanging up, I gave a full-body shudder. Ugh. Jeff. Jeff and my mom. I did not want to think about it anymore. That ship had sailed. Sailed, sailed, sailed, and fallen off the rim of the world, as far as I was concerned.

Please God, let it truly be over.

A cold nose touched my foot. I looked down to see Gracie. I sank to a crouch and hugged her large, hairy body. Wolfhounds were not small, and Gracie was taller than me if she stood with her paws on my shoulders. But she was the gentlest, most skittish of giants, a soul as shy and sweet as existed on earth. My chest loosened as I hugged her.

"I'm okay," I told her, letting out a shaky breath. "Just some bad memories. But we don't need to go there, do we?"

She licked my face. I felt a gush of love for her. Of all my animals, Gracie was the most sensitive, the one who couldn't stand to see anyone or anything in pain. Which reminded me of Duke.

"Let's go see how our boy's doing. Okay?"

Gracie trotted after me into the living room. Duke was still in his crate, but he was lying with his head and forepaws out of it now, on the floor. A literal reflection of him coming out of his shell.

"Hey, buddy." I sat down cross-legged a foot from him, and Gracie stood by. She nosed at his ear once.

Duke lifted his head and sniffed at her, gave her a little lick on the chin. I smiled. "So what will it be today, huh? Chicken or chicken? Or, on our regular house menu, we've got kibble."

Duke's ears perked a little, and he shifted forward about a half inch and gave me doggy eyes. I had no illusions this invitation was in response to anything other than the word *chicken*, but it was still progress. I held out my hand, palm up, and gradually moved it towards his nose. He sniffed it for some time, probably detecting traces of my animals and the coconut hand soap at the kitchen sink. Then he touched it once with his nose.

I gave him a gentle stroke on his head, and when he didn't pull away, petted him there, scratching his ears and rubbing my thumb between his eyes. Something dark flashed across Duke's face, and he began to pant. I pulled my hand away. But after a moment, Duke inched forward a hair more, requesting the renewal of attentions, so I petted him again.

"You're thinking about your dad. It hurts, I know," I said. "But it'll get easier, with time. I promise."

Just when I thought Duke was about to inch out farther, someone knocked on the door. It startled me and sent Duke to the back of his crate. Gracie disappeared and Leo and Ferdinand set up the Hallelujah Chorus in the hall.

"Fuck," I muttered, pushing to my feet.

I wasn't surprised when I peeked out of the window to see Sheriff Thompson. He was the only person who'd come knocking on my door, especially at eight at night.

I opened the door wide, letting Leo and Ferdinand have at him with their greeting. If he didn't like it, he could stop coming over here.

But a smile crossed his weary face, and he squatted down to give both dogs pets. "Hey, guys."

He sounded so tired, I felt a stab of pity.

He glanced at me hopefully. "I brought something for Duke."

He did? My defenses melted a little. And I couldn't leave him exhausted on my doorstep covered in animals. "Wanna come in for a minute?"

"I don't want to bother you."

"No, come in. I don't want Fudge to get out." I pulled him inside and shut the door.

"Fudge?"

"A kitten. She's currently obsessed with dreams of the outside world."

"Ah." For a moment, exhaustion blanked the sheriff's face, as if he'd forgotten where he was and why. Then he blinked and held something out. "Anyway, I went by Mike Bressett's room and got this T-shirt from his laundry basket. I left a note for his relatives explaining. I'm sure it's fine."

It was a white T-shirt. I gave him a grateful look and took it. I went into the living room and kneeled by Duke's crate. "Duke. Look what Sheriff Thompson brought you. Something of Mike's."

He was cowering, pressed up against the back of the crate. Probably the strange man's voice had set him off. But I just held it out, keeping calm, and he sniffed the air. He knew the scent, because he slunk forward and grabbed the T-shirt from my hand and moved back into the crate with it, sniffing it furiously. I heard the thump of a tail-wag.

I stood and saw the sheriff in the living room doorway. "It's a hit," I said. "Thanks for getting that."

"No problem. Anything to help. Well."

He stood there all kinds of awkward. This would be an excellent time for him to leave. But I couldn't help myself. "Would you like some coffee? Decaf? You look ready to keel over."

"I do?" He gave a sheepish smile. "Long day."

"I bet. Sit down. Ignore the dog hair. Coffee or tea?"

"I don't want to put you to any trouble."

"I'll make coffee," I decided.

I made us both a cup of decaf and sat at the other end of the sofa. The sheriff sipped his and looked at the crate. Duke had his head out again—not as far as before, but he wasn't hiding in the back either. He lay with the T-shirt between his paws and stared at the sheriff. I thought he remembered him from Sentinel Rocks, but he didn't appear threatened by him.

"Duke seems better," the sheriff said.

"He is better."

The sheriff looked at me hopefully.

"Not ready to take out yet. Soon, maybe."

The sheriff was disappointed, but he nodded. I found it a point in his favor that he didn't argue. Instead, he yawned, a real jaw-cracker.

He covered his mouth. "Sorry. That's—sorry."

"Hey, Ferdinand farts in my face all the time. I'd say my tolerance for weird body stuff is pretty high."

The sheriff gave a sheepish grin. "Well, I promise not to fart in your face."

"Thank you." I smiled. "You've been putting in long hours, huh?"

He nodded. "Haven't grabbed more than a few hours of sleep since this began. Even when I have the time, can't shut my brain off."

"Do you want to talk about it?" I felt my face heat at asking. But I was curious.

He looked conflicted. "I'd like to. My deputy is overwhelmed and a newbie. The ISB—they're the people who are supposed to investigate crimes in national parks—they're busy with some right-wing standoff in Idaho. To be honest, I could use some help. But I can't get into the details of a case with a civilian."

But oh, he wanted to. Badly. It was in the way he leaned towards me, in the gritting of his teeth, as though holding back the words by force. I offered him a compromise. "Don't spell out the details, then. But maybe generalities? Might help to have a sounding board. Besides, every creature I ever talk to lives in this house. And they don't tend to spread gossip."

He considered it for a moment. I waited. He'd either talk or not, it was up to him.

He began to speak, haltingly at first. "The problem isn't a lack of suspects. We have lots of those. But it's confusing as hell. Certain things happened post-mortem, and maybe the body was moved. But moved from where? I think we've eliminated one guy, which helps, but something happened that night at Sentinel Rocks that involved a lot of people based on the, um, evidence we found. But we don't know if it's just, like, kids partying, maybe before the murder, or if it's something more sinister. Some kind of ritual? Then there's the Makah angle. You said yourself Jimmy Bowie is a suspect."

"Definitely a suspect," I agreed. "But that doesn't mean he did it."

"Exactly. I haven't found him to question him, and

anything to do with the Makah is… delicate. They have their own tribal police, so we can't exactly go in and grab their people to interrogate. But I don't want to get the tribal authorities involved unless I have something solid, especially not with Charlie Bowie heading the council. Still. Gotta do my job."

God, it did sound like a tangle. I didn't envy him.

"I drove to town today and noticed a bunch of Bigfoot people," I said. "But I take it Sasquatch is not one of your suspects." I hoped a joke would lighten the mood. But given how laconic I was, it probably didn't come out that way, because the sheriff frowned.

"Yeah, that's a whole other shit show. It's taking up all my deputy's time just trying to keep lookie-loos away from Sentinel Rocks. And Abby and Rowan—the park rangers—are busy herding Bigfoot hunters crashing through the woods. Unfortunately, I can't arrest people for posting about the murder on social media."

"Do you want me to poke around the rez a bit more? Maybe talk to Jimmy Bowie?"

Now the sheriff was worried. "I can't ask you to do that, Mr. Russo. It might be dangerous. If he gets wind you suspect him…. No. Better not."

"Tiber," I said.

He blinked at me and gave me a shy smile. For a moment, he looked like a little boy. "Call me Gabriel. If you're gonna be my sounding board and all."

"Gabriel." The word sounded too good on my

tongue. And damn, he was handsome slumped there on my couch, all dark hair, and soulful dark eyes and end-of-day stubble. And I liked him better like this—tired and vulnerable. It was less easy to resist than the hard-ass cop who'd first knocked on my door.

My stomach fluttered. Not good. I searched for a distraction and picked up Leo, who was sitting at Gabriel's feet and staring at him adoringly. I put him on my lap and scratched his back. "So. Are you from Prophet?"

He sat straighter. "Yeah. Grew up here. My family is here. I left for college and only moved back a year ago. Worked for the LAPD for a time."

"Must be quite a change—LA to sleepy Prophet."

His gaze shifted away and darkened. There was something there, something very much not good. Had something happened in LA? But Gabriel only shrugged. "Prophet is a good town. The people are eccentric but, historically, it's been an artist's community, so it's fairly liberal. That works for me. Not that many small towns would want a gay sheriff."

He gave me a look when he said that, as if checking for my reaction.

I nodded. "I knew you were gay thirty seconds after you arrived at my door the first time."

"Really? How?"

"The way you looked at my feet."

He snorted out coffee and wiped his face, laughing.

"Jesus. You really are scary with that reading people stuff."

I couldn't stop a pleased smile, giddy at the compliment. "Well. It is sort of my job. To read animals, anyway."

I'd done a lot of thinking about what he'd said after we'd talked to Charlie at the rez, about how I was good at reading people, too. My first instinct was to deny it. But when I thought about it, there was definitely crossover. Tics. Tension. Tells. After all, humans were animals, too. Or maybe it was just because I'd trained myself to notice the smallest reactions in animals that I noticed more than most people.

Of course, homo sapiens could be duplicitous as fuck.

"You'd make an excellent detective," Gabriel said.

"I already am a detective."

He flushed. "I mean a homicide detective."

I grimaced. "I decided not to be a vet because I couldn't stand to have my day filled with animals in pain. Or, god forbid, having to put them down. Ergo, I don't think I'm cut out for homicide."

"You almost became a veterinarian?"

"Yeah. Both my parents were vets. They had a clinic near Portland. My mom just retired and sold it, actually."

"That makes sense." He nodded. I thought he

wanted to ask me about my dad, who'd passed away, but thought better of it.

"So…." he hesitated. "I thought maybe my gaydar got a little ping with you too. No offense intended if I'm wrong."

"You're not wrong."

Gabriel stared at me and his energy, the whole vibe in the room, grew thick and heavy. Weighted. Warm.

Crap.

I stood abruptly, huddling Leo to my chest. "You really should go home and get some rest."

"Yeah. Yeah, I should." Gabriel stood then took a step towards the front door and stopped. "Thank you. Thanks for the coffee and the, uh, talk. I needed that. Both."

"You're welcome. Guess you know where I live if you need to talk again."

Ugh. Such a stupid thing to say. *Clearly.*

I walked him to the door and said goodnight without meeting his gaze.

I locked the door after he left. And, on second thought, I threw the security chain too.

Chapter Thirteen

Gabriel

SLEEP WAS A LONG TIME COMING, too much in my head, too many thoughts in my brain, too many puzzles. The hopeful side of me expected the video would prove that Hillesden would remain the suspect, but the more realistic part of me already knew he was innocent. He was obsessed with Bigfoot, but he wasn't a killer—at least, that was what my gut told me. By the time I fell asleep, I'd come to terms with losing Hillesden from the board, and made a little sense of the questions I'd ask the campers who'd had the run-in with Mike—assuming they were still at the Applecross camping area. I knew what I'd be searching for in the morning, all apart from that insistent nagging fact about the blue chicken, which made absolutely no sense at all.

The chicken followed me into my nightmares, the body, the *X* carved into Mike's chest, and somehow in my sleep I was seeing monsters and running from them and shouting for help. When the nightmares twisted to the things I'd seen in LA I woke drenched in sweat, blinking in the darkness, my breathing harsh, and when I checked the time it was four a.m., and less than an hour away from first light. I laid back, but even the exercises I could use to still my thoughts couldn't erase the craziness of the nightmares.

Dawn, we meet again.

I showered, made coffee, and was out of the house as the sun rose, and heading for the office. It was Sunday, but with a murder investigation going on, there was no such thing as a day off. To his credit, Devin was there waiting, a thermos under his arm, looking as if he had all the energy in the world. I admired the twenty-three-year-old's passion for the job and couldn't help but wonder why I'd let so many things happen to me that made me feel old at thirty-two.

"Morning, sir! I have more coffee." He waved the thermos at me and filled my travel mug without being asked. When he'd done his as well, he settled back in his seat, carding his fingers through his blond curls and giving me a smile.

"Thank you."

"So I have more news, on Jimmy Bowie, from Abby. She didn't think much of it before because we were focusing on the video, but she wanted to point out that Jimmy doesn't have much love for the rangers here —all tied up in the tribal dispute, I imagine? She caught him and another guy vandalizing the station last summer, scrawling slogans about land-stealing and such. His grandfather Charlie got him off with a promise of working around the place. Abby said he did good work when he was there, but she wanted you to be aware he had a grievance."

"Jimmy Bowie. Okay." Tiber had told me he was a suspect. Now I learn he'd been caught vandalizing the ranger station? I felt a stab of excitement.

"Yep."

"Can you add him to the board and—"

"Already done."

"When?"

"I got here early."

"It's early now."

"Earlier," he qualified with eagerness in his tone. "I want to know everything, and I want to do it right."

"I like your initiative."

He grinned at me, then turned serious. "So what's our plan?"

"Get up there, locate the van, ask questions."

"Find the blue chicken?"

I thought he was joking, because that bird had to be long gone, but the kid was earnest and focused.

Chasing blue fucking chickens.

What next?

THE DRIVE to Applecross took us deeper into the forest, and a small part of me considered maybe we should have brought Abby with us so we didn't get lost. But, well-signposted, the road was easy enough to drive, mostly gravel, overgrown in places, and properly off-road. There were a few twists and turns, and every so often a gap offered breathtaking views of the white-capped Olympic mountain range, a reminder of the beauty of the place we lived. Devin was quiet next to me, but when the road widened to the parking area, it was him who pointed to the sole van in the corner.

"VW van. Just like on Mike's video."

"And you pulled the details?"

"Belongs to a Mr. Kevin Lomax. I haven't been able to get hold of the owner, unknown number, but found a website where his company rents vans. So I assume this is a rental."

"Or Mr. Smith is Kevin Lomax," I warned.

Devin's eyes widened. "Yeah, sure. I didn't think that at all."

"We have to be open to all possibilities."

I pulled the car around to park behind the van, blocking it in, although imagining it racing away and there being a car chase on these roads caused a hysterical bubble of laughter to rise in my throat. Devin shot me a look.

"Tell you later," I explained, and then schooled my features as we climbed out. Devin moved toward me, just a few steps back, and together we headed for the door. The van had seen better days, paint peeling, faded stickers in the window, a general air of disuse hung about it, and I hoped the engine was in a better state than the bodywork.

"No sign of the chicken," Devin deadpanned.

"Nope." How would we catch it even if by some miraculous twist of fate, we found it? My thoughts wondered. Maybe Tiber was a chicken whisperer, the same as he was for dogs and cats and tortoises. I imagined him crouching down and waiting for the chicken to fall under his spell.

The same spell that was capturing me.

Somewhere in a break in my fevered dreams last night, while I was staring at the ceiling, I'd imagined myself asking Tiber to meet me for a coffee. Not to discuss the case. Instead, it made me smile to think of learning more about him, of talking for hours, and then holding him close and kissing him. He pulled protective instincts out of me, but there was also a strength in him I was attracted to, a stubbornness that intrigued me, and I recognized the flicker of caution in his eyes that he covered up with sharp words.

"Should we knock?" Devin asked, and I realized too

slowly that I was staring at the van, and my thoughts were all the way back at Tiber's place, on his couch.

"Of course." I knocked, but there was no answer, so I stepped back and away, and peered into one foggy back window to a counter full of boxes. "Look around," I instructed in a whisper, "maybe ten feet into the trees, in a circle around here."

With a mock salute, Devin slipped away, and this left me standing like an idiot, waiting for someone to be home. I caught the scent of weed, not an unfamiliar smell up here, and followed my nose to the other side of the van. There was still no sign of anyone there, but the driver's side window was slightly open, and the scent grew stronger as I got closer. Faded stickers covered the door, but the ones I could still make out were concerning. Hateful slogans plastered the side, along with some religious iconography that was peeling off. There was a red-on-white cross I recognized as a white supremacy symbol, a skull and crossbones, a *Gods, guns, and guts* logo, and a Confederate flag.

"Nice," I muttered to no one. I already had an impression of who the people in this van were, and all of this amped up my suspicions that none of this was good. The paint was peeling, there were rust marks at every join, and the wing mirror was held together with clear tape, glass cracked on the edge but still roadworthy from a legal point of view. A tiny spider was right in the middle, sitting there minding its own business. I didn't like spiders much, but I couldn't fail to appreciate the intricacy of the web there.

"What the hell are you doing?" someone demanded.

I spun to come face-to-face with the person from Mike's video. Broad as hell, with a shaved head, bushy beard, and piercing blue eyes. Tattoos covered his bare arms, and he had a pistol holstered at his hip. Worst of all, his T-shirt proclaimed that he oiled his guns with liberal tears.

Perfect.

Just what I needed today.

I extended a hand, which he refused to shake. "Sheriff Thompson." I introduced myself, and he didn't give me his name. I wasn't at the point where I could demand his ID. Probable cause was a thing, and experience told me that asking him to prove who he was might end up in a *situation*. "And you are?"

Again there was hesitation, and he glanced at the van, and then back at me. "Lewis. Lewis… Smith. Mr. Smith."

"Not Kevin Lomax?"

He narrowed his eyes at me and rested his hand on his belt near his weapon. "He's a friend, lent me the van."

"Hands away from your weapon, please." I stayed calm, my hand nowhere near my gun. My experience with gun nuts was that they open-carried to make a show of their beliefs more than anything. It also made them feel tough. But although it might be a security blanket to him, it was one that could kill. I wasn't taking chances.

"I have a permit," he said, and his eyes gleamed with something, as if he was daring me to call him on it.

"Of course," I agreed, "but I think this would be more comfortable if we both kept our weapons out of it."

He rolled his eyes, but he did at least move his hand.

"Mr. Smith, I'm with the sheriff's department in Prophet, just back down the road."

"I've seen it," he said, and eyed me with distaste.

"I just had a few questions for you regarding—"

"No comment," he said at such a speed that I knew he was in defense mode. *Stay professional.*

"Mr. Smith—"

"I'm parked legally, abiding the law." He crossed his arms over his chest and stared me down. Someone had evidently told him that when faced with a cop, it was shoulders back and throw constant denial.

"Legal, sure." I remained civil, even encouraging. "I'm not here about parking—"

"Well, you've got no grounds to harass me." His eyes narrowed, and his hand curled into a fist. His arm flexed and a tattoo of a snake widened with the movement.

"You're right. I'm not here to check what you do in your own time, I'm here to ask you about an incident with a park ranger…" I pulled out my notebook, as if I didn't recall every moment of what I'd seen on that video. Would Lewis trip himself up with an I-didn't-touch-him defense and then stumble over his words? To have him give us that connection would be so damn easy, but Lewis wouldn't meet my gaze, and he cleared his throat.

"What?" he asked.

"Could you give me some more background for our records regarding the conversation you had with Ranger Mike Bressett at the Green Rocks camping area where he asked you to relocate?"

He blinked. "At Green Rocks? Oh yeah, I was minding my own business, and he gets up in my face." He scowled at me—he'd gone into immediate defense mode again.

I pretended to refer to my notes. "I believe Ranger Bressett had concerns over the fact you'd parked for an extended stay in a two-nights-only camping area?"

Mr. Smith bristled, but nodded. It was clear he'd decided he wasn't saying anything at all.

"Was this a *heated* debate?"

He rolled his eyes, opened his mouth, and then shut it again.

"Mr. Smith?" I encouraged. "It's probably best you explain from your point of view."

"I know my rights," he snapped after a moment. "The ass didn't show me ID. Hell, he was messing with me without cause. So I overstayed a couple nights. I'm an American, and I was parked on American soil. I told him so."

Devin appeared behind him and caught my gaze with an added shrug. He'd found nothing and there went my expectation that Devin might locate random magical evidence that would pin a murder on Lewis here. He sauntered around the van and came up next to me, and Lewis spared him only a quick suspicious glance.

"Sorry, I was watering the trees," Devin used his best aw shucks tone, but Lewis ignored him.

"We're interested in anyone who spoke to the ranger on or around Wednesday evening, the twenty-first."

Lewis' eyes widened, and then his cunning expression made my chest tighten. "I haven't seen him since he warned me off of Green Rocks."

"Can you tell me where you were Wednesday evening?"

"I was right here, in my van with my wife," Lewis snapped. "Get out here wife!" He bellowed so loud I bet the people back in Prophet would have heard him.

"This would be four nights ago. You were here at Applecross? When did you arrive?"

"Moved here that morning. Hey wife, get out here!"

"Hello?" A woman stepped out of the vehicle and Devin tensed. She was blonde, waiflike, nervous almost, the direct opposite to her blustering husband.

"Tell them what we were doing four nights ago."

"Here, reading, sleeping, just like always," she murmured, and cast a frightened look at her husband—at least she looked frightened to me, but maybe I was reading too much into things.

"Get back in the van." Lewis snapped.

She didn't even question it as she turned to go back inside.

"Wait a moment, Mrs. Smith? Can I ask you a question?"

"Why you gotta ask her anything? I already told you we were here. Four nights back, in the van. Right, wife?"

I really didn't like the way he called her *wife*. It was as if she had no identity other than that. "Sleeping?" I asked her for confirmation.

"You deaf?" Lewis snapped—hell he was doing nothing but snapping, the tension in him growing.

"Sleeping, we were reading, and then we slept." Her eyes widened as if she'd said more than she was supposed to.

"Fuck's sake, get your ass back inside," Lewis ordered, then rounded on me. "You got no right questioning my wife."

I ignored him, even if he took a small step toward me. "Mrs. Smith, I'm specifically referring to the evening four nights ago. On Wednesday twenty-first."

She shot Lewis a glance. "Sleeping." then she

dipped her chin and mumbled. "Together. He was with me. I was with him."

She shot Lewis a glance that spoke volumes, the kind that spoke volumes as if she were saying, *did I do that right?*

"Yeah," Lewis said, and this time he headed for the van, "So unless you wanna arrest us, or you got a warrant or something, you can go."

A warrant? An arrest?

I wish.

"Can we see your ID?" Devin blurted.

My stomach clenched. The type of gun-wielding wannabe tough guy like *Mr. Smith* weren't always amenable to casual showing of their IDs. I was right.

He turned smug. "The police can never compel you to identify yourself without reasonable suspicion to believe you're involved in illegal activity," he gave his interpretation of the rule book.

"You're quite right, sir." I knew the value of making the man think he'd won, so I got there before Devin could push him further. Still, I waited for Mr. Smith to get into self-righteous mode, maybe say something incriminating, call for a lawyer, or start a fight. I didn't know what I was looking for him to do—this was miles from where we'd found Mike, but there was something nagging at me about this man and I didn't want to leave.

Devin said he'd found nothing in the vicinity, and

nothing that might show Lewis had a connection to Mike's death. So far, this visit was one big, fat dead end, and the disappointment grated on me. Not to mention the rain had started up again, heavy, and hard, collecting in the trees and dumping entire buckets of the wet stuff down on us. Lewis crowded his wife back into the van and went inside before shutting the door on us. We heard shouting, and the vehicle rocked a little, but we had nothing.

"Fuck." I muttered. "Coffee?" I asked Devin.

"Sure."

I tossed the keys to him. "You drive."

"Sorry about the ID thing," Devin murmured.

I shook my head. "It's all good. One time out of ten you might get someone who showed you their ID; Mr. Smith would never be one of those."

I was tired, wet, and knew for sure something wasn't right. There'd been a run of people touring the parks with their vans and ending up living from day-to-day, but this wasn't like that—Lewis and his *wife* were just the wrong side of normal, and I had to think hard on possible unconscious bias, and ignore the call to knock on the van door to ask more questions. Just because he was a middle-aged white man with a weapon and questionable values didn't mean he was guilty of murder. The hardest part of any law enforcement job was attempting to see all sides, when really what I wanted to do was accuse Mr. Lewis Smith of something. *Anything.*

. . .

WE CAME BACK to find Will Abraham waiting for us at the office. He was Makah and a member of the tribal police who were an active part of our community. I'd had several long conversations with Will over jurisdiction in the months I'd been sheriff, getting to understand boundaries. We weren't friends but we were respectful of each other's positions, and by silent agreement, we stayed out of each other's way in anything connected to the law. It had worked well for us so far. Still, we'd never had a murder on our doorstep.

We shook hands, and I took him into my office, rather than the small incident room, for obvious reasons, and he took the chair opposite, which left Devin propping up the wall. A frown creased Will's forehead, his dark eyes narrowed on me, and not for the first time I considered how attractive the man was, with his dark hair and his high cheekbones, and warm-toned skin. All I knew about Will was his professional reputation—he was good at his job, and fiercely protective of the rez. Hen told me he'd not long back broken up with a man who'd worked with the tribal police for a year but who'd returned to the city. It happened just before I'd started here as sheriff, and I didn't know the full story, but Hen admitted Will was a difficult man to get information out of, and not even she could get a handle on the enigmatic tribal cop.

"Had Charlie tell me you were harassing him," Will began, and held up a hand when I opened my mouth to defend myself. "I'm just telling you what he said. He wanted to get things off his chest, and understands it wasn't an official visit." Will stopped then and waited. He was good at waiting for me to fill the space.

"And?" I asked after a pause, because I had so many questions, but none of them were appropriate for me to ask when he had his line in the sand, and I had mine.

"Off the record?" Will asked as he settled back in his chair and blew on his hot coffee.

Oh wait, this sounded interesting. "Of course."

Devin stood away from the wall. "You want me to leave, sir?"

Will waved a hand. "You'll get briefed, anyway. May as well stay. It's like this; Charlie is concerned, based on his previous experience with outside law enforcement, that you won't investigate much past looking at the Makah for any trouble."

"That's not true."

"I reassured him that's not the case, but his grandson's record means he fits into your suspect pool a little too easily, and that concerns Charlie."

Jimmy was definitely a suspect given what Tiber had sensed from him. And then what Devin had added this morning. He was dead center on my list to talk to, but it wasn't because he was Makah, but because of what others told me.

"Does it concern you as well?" I asked.

Will kept his gaze steady, and generations of hurt and pain filled his heavy sigh. Trust broke easily when centuries of history colored the present. "Jimmy presents as a perfect candidate for arrest, and yes, it worries me."

I didn't take offense with Will. He and I didn't know each other well, even though I'd grown up here. I'd done nothing to prove to Will I was someone who would do anything to make sure things were done properly.

"I promise you we're following all leads," I said.

After a pause, Will nodded. "As a professional courtesy, I'd like a heads up if you intend to come onto tribal land again."

"Of course."

We shook hands, and he left, taking one of Hen's muffins with him.

I had the feeling I'd be seeing him soon. Jimmy Bowie was top of my list now, alongside Mr. and Mrs. Smith. And I hadn't crossed off Hillesden the Bigfoot hunter, not to mention any other random people we hadn't even considered yet. Something about the New Age group staying at the hotel scratched at me, but it wasn't a fleshed-out thought—and it was hard to think of Madame Borschski committing murder. Hell, she was my grandmother's age.

"I have a question, sir?" Devin asked, as we went

into the incident room and stared at the board some more. "How can I make sure that my feelings don't impede the process of law, when all I wanted to do is arrest Lewis Smith just to wipe that smug smile off his face?"

I side-eyed my rookie for practically reading my mind, and wished I had an easy answer.

"Follow the law, trust the process, learn," I instructed.

He nodded as we considered the photos on the board in silence.

All I could think was that I'd love to have one solid lead.

Chapter Fourteen

Tiber

GRACIE WOKE me up on Monday morning, her tongue slick on my face. I blinked awake, trying to get my bearings.

"You need to go out?" I slurred.

Gracie hadn't been sleeping with the pack the last few nights. She'd been out in the living room with Duke. Now she was standing on the bed, looking at me expectantly. She gave a low woof.

"What is it? Is Duke okay?"

Alarmed, I scrambled from the bed, pulled on a pair of sleep pants, and followed the click of Gracie's nails out into the hall.

Duke's crate was empty. Gracie didn't pause, and I followed her to the front door. Duke was standing there staring at it, his posture rigid, and Mike's white T-shirt clutched in his mouth the way some dogs carry around their favorite toy. He glanced at me, then back at the door, telling me what he wanted. He pawed at the door in case I was dense.

I was a little confused because Duke went to the back door for a potty break, just like all my animals.

"Okay, we'll go out. Just give me a minute." I slipped on some old tennies I kept on a shelf by the door and clipped a leash onto Duke's harness. We went out, Gracie trotting after.

I never worried about having Gracie on leash when we were anywhere near my house. She wouldn't leave my side for love or money, and the road I lived on only had sparse local traffic and was surrounded by woods. But I wasn't sure about Duke. I sensed he would take off if I let him.

He squatted on the front grass to urinate. As soon as he was done, he pulled me to the road and to the right, toward town, straining on the leash.

"Be gentle, Duke," I said. He kept pulling.

I considered what he was telling me. He was at least three years old, so I'd bet he typically wasn't a puller on leash. He was desperate to go somewhere. But where?

I let him pull me for a while to see if maybe he'd caught scent of a deer or rabbit and would head off into the woods. But no, he kept going down the asphalt road.

Where was he headed? He didn't seem fearful at the

moment. More intent. This was progress—that Duke would leave his crate at all. But what did he need? Was he looking for Mike? I was certain he knew Mike was dead—he'd been grieving too hard the past few days for me to think otherwise, not to mention I'd gotten that intuitive flash from him about it.

Did he want to go back to Sentinel Rocks, the last place he'd seen Mike? Or their home? Maybe he just wanted to get closer to Mike's scent. Hell, even Mike's body.

Or could he, possibly, be after Mike's killer?

No. Dogs didn't think that way. They weren't vengeful, and especially not labs, a friendly breed if ever there was one. One thing was sure, Duke was about to yank my arm off, and I wasn't prepared to walk all the way to town.

"Duke, stop," I said.

To my surprise, he stopped and sat.

"Stop? Is that a word you know?"

Duke gave me a funny look over his shoulder, as if to say he was already stopped. Okay then. That was a good tool to have. *Thank you, Mike.*

I squatted down next to Duke at the side of the road. Gracie poked her nose in close to join the conference. Duke's gaze remained fixed at some distant point toward town.

"Duke," I said. "*Duke.*"

His gaze shifted to mine.

"Are you looking for Mike?" I asked gently.

Duke's tail thumped once at the name, but only once. He stared back down the road.

Yeah. He loved Mike, but he knew he wasn't about to see him.

"Do you want to go home?" I tried.

He didn't respond. I waited for an intuitive flash, but all I sensed from his mind was urgency. Hmm.

"Do you want to go for a ride? Want to go in the car?"

At this Duke met my gaze, tail wagging hard, and turned back for the house. When he reached the end of the leash, he stopped but he was quivering with anticipation.

I stood and let him lead the way back to the house. So he wanted to go for a ride. Why? Was he that desperate to get away from my place? I didn't think so. It could be that Mike often took Duke for car rides. Some dogs loved going for rides almost as much as they enjoyed going for walks. But this felt like more than a simple pleasure. This felt like a mission. Maybe Duke would give me more clues along the way.

Back at the house, Duke didn't want to go back inside, pulling towards my Subaru Outback, which was parked in the driveway. But I lured him into the house with a promise of breakfast. I fed the troops. Frank was waiting at the sliding glass door, and he was exceptionally happy to receive his bowl of veggie parings. Everyone went out into the back yard to do their business. I took my time to shower and dress, and when I let the dogs in, Ferdinand and Leo danced with giddy expectation of a walk.

"Sorry, boys, but you need to stay here. I've got business with Duke this morning."

Leo barked.

"Come on, Leo. You know Duke needs some extra attention right now. I'll be back in an hour or so. And no chasing Fudge while I'm gone."

Ferdinand licked my hand to tell me he understood, but Leo sulked. I swear, that old dog was such a toddler. I promised him some one-on-one time when I got home, stroked his silky ears, and then left the house with Duke. He still had the T-shirt in his mouth and, man, I wouldn't take that piece of cloth from him if my life depended on it.

It reminded me of how nice it had been of Gabriel —*the sheriff*—to bring it by. And that reminded me of how we'd sat on my couch and talked. And of how things had gotten awkward when I'd admitted I was gay.

What had I been thinking, inviting him inside like that? I had to tread carefully there. *No more men, ever.* That was the rule. And, while it would be nice to have a friend in town, especially someone else on the rainbow spectrum, it was too dangerous to get any closer to Sheriff Gabriel Thompson. He was attracted to me. And my body reacted to him. And that could *not* be allowed to progress.

Hadn't I learned my lesson with Jeff?

When I opened the car door, Duke leaped up onto the passenger seat. He bonked the window with his nose until I started the engine and lowered it. He stuck his head out, T-shirt clenched tight in his teeth. He was doing better, but this morning he had an intensity that worried me a little.

So much for being able to read dog's minds.

"Where shall we go?" I asked Duke.

He didn't answer.

I drove down to Prophet's Main Street. It had a quaint downtown with a funky 1900s vibe, spruced up by the local business owners. I drove around the block and up and down the commercial district several times. Prophet had long been an artists' community, and a small gallery on Main carried paintings and sculptures by locals and had a rainbow flag out front. As I drove by, I noticed their current window display featured a gorgeous painting of two white wolves standing on a rock amidst foliage so green it glowed. That must be a new one by Libby Smith, Prophet's famous wildlife painter. I'd never met her. But damn, that was one sweet painting.

Duke stared out of the window intently as we drove. I watched for indications that he wanted to stop, but I didn't see him react to anything particular.

Then I noticed a crow perched on a parking sign in front of the town's coffee shop, Grounds For Joy. It might mean something or, more likely, it might not. But hell, I could always use a coffee. I turned into one of the diagonal parking spots along Main and rolled the windows up. "I'll just be gone a minute," I said. "Stay here."

I locked Duke in the car and went inside.

Grounds for Joy was a cute place with red brick walls on both sides of a long room and displays of baked goods in the window. There were a half dozen small white tables and chairs, a counter with more baked goods in a glass case, and gleaming silver coffee apparatus. There was only one older couple at a table having coffee and pastries, which meant I got the undivided attention of Jill, the woman who worked there.

Jill looked to be in her mid-twenties, had cartoonishly huge blue eyes, and wore her thin brown hair in waifish little pigtails that stuck out straight on both sides of her head. She gave me a warm smile.

"Hi, Tiber! Haven't seen you in a while."

"Yeah. Been busy." Honestly, it was cheaper to make coffee at home. Besides, I never left my house before the afternoon, if at all. "I'll take a Grande latte with soy milk please. Double shot."

"No flavorings?"

I shook my head. "Coffee and sweet doesn't mix for me."

"And that's why you're so thin!" she said cheerfully.

She meant it as a compliment, but my hand went to my ribs self-consciously. Cold fingers ran up my spine.

You look like a fucking wraith. Why don't you eat properly? You don't take care of yourself, Tiber. I have to constantly look after you.

Fuck you, Jeff, I told the vicious memory.

"So how's it going?" Jill asked over the sound of steam as she made my coffee.

I forced my brain back to the present. "Fine. How're things here?"

"Oh, you know. Serving the crazies and oddballs as usual. That's Prophet."

The words lightened my heart, and I took a deep breath. Yeah, *everyone* was weird in Prophet. Which was maybe why I felt so at home here. "Crazy good, though. Right?"

"Of course." She brought me my coffee and a smile. "Wouldn't be anywhere else."

I paid her, thanked her, and had just turned to leave when the front door swung open with a tinkle of the bell. Eight people crowded in. They struck me as tourists, though the reek of patchouli and cannabis would be right at home on some locals.

The woman at the head of the group had hair dyed jet-black framing a wrinkled face and hard, hard eyes. I took a step back involuntarily, out of their way. Something about her unnerved me, and there was a tall man at the back of her group who made my skin crawl.

But then she saw me and her face transformed, taking on a benign and friendly energy. "Oh, hello!" she greeted me. "What is that, coffee?"

"Uh—yes."

She wagged her finger. "That's so bad for your chakras, you know. Have you tried the Chai here? Is it any good?"

"I haven't."

"Well, I guess we'll just have to find out for ourselves then, won't we?" She gave me a syrupy smile. "Have a blessed day, Earth brother!"

Earth brother? For fuck's sake. White people could be so clueless. I shook my head and made my way to the door. I felt the creepy guy's eyes on me, but I didn't look at him.

Ugh. Tourists!

As I approached my car, I saw Duke had his front paws on the window, nose pressed to the glass, and was staring at the coffee shop. I assumed he was waiting for me. That surprised me, since we hadn't had long enough to bond in a way that would make him possessive. That behavior was something Leo would do. But perhaps I represented safety to him and he was frightened parked on the street alone?

But it turned out it wasn't about me. When I got in

the driver's seat, Duke couldn't care less. He remained pressed to the glass, staring at the coffee shop door.

"What is it, Duke?" I asked, putting my cup in the holder. "Did you used to come here with Mike? He's not inside, baby. I'm sorry."

Duke gave a frustrated bark, and I noticed he'd even dropped the T-shirt. It was now lying by his paws on his seat.

"It's okay, buddy." I stroked his back, but he didn't relax.

I started the car and eased back, keeping one eye on Duke. His focus didn't drop until Main Street was far behind us.

So I ended up driving over to Neah Bay. I argued with myself about the wisdom of it. Gabriel had been very clear when he'd told me to stay out of it. But he'd also admitted how difficult it was for him to make headway on the rez. And I knew it'd be much easier for me—being native, a stranger, and not the Law—to get info.

As for his fears about Jimmy getting violent, I didn't disagree. But I wasn't about to lay the fifth degree on the guy. Surely I could read the room enough not to make Jimmy suspicious.

Nothing up my sleeve. Honest.

And anyway, a walk on the beach might be good for Duke. And I doubted Mike had spent any time on the rez, and therefore it wouldn't be triggering for him.

Lame excuses R Us.

———————

WHEN WE PULLED up at beach parking, Duke's head was out of the window, as it had been the whole drive. He looked around, panting lightly.

Panting could mean various things. It could just mean he was hot. But, in this case, it was a sign of anxiety. It was low-level, though—so much better than it had been. We sat for a bit with the engine off, just taking in the view. Adjusting. In front of us was a swatch of rocky beach and the beautiful bay. It was overcast, the sky chalk-white. But it wasn't raining.

"Want to go for a walk?" I asked Duke.

His ears perked up, and he put a paw on the door. That was good enough for me.

I got out and fetched Duke from the passenger side, clipping on a leash. We walked down the beach a ways, lured on by the beauty of the landscape. Neah Bay was famous for towering rocky structures out in the water, and today they looked brown and pitted in the diffused light. The waves were minimal, lapping on the damp sand as we picked our way past assorted seaweed and flotsam left by the tide. I watched out for sea urchins. They were the same level as the sand and would spit if you stepped on them. Couldn't blame them.

I was lured on, too, by Duke's steady trotting. It had

to feel good to him to move after a few days of being so still. Retrievers were an active breed. His paws glided along, even if worry lurked in his eyes and his head was on a swivel to make sure no one was getting too close. He stuck near me and didn't pull on the leash at all.

There were some tourists on the beach, people engaged in their daily walk, and a few Makah families sitting on blankets on the sand. But it was far from crowded, and we had no trouble keeping our distance.

This was good for Duke. Getting some exercise, fresh air, and doing something as normal as taking a walk. But he was still exhibiting fear and he probably would for some time.

We turned around and were almost back at the car when I spotted Jimmy Bowie. He was sitting on his motorcycle in the same spot he'd been before, but he was alone this time. He was watching a family of three —two parents and a pretty older teenaged girl—who were sitting on a bench near the parking area eating sandwiches.

So that was why he hung out here, I realized. Trying to pick up girls. Given his looks, I'd bet he did pretty well for himself.

I stopped walking, bringing Duke in close and stroking his head. I had a decision to make. Duke hadn't noticed Jimmy. His gaze was fixed on some people walking along the water.

The protective part of my brain wanted to steer clear

of Jimmy if there was any chance of triggering Duke and setting back his progress. But Sheriff Thompson—Gabriel's—face came into my head. He'd been so tired and frustrated last night. And I pictured, too, Duke's owner, Mike Bressett, whose photo had been in the news. He deserved justice. And if I could bring a speedy end to this, shouldn't I? Hell, getting the killer into custody might even save another life.

Resolved, I started walking again, veering toward Jimmy. I watched Duke, and if he freaked, we were out of there. But his demeanor didn't change. I could swear he glanced at Jimmy, but he looked away again with no particular reaction. I dared to move a little closer. And then whatever caution I might have employed went sideways when Jimmy saw me. He rose from his motorcycle seat and came towards us. I froze, unsure what to do. Running away would seem suspicious, and it was too late to pretend I hadn't seen him.

Duke stood there, staring at me as if wondering why we'd stopped.

"Hey you," Jimmy said, tone flat. "Navajo." He approached and stopped a few feet away.

"Hey," I said, my attention on Duke.

The dog walked as far away from Jimmy as he could get on leash and sat down, facing him to keep an eye out. But it was the same sort of avoidance and wariness of other humans he'd displayed all day. He didn't seem agitated.

Maybe he didn't recognize Jimmy? It had probably been dark during the attack. But surely he'd smell the same, sound the same.

"Thought you had one of those little shit dogs. What are you, a dog walker or something? Dognapper?"

The sneer in Jimmy's voice said he was trying to egg me on now because I wasn't giving him the time of day. So I looked him in the eye.

That little shit dog could kick your ass, I thought. But I shrugged. "I have a couple of dogs. This one—" I almost said *this one is Duke*, but thought better of it. What if Jimmy had known Mike and recognized the name? "—this one is a foster dog."

"Whatever. So are you staying around here for a while then, or what? Thought you were just passing through."

"I'm gonna hang for a little while. What is there to do around here?" I tried my best to sound friendly.

Jimmy snorted. "Around here? Nothing." But he gave me an assessing up and down. "Me and Ben'll probably hit King Fisher's tonight. That's a bar in Prophet."

"Cool. Maybe I'll see you there, *Jimmy.*" I said his name loudly. Duke was looking away, now scrutinizing the family at the bench. I clicked my tongue to get his attention. When he met my gaze, I prompted. "Wanna say bye to Jimmy?" I pointed. Duke followed my finger and gave Jimmy another glance. He huffed a breath and scooted back an inch more against the leash.

No, he didn't want to say squat to Jimmy. But he wasn't afraid of him either.

"Dude. It's a dog," Jimmy said with a verbal eye roll. "Anyway, whatever. See ya." He walked away, taking out a cigarette.

Holy fuck!

I dropped to my knees and gave Duke a hug, excitement making me shake. "Duke! You did it!" I whispered. "Good boy! What a good boy."

This brilliant dog had just eliminated his first suspect.

Chapter Fifteen

Tiber

I DROVE from the rez straight to Main Street in Prophet and pulled up in front of the sheriff's office. I'd never been inside, but I'd seen it in passing often enough.

Since I'd managed to park in the shade, and the day wasn't too hot, I cracked the window a few inches and left Duke snoozing in the passenger seat. "I'll be back in a few minutes," I told him. He opened one eye to look at me and then went back to sleep. He'd been so hypervigilant during our outing that he'd exhausted himself. I wanted to get him back home where he could have some quiet time in his crate, but first I had to talk to Gabriel.

The sheriff's office reception area had a counter where an older woman with white hair and glasses typed away ferociously. She glanced up at me and stopped typing. "Oh, Tiber Russo! Hello." She gave me a welcoming smile.

I blinked at her. "Uh… hi."

"I know. We've never met. I'm Henrietta Wilkes, but everyone calls me Hen. Only, working here at the sheriff's office, as you can just imagine, I know everyone in town—by name and face if not by encounter. How are all your animals? Oh! How's Duke doing? Poor thing."

I wondered who had been talking about me. I hadn't exactly been a social butterfly since moving to Prophet. Had Gabriel said something?

Of course, Duke was related to the case, so why wouldn't he? Still, something about the way Hen regarded me—a kind of knowing look—made me think there was more to it. I decided to ignore that for now.

"Duke is doing better. Is Sheriff Thompson in?"

"Is this visit related to a case or purely personal?" she asked, placing her fingers on the keyboard as if she were about to log my response.

"I—"

"Hen!" Gabriel came charging out of an office. He gave the woman a warning glance. "Right this way, Mr. Russo." He motioned with one hand, and I followed him into another room. He shut the door.

So this was his office. It was very functional. There was a large wooden desk, white board, bulletin board with various *WANTED* posters, and a window that probably overlooked Main Street but had the blinds closed. One wall was loaded with certificates and photos. The photos were of the Prophet Sheriff's Department over the years, various small groupings of uniformed personnel lined up in front of flags. None of them showed Gabriel. I glanced at his desk. No family photos there, either.

"Have a seat, Tiber." Gabriel grabbed a sculpted office chair with black fabric cushions and pulled it out a little before moving to sit behind the desk.

"That's okay." I was too excited to sit. Now that I was in front of Gabriel, the thrill of Duke's recent revelation came back. I had to tuck my hands into my front jeans pockets to keep from wringing them.

Gabriel watched me curiously. "What happened?"

I tried to keep my voice level. "So Duke wanted to go for a drive today. As in, he literally pulled me out of the house. I brought him down to Main Street in my car, but he didn't react to anything specific—"

The way he'd acted when I'd gotten into the car at the coffee shop popped into my head, but there wasn't much to say about that.

"—so I ended up driving to Neah Bay, and we took a walk on the beach."

Gabriel's eyebrows went up. He settled farther back in his chair, but his hand clenched anxiously on the desk.

"—and guess who we ran into? Jimmy Bowie. He came up to talk to me since I met him that one time. And Duke didn't go ballistic or even react to him. So score one for Duke. He's done his first *line-up* and Jimmy is clear!"

I was breathing hard by the time I finished. I was so proud of Duke and so excited I was sort of hyperventilating. But Gabriel did not mirror that back to me. He didn't seem excited at all.

He frowned, started to say something, stopped, drilled his finger on his desk. "Can you describe exactly what happened?"

I was disappointed, but I figured I'd been too vague. So I went through Duke's responses again, from walking on the beach through our encounter with Jimmy, in more detail, ending with how I'd made sure Duke looked at Jimmy and repeated his name several times.

But the grim expression on Gabriel's face didn't budge. He wiped his face with his hand in a gesture of frustration. "Okay. Thanks for letting me know."

"You don't believe me," I said, my heart sinking.

"It's not that."

Yeah. Yeah, it was. A blaze of anger and an unexpected sense of betrayal overcame me. "Fine. Whatever. Just don't ask for my help again."

I turned to storm out, hurt because I thought we had a connection, but I didn't get far when Gabriel got to the door first and put a hand on it. "Wait. Tiber. I didn't say that."

I refused to look at him, glaring at the wall. "Why did you ask me to get involved if you think I don't know what I'm doing? You're the one who wanted me to help Duke get better so he could identify the killer!"

"I know. Can we just... I have some questions. Would you please sit down?"

No, I wouldn't sit down. But I did turn away from the door. I folded my arms over my chest, still pissed.

Gabriel shook his head. "It's just... I learned some things about Jimmy that were incredibly incriminating. I thought... I thought we finally had a good lead." He began to pace, frustrated. But his tone wasn't accusatory. More disappointed.

I shifted onto my other leg but kept my arms folded. "Well, I'm sorry. But I'm guessing the point of this exercise is to find the actual killer. Not just to pin it on someone because you can."

He stopped pacing to look at me. "Of course not! Christ. Just... I trust your assessment. I do. But... is there any chance Duke didn't recognize the killer? It was probably dark when Mike was attacked—"

"Dogs have much better night vision than we do. Not to mention their sense of smell."

"—right. But what if Duke wasn't close to Mike when the attack happened? Maybe he was off doing his business or chasing a squirrel. Or is there any chance trauma might have wiped Duke's memory? Or that he was too afraid of Jimmy to react? The way sometimes people freeze up? I've seen that happen in line-ups."

He was asking good questions, and in a reasonable tone of voice. I felt myself relaxing a little. "If he'd been that afraid of Jimmy that he *froze up*, I would have seen it. That's not what he did. He literally did not care about Jimmy any more than he did anyone else on the beach."

Gabriel nodded reluctantly. "Okay."

"As for not seeing the attack, or not being close to it, I doubt it. Duke would likely stay close to Mike if they were jogging together and Duke was off-leash. Otherwise, Mike wouldn't have let him run free like that. But even if he wasn't right next to Mike, he would have heard the attack and come running. Duke would have tried to stop it. Besides, he didn't recognize Jimmy's scent or voice either."

"Right," Gabriel sighed. He slumped to sit on the edge of his desk.

"Let me ask you this," I said, "if Duke was a person, the only eyewitness, and said someone in a line-up didn't do it, would you believe them?"

He looked up at me sharply. "It's not a matter of believing. I mean, if they really were convinced, I probably would believe them. But the more important thing is that it would mean there was no case, whether they were right or not."

I nodded. "Well trust me when I say that Duke's

senses are ten times that of any human witness. And he said Jimmy didn't do it."

Gabriel wiped his face again, but he nodded. "Okay."

It was a simple word, but I could see in his body language, his eyes, that he meant it.

I got a lump in my throat. I felt foolish. I'd overreacted when I thought he didn't believe me, and I was overreacting now in the opposite direction. What was up with that?

But it meant something to me. It did.

A lot of people didn't take me seriously. Jeff, for one. He'd always made fun of my *"stupid pet tricks,"* as he called them. And he'd implied I was somehow fleecing my clients. That I just made shit up.

It mattered to me that Gabriel respected my word. Maybe it shouldn't, but it did.

"Thank you for doing that, Tiber." Gabriel stood and put his hands on his hips, regarding me. "It's much faster than I expected to get anything from Duke."

"Duke's progress is all his doing."

Gabriel shook his head. "You've provided a safe environment. And you led him through what you did today. I truly appreciate it."

"Is there anyone else you suspect? I mean, I don't want to push Duke, but if the opportunity came up, like it did today…."

Gabriel was torn. "I can't give out any specific

names at the moment. But would you be available for a ride-along at some point if the circumstances warrant it? Honestly, it's not just Duke's judgement I trust."

My face burned. "Yeah. If I can help.....,"

"I know where to find you." Gabriel smiled.

The door opened and Hen stuck her head in. She looked from the sheriff's face to mine and back again. "Muffins, anyone?" she asked.

Chapter Sixteen

Gabriel

I'D NEVER TURNED down a warm muffin, but I was so damn tempted to throw the ones Hen placed on my desk out of the window.

Only because Hen was now in the room with us, and Tiber used the interruption as an excuse to escape and I had more I wanted to say to him.

"Thank you," I heard him say as he slipped out of the door, and you'd better believe I was up and out of my chair in an instant, winding past a smirking Hen and then stopping.

"I'm taking a break," I advised her.

She raised an eyebrow, and I rolled my eyes—that was a hell of a lot of non-verbal communication.

"You can leave the muffins if you like," I said.

She bit her lip as if she was keeping back a laugh. "Sure."

I grabbed my coat—no sign of Tiber—and dashed out into the pouring rain, waving at him as he closed his car door. I'd caught his attention, but he was still buckling up.

"Coffee?" I mouthed, and made the sign of drinking from a cup.

I called it a win that he didn't start the engine, but a worry that he didn't immediately get out of the car, and I counted down from five before I casually strolled over to ask him again. I was almost at the door when it opened.

"Did you want me?" he asked with care.

Oh yeah. I kind of did. I wanted to talk to him, and hold him, and kiss his nose, and run my hands through his long dark hair. I hadn't felt stirrings of attraction like this about anyone since I'd been in LA, but Tiber was there in my head, and I caught the way he glanced at me.

I wished I could read his expression.

"Do you want to get a coffee?"

"We just had a coffee," he picked up something and waved it at me. "I got a muffin too."

"I'd like to ask you…" I stopped when the lie caught in my throat. "I'd like to talk to you about things that aren't murders and witnesses."

He looked at the passenger seat. For the first time I

noticed Duke was in the car. He was zonked out, curled up on the seat with Mike's T-shirt under his head. *Way to be observant, Gabriel.*

"I guess it's okay to leave Duke for a few more minutes." He tilted his head towards Grounds for Joy across the street. "If you meant now?"

"Yeah. I'd like that," I murmured, and winced when a raindrop slid down my nose and dripped off the end. There must have been something amusing in me doing that because Tiber smiled.

"Okay."

He clambered out, locked the car, and pulled up his hood, and together we darted across the road to the coffee shop and slipped inside as someone came out. I recognized Louise from the doctor's office, so I assume with her and Hen on the gossip line, then us having coffee would be all over town in less than an hour.

I guess it was better to have that than the anonymity of the city and the secrets of being undercover.

We hovered by the counter; he ordered a hot chocolate with cream and marshmallows; I went for my normal straight black coffee, and then it was a matter of taking said drinks to a table, and we headed to the seats behind a large display of Bigfoot merchandise—the irony wasn't lost on me at all.

We'd removed our coats, and settled in our seats, and I passed some conversations starters through my thoughts, but nothing came to mind. I think I'd lost all my skills when I'd been pretending to be someone else, and they hadn't come back to me yet. I could easily drop into character as my undercover alter ego, Zachary Owens, but when I tried to find the real me, I felt brittle.

"Did you have some more questions for me?" Tiber asked. "I mean, there's not much more I can give you."

"This isn't about the case," I said, far too quick, so much that I startled him—way to fuck this up. "I just thought that you… that I… Jesus." I scrubbed my eyes and then laughed. "I like you. I'd like to get to know you more."

"Like a date?"

"Sure."

He winced. "I don't date."

"Oh." *Well, damn.*

Silence.

Tiber examined a marshmallow, poking it with a spoon so it went under the chocolate and then bobbed up, each time a little more melted, and I was lost over what to say. What could I talk about that would push the onus for chatting over on Tiber? Maybe if I listened to him, then I could find the bits of me that weren't sheriff, and weren't LA Cop, and surprise even myself. Dogs. I could talk about dogs. I liked dogs. I'd even thought of having a dog. This was safe ground.

"So you've always liked dogs, then. I mean, to want to be a vet, I guess you have to?" *Lame. So lame.*

"All animals really, but I've had more of a pack since I settled here in Prophet. My previous, er, *roommate*, wasn't a fan."

"What made you come to Prophet?"

He shrugged, and then quirked a smile—a cute and sexy smile. "I drove up to check out the Olympic National Park and fell in love." He made it sound so simple, but then Prophet was home to me, and I couldn't disagree that it had a certain peace. "What about you? "he asked. "Why did you come back home after living in LA? Not that I think you made the wrong choice at all—I hate LA"

I wondered how much of my story he knew. Was he aware that the family split I'd caused had left me on the outside looking in? Did he understand that despite all of that, the town still called me one of their own? Had he seen how cautious people were to mention my family around me?

"Things went badly wrong. I was... unhappy. I'd left here thinking I'd have this bright shining career, then messed that up, broke apart. Home seemed like the best place to get my head straight, but when I came back, too many things had happened. My dad died, and I wasn't here. The twins were born, and I was there for that, but not for when they talked, or walked, or became the little people I want to be Uncle Gabriel for. You know I have a niece and nephew, right?"

"Not really—I'm not exactly in the loop when it

comes to local gossip."

I saw his expression change, a hint of sadness or maybe resignation. I didn't want him to feel sad. "I came home to fix things, but I think maybe it's impossible."

"I get that," he said, and scooped up some cream, licking it from the spoon. He didn't do it to be sexy, but the way his expression changed, as if that cream was the best taste in the entire world, a soft sigh escaping his lips—I was hard and needy and wanted to lean over and kiss the cream from his mouth. "Sometimes the past was so twisted up, that it's impossible to think about a future. At least you came here to do good things," he added the last and then smiled at me.

Oh god... that smile...

"I was away too much. Things fell to one side. I messed up, but my reasoning for staying in Prophet is to find... peace I guess, and also that if my family see me enough, they might forgive me."

"That's what families should do."

"Yeah."

I felt shaky that I'd even touched on the reasons I'd come back to Prophet, but something about Tiber made me want to share at least something of the real me, and to ask him real questions.

"So why no dating?" I asked innocently, and I didn't have to be a cop to see the shutters falling in Tiber's eyes as he hurried to shove all his secrets away.

"I can't. I'm not... I don't..." He pressed his lips tight. "I've had shitty experiences with it, to be honest. And one extremely toxic relationship. I'm not going there again. I can't."

I remembered what Hen had relayed about the local gossip. *A badly broken heart.* It sounded not so much broken as crushed under someone's boot. "I'm sorry to hear that, Tiber. But it doesn't have to be like that."

He shook his head again, his expression stony. He wasn't playing coy. He meant it. I wondered who'd been such an asshole as to be cruel to this beautiful, gentle man.

"How about we just get coffee then, and see how it goes?"

"What?" he shot me a look. "No. I said, no dating."

"Coffee isn't dating," I lied.

He stood then, abruptly, his chair hitting the display, a handful of Bigfoot stickers tumbled to the floor, and he picked them up with a guilty expression. Then he pulled out some cash and dropped it on the table. Now he was flustered, angry, sad? Jeez, I couldn't tell.

"Wait, I'm sorry, whatever I did I—"

"You did nothing," he said in a low voice low despite the only person in the shop being the owner herself— Glenda—who barely heard orders, let alone heated discussions. "I'm sorry. I just... can't."

"Tiber—"

The door closed behind him, which was a good

thing because I didn't know what I was going to say, anyway. By the time I dropped cash of my own and hurried to the door, my arms twisted in my coat, I saw his car vanishing around the corner and when I darted out, I just about missed crashing into my brother, who sidestepped to avoid me, and then carried on.

I was about done with the silent treatment.

"Sam wait! How are the kids? And Lori?" I called after him.

"Fine," he said and kept walking, heading for the mercantile.

No. Not this time. I couldn't let him just go without at least getting him to understand I had my reasons, and that I had to get him to accept them at face value. I jogged to catch up, grabbing his arm and yanking him under the shelter of a tree, pulling him back until we were out of sight of prying eyes.

"There was a reason I couldn't come home. I was so deep in everything—"

Sam shook off my hold. "You hated Dad, you didn't care about me and Ezra, that's all."

"That's bullshit. I love you and Ezra, you're my little brothers." I didn't address the Dad part. I never hated him, I just hated what he believed in, when religion ruled his every thought. We'd argued all the time, butted heads over most things. He wanted me to stay at home and work the family business, he wanted me to marry and have kids, and he certainly didn't want me to be gay because in his eyes that was against God's word. "I never hated him, but his beliefs and how he just never accepted who I was and—"

"You killed him by leaving."

I reared back in surprise. Hell, that was some accusation, and a new one thrown from Sam.

"Me leaving didn't kill him, so don't you do that. Don't lay it on me!" I snapped.

Sam took a step away from me and winced. Sam had heard the fights, heard our dad tell me he didn't have three sons anymore, told me to pack my bags and leave. What did he expect me to do? Did I regret it as soon as I left? Did I miss my brothers? Did I hate myself for being so damn stubborn? Of course, to all of those, but hindsight was a wonderful thing, and the Thompson family was stubborn.

"I didn't mean—"

"His heart killed him, bitterness killed him, but having a gay son didn't kill him."

We stood in silence, both on the edge of temper, but it was Sam who thought he had the most to say, and after that pause he went straight for the jugular.

"You could have tried to stay for your brothers. Ezra was only ten, and you didn't stay, and then Dad died and you never came back to help me." Sam shouted in my face, then lowered his voice. "You never even tried."

"I love you and Ezra. You're my brothers. And Lori and the kids. You're all the reason I came home."

"I was on my own," Sam said, his voice choked. "Dad died, and you were nowhere. You weren't here." He shoved me then, and I stumbled, my back against the trunk of the tree. "You left me to deal with Ezra, you left me with Dad who was ill for months, you left me to deal with the horses, the cabins, the stables, our tours. Hell, I watched our family business lose money every single day because I couldn't do it all." He shoved me again. "Because you. Left. *Me*."

I caught his hand, but he wrenched it away.

"I didn't mean to. I should have come back, but I couldn't." I was so torn over wanting to tell Sam everything.

Sam waited, tilted his head as if he was examining me. "Why?"

"Why what?"

"That's all I'm getting? You say you were stubborn, say you should have come back, and then you stop. Is that all the explanation I'm ever going to get?"

"I want to tell you more, but I promise as soon as I can let you know, I will—"

"I'm your brother!" he snapped, and then he stalked away.

And I let him go.

I'd upset Tiber, given Sam nothing, and in doing so, both men had left.

This day was so messed up.

Chapter Seventeen

Tiber

THAT NIGHT when I went to bed, Duke padded into the
room, followed by Gracie. He stared at me with big
brown eyes.

"You want to sleep with us?"

This invitation made Leo snuggle closer to me,
defensive of his spot.

"You can come up." I patted an empty spot next to
my leg. Ferdinand liked to sleep on the spare pillow
closest to the window, Patch and Fudge lay together on
a cat bed on the dresser where Patch could watch over
his kingdom, and Renfield snuggled under the covers in
his open cage in the corner. Everyone had their spot, but
there was always room for one more.

Well, as long as the *one more* had fur.

Sheriff Gabriel Thompson wanted to date me. *Me*.

I'd told him no, of course. But I felt sort of sick about it. Unsettled.

And, lying here in bed with a zillion animals... horny.

I was twenty-six years old and male. Apparently, no matter how bad your past experiences were, it didn't kill your libido. At least, it hadn't mine. I was attracted to Gabriel. Physically. Well, fuck. He was one fine-looking man, and it turned out I wasn't immune to the warmth in his eyes or the way he treated me with respect.

But Jeff had seemed great too, at the start. And I hadn't even gotten over my last disaster of a relationship. I'd moved to Prophet as a fresh start, a haven. To get away from a guy who wanted to control me. The last thing I needed—the absolutely last fucking thing—was to get involved with someone here and have that go to shit.

Because then what would I do? This little house and yard were perfect for the animals; perfect for me. I wouldn't risk that. And Gabriel was the goddamn sheriff. If it went bad, he could make my life a living hell. Call up any number of citations I was breaking with my little home zoo or whatever. Stalk me. Beat me. And I wouldn't even be able to turn to the cops for help.

"Is it legal to keep something like that as a pet?"

He'd said that the first time I met him about Frank. Hello? How much of a red flag was that?

And then there was the fact that I hadn't desired anyone since I'd left Jeff. So my body might get ideas, but the rest of me did not need the complication.

This had to be a working relationship only. End of story.

I mean it.

Please, God, don't let me fuck this up.

Duke jumped on the bed, followed by Gracie. The pair of them settled near my feet. The rain was loud on the windows, on the roof. I pushed down my hormones and turned out the light. I was too tired to deal with getting off. Tomorrow, in the shower.

I was fine being alone. *Just fine.*

One of the animals sighed or maybe I dreamed it.

I was on a country road at night, and it was pouring rain. I was trying to walk, trying to get somewhere, but the rain kept getting in my eyes, stinging, and blinding me. I wiped at them, trying to clear it away, but it was thick. Thick and sticky.

I looked down at my hands. There was moonlight despite the rain, and I saw my hands were covered with something dark. I rubbed it between my fingers.

It was raining blood.

Panic and fear came over me. I suddenly remembered where I'd been going. I had to hurry! I began to run. I had to get there in time. Had to!

From a distance, I heard her scream. You think deer can't scream. But let me tell you something—they can.

And it's a sound you never want to hear as long as you live.

The doe was screaming. She was screaming and screaming.

I had to get to her. I had to move her babies off the road so she wouldn't get hit. I ran so hard, I couldn't breathe. Then I saw her up ahead. She stood on the two-lane tarmac over two small, limp bodies, and she was screaming.

I'm coming. I'm coming. Gotta drag the fawns off the road. Poor things. Poor, poor things. It was so wrong, so *horrible and awful and wrong*. And Jeff laughing. The doe will never leave them. She won't leave the road while—

Her silhouette was suddenly illuminated by the lights of a huge, approaching semi-truck.

No! No, stop! Please!

I woke to Leo licking the tears off my face.

Chapter Eighteen

Gabriel

THE CALL to my old boss was an early one, but Lincoln McGinnis was an early riser, and I knew he'd be sitting at his desk, just the same as I'd always known him to be, fueled by caffeine and hope.

I knew the coffee would be thick and sludgy, and that the hope was for the guys under him to come home safe.

"LAPD. McGinnis," he answered gruffly.

"Lincoln! It's Gabriel."

"Gabriel, dude, how's it hanging?" Never let it be said that Lincoln was a serious boss. He was the king of gallows humor and one of the best men I'd ever met. We weren't friends outside work, we hadn't kept in touch for many reasons since I'd left LA four months ago, but I respected and admired the way Lincoln ran his team.

"Good," I lied.

"You coming back?" he asked, and there was that hope again.

"Nope." I kept my refusal light and forced all the demons wanting me to say *fuck no* to one side. Lincoln was one of the few people who knew the full story of my time undercover, and it wasn't pretty. I knew he'd wanted me to stay with his team, but also he'd understood when I'd turned in my badge and gun.

"Okay, well, if this isn't a call about how you miss us so much you want back in, then, how goes the wild west, sheriff?" He snorted at his own joke.

"It's going." I waited a moment, then leaped straight in. "What's the latest on Cyrus?"

Lincoln gave a heavy sigh. "Still behind bars, survived three attempts on his life so far. I wish he'd die already," he added with a huff. "Give closure to those he hurt.

Amen to that.

"Still no chance of him getting out, or reaching for outside help, or hunting me down or—"

"You died. Your identity as Zachary Owens died. All roads point to Zachary being dead. Why are you asking?"

Relief unfurled inside me, but I still had to ask the other question, and this one far thornier. "Linc, just…

I'm here with my family and I want to…" *tell them
everything.*

"I see. Gabe, look, this happens. Especially when
you've been undercover for so long. You know why we
advise against it."

"To keep them safe, I know. I get it. But he's in jail,
his networks are gone, he's nothing, and my identity is
dead, so how can it hurt?"

"Family taking it bad?"

Now it was my turn to sigh. "So freaking bad, you
wouldn't believe."

"It's your decision, Gabriel, but you know what you
signed up for when you joined the team, so be mindful
of what you say?"

"Yeah. I will. I'm not even sure I'm going to say
anything. Maybe it's better I keep everything inside."

"Look, Gabe," he'd lowered his voice as if he
wanted this part off-the-record. "Family is everything,
and sometimes secrets are acid inside us. You don't
have to be specific, but they need you as much as you
need them. That's all I'm saying."

There was a clatter on his end, and he called hello to
someone whose name I didn't know. The special ops
undercover team had a high turnover. "Gotta go, but
think on what I said. Yeah?"

"Thanks Lincoln. I will."

Hen arriving made me cut the call, and with a
hurried goodbye, I was opening work email and gave

Hen a smile as she refilled my coffee. Luckily she had to answer the phone. I got past her and then locked myself in the incident room, slumping into a chair and staring at the boards as if doing that would produce an answer to real-life problems and a solution to the case all at the same time.

Anything to distract myself from my conversation with Lincoln.

The coroner had sent through a more detailed report. Mike had died from the blow to the head, which was enough to cause brain damage and internal bleeding. The crack in his skull suggested someone had punched him with a powerful blow.

I scrubbed at my eyes; It wasn't her fault, but I hated she was so specific.

One good point was that she'd made a note about a tan line on his left wrist consistent with him wearing a watch or a metal bracelet, so that lined up with the watch I'd seen in the video, although we couldn't find his phone, or anything on his laptop that tracked his steps.

This was one frustration after another. I could put a call in with everyone who might track steps, but that would take time, and involve warrants, and even though I asked Devin to get the ball rolling, it could be weeks before we got any decent data.

In her conclusion, the coroner ruled Mike's death as probable homicide.

What I'd expected, but hard to see all the same.

Someone knocked sharp and certain on the door.

"Fire, sheriff!" Hen called from outside.

I hurried out, my head full of my town being destroyed, to find Lucas Quinnel grinning at me and not looking at all as if he was worried about a fire. He was one of four volunteer firefighters in the area, and if there was an incident, he shouldn't be smiling, right? Unless he was under the influence of an adrenaline rush.

I'd seen it before—people standing and grinning as their worlds burned.

"What? Fire? Where?" I asked, and raked my gaze over Lucas, checking for damage, smoke, burns, whatever might show what we're facing.

"A small one," Lucas said. "Over at the hotel, room three, the dormitory room with the bunks. Dealt with, but there's something odd, and I need you to come down and look."

"Sure," I glanced at Hen, who nodded that she'd mark me as out, and then followed Lucas out of the station and over to the hotel. All too soon we were at room 3, Daisy hovering outside the door and wringing her hands.

"It's my hotel! It's mine! They could have burned down the whole thing!" she wailed. "I told them, no damage, and look what they've done! You need to arrest all of them now!"

Lucas ushered me in, and the smell of burning hit

me, only there wasn't much evidence of a fire, apart from a burn mark on the floor. I took stock of that, and the eight people perched on seats and the bottom bunks staring forlornly at the floor. Well, all apart from two, Madame Borschski, the New Age seventy-year-old with her black and purple skirts, which were singed, and the guy who'd stared at me when we last met.

"Okay, what happened here?"

"We were welcoming the dawn, and—"

"Shhhh!"

"It was an accident—"

"Say nothing!"

I waited until the clamor died down, gleaning nothing at all.

"Lucas?" I asked our firefighter, who appeared to be keeping back laughter.

"Automatic alarms alerted us to the fire." He pointed to the ceiling and the flashing light. "We located the burn, which the guests had actually extinguished by the time we got here, carried out our checks, and then called you."

"It's the man with the purple aura," one of them muttered.

"I still say it's scarlet."

"Madame says it's purple, so it's purple."

Lucas turned to face me, and bit his lip, but couldn't stop a snort of laughter he covered up with a cough. "The   occupants   were"—he   coughed   again—

"undertaking a ceremony." He shook off the smile and tried his best to look serious as he turned back to the group. "We're all clear here, so I'll leave you to talk to the sheriff."

Firefighter Quinnel left, and I folded my arms over my chest.

"Arrest them!" Daisy demanded from the doorway. "Burning things on my property, and only paid until tomorrow. I bet they were going to burn and run! Oh my god! They were going to burn down the entire building! And me inside it! Murder!"

"It was one chicken," Madame Borschski defended.

Huh? I blinked at her. "You were cooking a chicken? In the middle of your room?"

Madame Borschski wrinkled her nose and shook her hand so hard all her bracelets jangled. "It was a ceremony," she said, but didn't elaborate.

"Arrest them!" Daisy shrieked.

I shot her a frown of warning. "If you could wait outside, Ms. Simmonds," I encouraged her, forcefully.

She seemed as if she was going to protest, but then she backpedaled and vanished out of the door, all while muttering under her breath. I turned to face the eight; six of whom refused to look at me. It was only Madame Borschski and that other guy who met my gaze, and their expressions were closed off.

"Where *is* the chicken?" I asked because what else

was I going to ask? Why was it that chickens were the bane of my life right now?

No one spoke, but then Madame Borschski pointed to a bag in the corner and I picked it up. The remains of an oven-ready frozen chicken were inside, along with the plastic it had come in, some black candles, and matches. I pulled out the carcass, two blue stripes on its breast, and noted that someone had taken a knife to it and split the chicken's breast neatly into four on the diagonal.

"I know I'm probably going to regret this, but can someone explain to me why there was a fire, and why I'm holding a bag of chicken?"

The silence was overwhelming. Then the man farthest from me whispered something to the woman next to him, and I saw Madame Borschski's composure slip into a frown she shot his way.

"Robert Parker," the timid guy who saw my aura as scarlet introduced himself. "We all paid good money for this, but I think maybe we were conned."

"Shhh."

"I agree," a woman said. "Seriously, two thousand bucks and we're reduced to a frozen chicken."

"The dawn—"

"I'm done with this." Robert raised his hand again, as if he was in a classroom. "All I wanted was to commune with nature, drink in the solstice's splendor, that's all."

"And you got what you paid for," the staring man said, and Robert went quiet.

"Can I get *your* name, sir?"

He paused a moment, then sighed. "Tom Dorman. I work with Madame Borschski."

"Mr. Dorman, what can you tell me about the chickens?" I couldn't believe I'd just asked that question, but the blue paint made me think of the connection to the birds Abby told me about. In all my training and experience, I never thought I'd be talking to someone about chickens in a murder case.

Robert huffed. "It's stupid—"

"It's symbolic," Tom interjected. "So you can shut your mouth and stay quiet."

Robert was cowed again, but the whole room was changing in tone with more murmurs of discontent.

"It's a mess. The whole thing is a goddamned mess and I want no part in any of it." Robert scrubbed at his eyes. "I told her it was madness."

"Told her what was madness?" I asked.

Tom glared at Robert, who did a brilliant impression of a goldfish and then went silent.

Madame Borschski gasped, but other than that single noise, it was silent again. I was feeling dizzy, not sure if it was the absurdity of what was happening here or the fragrance of weed that permeated everything. I placed the bag of chicken on the table and sat on the wide windowsill.

"What was madness?" I asked the room.

Robert was mute, but then another person, a younger woman with long green hair, put her hand up.

I tried my hardest not to mention this wasn't school.

"The solstice demanded a sacrifice, and the first chicken escaped and the second one, well it just up and got carried away by something in the woods right after we'd painted its head for the ritual."

"What ritual?" I asked, knowing that whatever I heard was going to freak me out.

"The solstice ritual, where we—"

"That's enough, Mavis," Madame Borschski interrupted. "It's private business between us and Beelzebub."

I'd heard enough and pointed at Madame Borschski. "You, stop talking." Then I pointed at Mavis. "You carry on."

"We can't find balance. Not until we spill blood," Mavis finished, but cowered as Madame Borschski glared at her.

The feeling that I was on the edge of something made the hairs stand up on the back of my neck and I made my way to the door and leaned there—blocking anyone from getting out. Then I pressed the button on my radio.

"Dispatch, get Devin down to the scene at the hotel."

"Copy sheriff. Was it a big fire?"

I felt bad for shutting Hen down, but ritual, blood, sacrifice, and the fact we had a body was making everything light up in my brain. I rested my hand on my weapon, just enough to show I was in charge in the room, and everyone stared at me. "Just get Devin, to me. Please."

"Copy that."

Mavis hummed, swaying gently, her shoulders knocking the woman next to her. "Everyone join in…" she encouraged.

Not a single person did. Not even Madame Borschski, who was looking less ethereal and floaty, and instead hard and watchful… I didn't know what they were a group of. New age religious? But where did sacrifice fit in? And why were they trying to invoke Beelzebub, because he was a demon, right? None of this made sense individually, but every point added together became more, and I would be stupid not to add each and every one of them to my list of suspects.

Devin arrived quickly, stopping at my side. "Sir?"

"I want you to stand in this room while I get to the bottom of the fire here."

The cacophony of responses was so loud that Devin took a step back.

"What?"

"No, we didn't—"

"It's frozen!"

"I'm not having this—"

Everyone tried to talk, but Devin stopped them with a loud whistle.

"Okay, okay. Settle down," he ordered.

I was impressed that he took control of the scene.

"No more burning in hotel rooms, and stay off the chicken thing, okay?" Despite my gut telling me something was happening here, I aimed for affable, and one by one everyone appeared to relax, even Madame Borschski and her friend Tom. "I'm sure we can smooth everything over."

Devin side-eyed me, and I ignored him.

"I'll leave my deputy here, and he can fetch you to me a few at a time for us to get details from you all."

"Don't see why I have to say anything," a young woman pointed out from the back.

Leaving Devin here was a way of making sure no one left, and I gestured for him. to follow me outside. "I'm getting Tiber, and Duke. Meet me at the cafe in thirty, bring Madame Borschski, her second, Tom, and that younger woman, Mavis. Something's not right and I have a hunch they are hiding something."

"You're going to arrest them? All of them?"

"On what grounds? Structural damage and painting a frozen chicken blue is hardly grounds to have eight of them in for questioning, so I want to try the Tiber thing first."

"Sir…" He paused and seemed uncomfortable.

"Spit it out, Devin."

"You're ignoring the collection of facts and instead you're relying on a dog?"

He seemed so confused, and I knew I was appearing crazy.

"I always work my hunches, and I think this will cut corners and allow us to at least get a feel for whether something connects them to the murder."

"Okay, but what do I do with them?" He seemed nervous. "What if they rush me?"

I clapped a hand on his shoulder. "I think you can handle it. Keep them in the room, stand at the open door, listen, watch, and I'll be back as soon as I can with Tiber and Duke, and I hope to hell Duke can give us an idea if they were involved and close this case before ISB even gets here."

"Sure thing, sheriff."

I'd been hoping in my heart that the next time I saw Tiber it would be to talk to him about what was so bad in his past that he didn't want to date. The selfish part of me wanted him to give me an explanation with issues where I had a solution that made everything right. I wouldn't ask him—it wasn't my place, and he could keep his secrets. I respected him for that.

Only, if a date wasn't happening then I'd take a work connection over nothing else.

I'd take anything that meant I got to see him again.

Chapter Nineteen

Tiber

TUESDAY MORNING I woke to the sound of rain. I fed the troops and stared out at a bleak, soggy day. Even in Portland, you'd get the occasional day in July and August that felt like February—rainy and cold. It happened more often than not here in the shadow of the Olympics.

Fortunately, I'd taken Gracie, Leo, and Ferdinand for a long walk the evening before after getting back from the sheriff's office. They'd needed it, and it had given Duke some quiet time in his crate.

I was doubly glad of it now, since it meant I didn't need to get them all out in the downpour. But I didn't have any work scheduled for the day either.

I spent a few hours cleaning. And not because

Gabriel might stop by at some point—for work-related reasons. There was always plenty to do in a house with this many animals.

I was still working on my bathroom when a chorus of barks rose up. I rinsed my hands, dried them, and reached the front door just as the knock came. I peeked out of the window. The sheriff's department's uniform and handsome profile made my heart pound.

I ordered the beasts to get back and slipped out of the front door to join him on the stoop.

"Hey," I said, feeling breathless.

"Hey, Tiber."

For a moment he stared at me, then glanced down at my feet, and quickly back up again as if remembering what I'd said about him staring at my feet the first time.

I raised an eyebrow at him.

Gabriel was flustered. "I'm not…. I mean…." He straightened his shoulders. "I wanted to ask if you'd be willing, and if Duke was up to it, if you'd help me out with something."

"Yeah. Of course. What's up?"

"I was hoping we might drive Duke over to the hotel together. There're some people staying there that are, well, suspects. I'd love to gauge his reaction to them. If you think he's up to it."

Was he? Duke had slept for hours after we'd returned yesterday, but he'd seemed okay last night. He'd sat by my feet while I worked on my laptop on the couch with all the troops around me, and he'd slept in my bed with the pack. If my nightmare had disturbed him, he hadn't shown it. But then, maybe he had nightmares of his own.

"I think he can handle going into town," I said. "But if you want him to check out a suspect, it would be better if I could gauge his reaction to them from a distance before we get too close. Would it be possible to do it outside?"

"I was thinking the cafe, but you have a point." Gabriel considered it. "There's a picnic table at the hotel. You could walk by there with Duke."

I looked at the sky, and a fat raindrop hit my nose. I raised one eyebrow.

He smiled, sheepish. "It's a covered picnic table. Like a little picnic shelter thing. Besides, it's just drizzling."

"Spoken like a true Prophetite. Okay, let's try it."

Gabriel seemed relieved. "Great. Thank you. Just give me a minute." He radioed his deputy, Devin, about the change of plans, then turned back to me with a little smile. "You know, I kind of feel like I have a secret weapon. Not sure I could explain it in court, though."

I shrugged, though I was pleased. "Court schmort. At least Duke can point you in the right direction."

"Exactly." He hesitated. "So… would now be a good time?"

I could tell he was anxious to go, but he was *asking*

me, not telling, which I appreciated. He needed my ready cooperation, of course. And Duke's.

"We can go now if you want. And ride with you?"

"Perfect."

"Just give me a few minutes."

My hands were shaking as I got changed. I took a moment to sit on the bed and gather myself. I hated that I reacted to Gabriel Thompson so strongly. But this wasn't about me. It was about Mike Bressett, and Duke, and maybe even helping to protect others from a killer. If it weren't for that, I'd extract myself from this… whatever it was. Shut the door in the sheriff's face. That handsome, too-tempting face.

I'd been doing fine on my own. I didn't need this.

It would all be over soon, one way or the other. Then I could go back to normal.

I put on a rain jacket, slipped a leash on Duke, and left the house. I was quiet as Gabriel let Duke and I into the back seat of the sheriff's department SUV and drove to town.

The plan he outlined was simple. He would drop Duke and me off at a small park across from the hotel, and then he'd get the suspects to walk out to the picnic table with him. I'd stroll by with Duke on leash. Gabriel didn't tell me anything about the suspects, and I didn't ask. Maybe he thought it'd be better if I had no bias going in.

When we got to the park, the rain had abated,

though the sky was dark and ominous. I walked Duke around the park's perimeter a few times to help him relax. But he was tense—more tense today than he'd been yesterday. His body was rigid, his ears alert, and he scanned the area for danger.

Was I pushing him too hard? I sat down on a bench and brought him close, scratching his back. "It's okay, Duke. What's wrong, buddy? I won't let anyone hurt you."

I got a flash of intuition from him. He knew this park. He'd been here with Mike.

That surprised me. This park was too small for anyone but—

Then it hit me. Gabriel had mentioned that Mike and Duke were staying in the hotel since he was new in town. I'd bet Mike had walked Duke over here to this park to do his business several times a day.

Crap! I wanted to kick my own ass. Why hadn't I thought of that?

Because you were trying to impress the sheriff with what Duke could do. What you could do.

Fuck me. Duke wasn't freaking out, but he was under stress. He didn't need this vivid of a reminder about what he'd lost. I was about to text Gabriel and tell him we needed to go when the front door of the hotel opened and he came out. Two women and a man, all carrying coffee cups, followed him.

They headed for the covered picnic table on the little

hotel lawn. I bit my lip and put my phone back in my pocket. Too late. It took me a moment, but I recognized the people Gabriel was with. The woman with the jet-black dyed hair and wrinkled face was the one I'd met at the coffee shop, the one who'd asked about chai tea. I didn't recognize the shorter, skinny, woman with her, but the taller man with thinning hair was the creepy guy who'd been in her group that day.

They were suspects in Mike's murder? Really? Why?

Duke took off, and my arm was nearly yanked out of its socket. His attention was laser-focused on the small group as they sat at the picnic table. He pulled me to the street, and I had to wrap the leash around my arm to get him to stop so I could check for traffic. It was clear, so I let him lead me across. He made a beeline for the picnic table.

My heart raced and my mouth turned into a desert. Shit. Shit. He knew these people. Was one of them the murderer?

The older lady was talking about something, waving her hands, as we approached. Gabriel nodded, listening, then he spotted me and Duke. His eyes went wide and he stiffened, his glance moving between Duke and the three strangers.

Gabriel's hand went to his waist. His gun?

Fuck. This could all go sideways fast. Because Duke was gonna do whatever Duke was gonna do, and the suspects might panic, and maybe there'd be running and shooting…. It was sheer fear on my part that made me ground my heels and pull back on Duke's leash. We were only about six yards from the picnic tables. The creepy man rose unsteadily to his feet, his gaze on Duke. His face went sunset-red.

His forward momentum halted, Duke barked. And barked. It was a high bark, incessant, and it reminded me of Leo telling off any squirrel that dared step foot on my deck.

The woman said something like "Young man, could you please remove that dog?" She didn't seem to recognize Duke, but Creepy Guy did. He eyed him with an expression that made me glad he wasn't within kicking distance. He seemed ready to bolt and, fuck, Duke's barks were painful, and he was pulling hard.

Gabriel drew his service revolver and raised his voice above the noise. "You—sit down! All of you, hands on the table, open and palms up Now!"

The gun was effective. Creepy Guy almost fell back onto the bench seat and all three of them put their hands on the table posthaste. Meanwhile, Duke kept barking at supersonic levels.

"That's it! I'm arresting you for the murder of—"

"Wait!" I shouted over the chaos.

Gabriel glanced at me, confused.

Fuck. I needed to calm this whole situation down. I

remembered the word Duke had responded to before. "Duke, *stop!*"

I said it loudly and firmly, with a matching quick tug-and-release on the leash. Duke fell silent then checked up with me as if surprised I was still there, he'd been so focused.

I put my finger to my lips. "Shhh. Quiet. I got the message. Quiet now."

Duke sat with a grumble and continued to glare at the three people at the picnic table, but he shut up.

I took a deep breath and looked at Gabriel. "Before you do anything—these three were there that night. At Sentinel Rocks. They were involved with it somehow. But they didn't kill Mike."

Gabriel blinked in surprise. He glanced at Duke, then back up to me. There was a question in his eyes, *are you sure?* I nodded.

"You can't prove we were there!" Creepy Guy said, his big hands still obediently splayed on the table. "No court's going to take a dog's word for it."

"Maybe not," Gabriel said. "But they'll take forensic evidence."

"They won't find anything!" Creepy Guy insisted, and smiled as if he'd won a prize as he puffed out his chest. I could sense the victory he was feeling, and it was slimy and nasty, and outweighed any guilt or sense of responsibility. He knew something. They *all* knew something.

"What can you tell me about the cross cut into Mike's chest?" Gabriel asked in a tone that suggested it was a throwaway question.

Creepy Guy's attitude changed, his smile slipping, and he stared around him as if he didn't understand the words.

Now it was the young woman's turn to speak up. "We didn't mean to—"

"Shut up," Creepy Guy snapped, and she subsided.

Gabriel watched the interplay, and his gaze settled on Creepy Guy. "I think we'll find the blade that cut the cross on Mike's chest will belong to you."

"What the hell? No, I—"

"In fact, I would lay money that forensics will match the cut with a knife in your possession. I'm sure it's in your hotel rooms or cars." Gabriel leaned forward. "Why don't I call up our local judge right now and get a search warrant? That's the beauty of small towns. I can have my deputy here with a warrant in about twenty minutes."

I could tell Gabriel was bluffing, but it worked.

The older woman slumped, and her beatific expression fell away, leaving an ugly sneer. "I told you to drop that knife in the lake, Tom!" She glared at Creepy Guy.

Creepy Guy—Tom—gaped at her. Yeah, she'd just thrown him under the bus. "I did not! You—! What knife?"

The skinny women rolled her eyes. "The one you said was a collector's edition *Lord of the Rings* dagger, Tom. Madame Borschski is right. You should have gotten rid of it."

The older woman—Madame Borschski—something or other—turned her death glare on Gabriel. "Yes, we were at Sentinel Rocks that night. We had a ceremony. One of the most important of the year. A solstice ceremony." Her tone dripped with disdain, as if Gabriel couldn't possibly understand.

"Go on," Gabriel said through barred teeth. "Tell me everything."

"Stop waving that gun around, and I will."

Gabriel hesitated. "Fine. But don't any of you so much as lift a pinky." He put the gun back into his holster. "Now talk."

"Madame Borschski had *chickens*," sneered Tom.

The lady in question gave him a dirty look. "Well, I meant to get a goat, but the person selling it changed their mind at the last minute. And then, provenance shone upon us and provided the ultimate sacrifice! It was the will of Beelzebub."

"To be clear, he was already dead!" Tom emphasized.

"You found Mike's body," I said, taking my cues from Duke. "This dog led you to him, didn't he? He was asking for your help!"

"He kept barking and barking," said the timid woman.

"And your name is?" Gabriel prompted.

"M-m-Mavis. Madame Borschski could hardly get through a single line of the ritual with all the racket."

"You assholes! Duke begged you to help Mike, and instead you *used* him," I snarled.

Gabriel gave me a warning glance. "I'd like to hear what happened from them, please."

He was right. I was probably doing something like leading the witnesses. Only I felt Duke's frustration so clear, and it was hard not to express it for him. I pressed my lips tight.

"We were at the sacred site and that dumb dog was there, barking and barking. I followed him to see what he wanted, just to shut him up," Tom complained. "That's when we found the body. Guy was already cold and stiff. There was no point in calling an ambulance."

"And we had to complete the ritual that same night. The gnostic calendar is very specific, you know," added Mavis.

Madame Borschski waved a bangled hand dismissively. "As far as I'm concerned, he was a gift, meant to be part of our ceremony. It was a great honor for him."

Honor? I pictured these nuts moving Mike's body and using it in whatever made-for-TV dark ceremony they'd dreamed up. They were sick! I kept my mouth shut, but oh how I glared. I wanted to let Duke go. Maybe he'd bite one of them. But he didn't need that grief, and it wouldn't make the sheriff too happy either, so I kept a tight grip on his leash.

Gabriel wiped his face with his hand. "You moved the body. To Sentinel Rocks?"

Madame nodded.

"From where?"

The two women looked at Tom. He shook his head. "I don't know. It was nearby. In the woods. Just lying there."

"You will show me where you found it," Gabriel growled.

"I can try. But it was dark." Tom shrugged.

Gabriel was pissed, his face pale. He was a bit scary when he was pissed. "We'll continue this down at the station. I want a full statement from each of you, and from anyone else who was there. And, by the way, you're all under arrest."

"We didn't do anything wrong!" Madame Borschski exclaimed. "Freedom of religion is a sacred right in this country."

Gabriel took out his handcuffs. "That may be. But how about tampering with evidence? Obstructing a crime scene investigation? Desecration of a corpse? Animal abuse? And that's for starters."

I pulled Duke to the side as Gabriel got the three people handcuffed and—complaining the whole way—

into the back of his SUV. He shut them in and came over to me. "I need to take them over to the station, but I can come back and give you a lift home."

"Thanks, but it's only two miles, and Duke and I could use the walk."

"Are you sure? It's no problem. I can lock them in detention for an hour."

"We're good." I looked down at Duke. We really were. His focus was on the sheriff's SUV and the people in the back. I could swear he understood what had just happened and felt some satisfaction at their arrest.

Poor boy. He'd tried to get them to help Mike, and what had they done? It made me furious.

Seriously, people are the worst!

A hand landed gently on my shoulder and I looked up into the prettiest hazel eyes.

"You're truly remarkable," Gabriel murmured. "How did you know that? That they didn't kill Mike?"

I shrugged. "Duke was pissed at them, but not afraid and not, like, rip-their-throats-out angry. He would have reacted differently if they'd killed Mike. It just didn't match the behavior I'd seen from him since I picked him up. Something really frightened him, and it wasn't these clowns."

There was more to it than that. An intuition about what Duke was feeling—that he'd trusted them and they'd let him down. But I could never explain it. I just knew.

Gabriel shook his head. "Well, I never would have gotten that confession without you. It was driving me nuts trying to figure out what happened. This gives me one huge piece of the puzzle, at least. So thank you."

My face heated at the praise. "Thank Duke."

"Thank you, Duke. You're a very, very good boy." Gabriel put out a hand to Duke, letting him sniff it, and when Duke didn't draw back, he stroked Duke's head. "Mike would be so proud of you."

Fuck. Time to leave before I started to cry. "So… good luck with that. Them. Let me know how it went."

"I will. Thanks again, Tiber."

And with a warm smile I wasn't sure how to interpret, he turned for his SUV.

Chapter Twenty

Gabriel

IT TURNED out that Madame Borschski, AKA Mathilda Mathews, was wanted in both California and Arizona for fraud, and when the Cali cops agreed to collect her later that afternoon, she was off our books, but in line for prosecution regarding the desecration of a corpse. Dealing with everyone else in the group, taking statements, meant it had gotten too late to go hunting near the lake for evidence now, so first light tomorrow, Madame Borschski's second, Tom, was accompanying us to show us where he'd found the body.

He'd turned from sycophant to disbeliever, and when he saw the levels that Mathilda Mathews had gone to fleece people of their hard-earned cash, he went straight through to wanting to help us with *everything*.

It didn't get us any closer to finding the murderer, given that evidence already pointed to the X being cut postmortem. Still, I wanted to find where he'd located Mike's body, and do a thorough search of the area.

With the New Age group and our resident Bigfoot expert, plus Jimmy, all eliminated from the actual murder, I was fast running out of people to suspect, and now Hen said ISB was calling, and I had this feeling about what they were going to say.

"Sheriff Thompson," I said, but all I could hear was background noise, the clack of a keyboard, and that empty echoing that made it sound like a cold call. "Hello?"

"Hello? Are you still there?"

"Sheriff Thompson speaking."

"Sorry, this line is bad... hang on..." The noise changed as the caller moved outside. "Sheriff, nice to talk finally. I'm Agent Hudson Reid with the National Park Service Law Enforcement Rangers. I understand you're in charge of the murder case. I've seen the final coroner's report, blunt force injury to the head, no intoxication, not much to go on. The rain didn't help." That was exactly what I thought when I'd read it earlier. "Do you have anything to go on?"

"We're working what we can, have a lead on where the body may have been originally."

"I've caught up with the case file, but things down here..." He paused for a moment, but I'd already heard the strain in his voice. "I'm your designated contact, and I hope that in the next few days, my team and I will be with you. Until then, store this number and keep me appraised of anything significant?"

Agent Reid had a team? I glanced over at Devin, who was filing paperwork. He was a good deputy, but the two of us weren't enough to be classed as a team of people, and we were doing a fine job of working this case on our own.

Still, more people would be awesome.

It was both good and bad that Agent Reid wasn't coming up to take over, hell, this far in I wanted to see it to the end, but also, I could do with more resources.

"Can you spare any of your team to work with me?"

"I wish I could, sheriff, if you saw what we were up against..." He cursed. "Right now it's chaos and all hands are on deck." Agent Reid was blunt and to the point, and my first instinct was to resent that, which quickly became something else when I hung up on the call. Relief. When it came down to it, I didn't want the ISB swooping in and clearing the case when it had been me and Devin who'd gotten us this far.

And Tiber and, of course, Duke.

I owed Tiber a thank you for that.

I wonder if he likes candy?

I should go visit Tiber and Duke, just to make sure Duke is okay. I could do that now, given Devin was on first shift watching the locked room where Tom lay on the super comfortable bed. Tom was the only one of the group in custody, given he was the one who'd found Mike's body, plus that he was so close to the fraudulent Mathilda Mathews. The rest of the group were in the hotel on a promise they wouldn't leave—but I had photos and names, copies of IDs, even if they did.

"I'll be back at midnight to relieve you," I informed Devin, and he glanced up from his book to smile at me.

"Yes, sir."

I headed straight for the grocery store, determined to pick up something that would give me an excuse to visit Tiber. I caught them a few moments before closing—no twenty-four-hour anything in Prophet. I grabbed candy —a lot of candy, and, given I'd eaten nothing since breakfast, a bag of chips. Plus I couldn't help but find the dog snacks, and hoped they were appropriate given they were packaged up. I had the feeling that Tiber made his own snacks for the dogs, and who knew if I was doing the right thing. Cat treats went in next, but I couldn't think what to take for a tortoise or a rabbit, so I checked Google, and after considering that I wouldn't know where to find slugs right now, I bought some lettuce and carrots.

Then I headed to my SUV, dumping my prizes onto the passenger seat, and wavered between leaving now or heading home to get out of my uniform before turning up at Tiber's door.

I'm just checking up on Tiber, right? There's no need for me to change.

I eyed the candy haul and the carrot tops poking out of the bag, and an unaccountable sadness washed over me as I checked the clock on the dash. Why was I second guessing myself?

Because if I go home, to get a shower and change into casual clothes, then there was nothing official about visiting Tiber.

Only, when I got to the end of the road, I turned left to head back to my place because I didn't want to visit Tiber while looking like day-old road kill. I stopped outside my two-bedroom house on its scrappy piece of land, feeling a swell of pride when I saw it, knowing that it was mine. Not that I ever had time to fix the small porch, or spend time in the yard, or figure out how to mend the front door, which creaked as if it had a starring role in a ghost story.

If I could stop the nightmares and actually get some sleep, then maybe I wouldn't lack energy, and I'd be up to fixing everything. The house *and* the relationship with my family.

Way to spiral, Gabriel.

I showered in record time, taking the time to choose my favorite T-shirt and jeans, because I wanted to feel comfortable, not because I wanted to impress Tiber.

That was a lie—I wanted to impress him, enough so

that he changed his mind and we could go out on a date or something. Friendship first though.

I needed a friend like Tiber.

What I saw in my reflection gave me pause, and I stared at the exhausted man facing me. I needed a haircut, I should shave, I needed sleep, and what I shouldn't be doing is traipsing over to Tiber's, sharing candy and spoiling his animals. After all, I needed to be back at the station in a few hours.

"What's the worst that can happen?"

Well, I guess Tiber could shut the door in my face, or ask me why I was visiting, or set his pack of dogs on me.

Or he could welcome me in, we could eat candy, talk about anything that wasn't the case, and maybe even when I had to go back to the station, he'd forget why we couldn't date and he'd kiss me goodbye. I knew which option I was hoping for.

I'd almost reached the car when someone whistled, and I turned immediately, jumpier than a box of frogs, but it was Sam, and he was standing by my gate, hands forced into his pockets. His expression impassive, not angry, or filled with cold dismissal.

"Can we talk?" he called over.

I jogged toward him, worry gripping me that something was wrong.

"What's up? Is it the kids? Lori?"

I'd drop everything to help, even give up on heading

out to Tiber's place to flirt. I was already regretting not being in uniform.

"Aaron," Sam said softly.

"Is he okay?" I glanced at my SUV. "Is it an emergency? Do you need the sheriff?"

Sam opened his mouth to answer, but just as quick shut it again, then shook his head.

"Then what? Is Aaron worse? I can—"

"You know how much I hate mac 'n' cheese." he interrupted.

My head spun at the change of subject. "Um, yeah?"

"It's Aaron's favorite, just like…"

I filled in the blanks. "Like me."

"Yeah, he asked me why I made it if I didn't like it, and I tried to tell him that it was just because he'd been ill and needed to eat something, but we debated it, like a dad does with their kid, y'know?" He stared at me. I didn't know, not having kids, but I nodded. "Anyway, somehow I talked about you liking it."

"You did?"

"And Aaron made me promise I'd come and thank you for showing him your prison."

I sagged against the small fence enclosing my front yard. "And you're here."

"Yep."

"Why? I mean, you could have just said you'd spoken to me. He'd never know."

"My son trusts me. I don't mess with that trust."

I winced, because he used to trust me, used to look up to his big brother.

"Okay, so…"

Sam cleared his throat and couldn't meet my gaze. "He said you carried him and he felt safe."

"Oh—"

"I remember that. I remember you made everything safe for me. With Dad. When he got angry and you got in between us and you took the brunt of it, and… yeah, you made me feel safe."

"Sam—"

"Tell me why you didn't come home. I don't mean the bullshit about how you can't tell me, or that it's best I don't know, or asking me to accept on face value you had reasons. I need more." He paused. "I deserve more."

My chest tightened, my heart hurt, and emotion strangled my words. Lincoln's words about being careful rang in my head. "I don't know if I can—"

"Never mind, this was a mistake," Sam interrupted, then turned away. Everything fell into place and all the secrets in the world meant nothing, next to being Sam's big brother again. I was too tired, my nightmares wrecked my waking hours, I was no further in this damn case, I felt like I was spinning out, and now Mike's death had become twisted into those night terrors that pulled me awake. I was over having secrets and it wouldn't hurt to tell Sam enough so I'd have him back in my life.

I needed that.

"Wait." I called and Sam turned back to me. I gestured at my front door. "Can we go inside? Please?"

He paused for a long time, until I thought he might not move at all, and then followed me in. He'd barely closed the door when I launched into things I never thought I'd tell a single soul.

"Nearly three years I was undercover working alongside ATF and the FBI, using a fake name, and I mean *deep* undercover, breaking up a human trafficking ring from the inside," I blurted.

He blinked at me. "No," he said with care. "You were *just* a beat cop."

I tried not to bristle at the use of *just* in that sentence. "I was top of my class, determined to be the best to show you and Dad that it didn't matter *who* I slept with, that I was still me."

"Hang on, what do you mean, Dad *and* me? I never said a thing about you being gay—"

"Exactly," I said tiredly, "you said nothing. I needed something from you, some hope that you could accept me for coming out."

He shook his head. "That's not fair, Gabriel. I wasn't old enough to stand up to Dad, but you were my big brother. Of course, it was okay, it was more than okay, it was everything to you, so it was everything to me." He carded his hand through his hair and gripped it hard. "All this hate wrapped up in the old man and he's not even here now. It's so fucking messed up."

"I meant to come back, but—"

"But you thought I wouldn't love you still? Why? Because you were gay? Fuck that."

"No." I said, then sagged. "Yes. Maybe. Only it all changed and I couldn't come back until I'd finished." How was it that I was losing control of the narrative here? *Tell him what you meant to tell him! For god's sake!*

"How did it change?"

"My LAPD partner died, he was a rookie, and I let him down when he got involved in things he shouldn't have... I can't..." fuck. How much could I tell him without him hating me forever? "I excelled in undercover, I trained, I was... I got lost in what I was doing, ended up messing everything up." My words were so jerky, and my chest tight with pain. Was this what it was like to suffer a panic attack?

Sam leaned against the door with his eyebrow raised. "Even undercover cops get time off, and we had nothing from you. Not a birthday card, nothing for the kids."

"Things went so wrong." My legs slid from under me, and I ended up on the floor with the stairs at my back. "I finished the job, but I lost so much of myself in grief and shame and pretending to be someone I wasn't. Sometimes I forgot my real name—I wasn't Gabriel anymore." I scrubbed my eyes and wondered if I could tell Sam any of the rest of this without crying. What would he say if I cried? I knew Dad hated it, said we needed to be men, and for all I knew in the past few years Sam had become the same person.

He headed to the kitchen and then returned with a paper towel.

"Here," he said, and thrust them at me.

"This is stupid. I don't mean to cry," I said, as yet another tear trickled down my face.

"Maybe you should," Sam muttered, and then crossed his arms over his chest.

"I desperately wanted to come home every second I had my different name. Sometimes all I could think about was stabbing the man I was with square in the chest, getting it over and done with, and running, but I couldn't. Too many others' lives depended on it, and that stubborn streak that made me leave for LA fed me enough to see it through to the end." Once the words started, they fell out. "I had to do what I did, but I can't tell you everything, because it could compromise you and Lori and the kids."

His expression softened, but he didn't talk.

"It would kill me if you thought less of me."

Silence. He at least unfolded his arms, but his hands were twitchy. "And when Dad died?" he prompted.

"I didn't even know he'd died."

"I contacted you."

"I wasn't there."

"They said they passed on the message."

"*They* lied. I had to keep you all safe and lose Gabriel Thompson completely and let my other persona run my life, otherwise it would all be for nothing." I scrubbed at my eyes before looking up at my brother.

"So, you were keeping us safe?"

"Yeah, in my own messed-up way."

"Like you always used to."

Emotion made my eyes even wetter, and I swiped away tears. "I'm sorry."

Sam went to a crouch in front of me and regarded me. "Are you seeing a counselor?"

I nodded. "Twice a week."

He placed a hand on my knee to balance himself as he stood with a neutral expression that could mean anything from giving me a hug to punching me. Finally, he offered a hand to me and pulled me into an awkward bro hug that was nothing like the kinds of hugs we used to share. There was hesitation in both of us, him not forgiving what I'd done, and me not sure anyone should forgive me at all.

"You came home to us after all," Sam mused. "I wish you'd told me day one instead of asking me to accept your reason for staying away, without knowing what happened."

"Shit, Sam. I have so many secrets, but I can't do this for much longer. There are cracks inside me now since I've come home." I pressed a hand over my heart. "I see the counselor, and right now with the murder at the Rocks, with *everything*, I'm good at compartmentalizing but this is bad." I *had* to concentrate on the case.

"Then don't do that. Let all the ugly parts out."

I couldn't help the snort of laughter. "I do that and you'd run in the opposite direction."

"And maybe I wouldn't," Sam murmured. His cell vibrated and after a pause he pulled it out, reading the message and then pocketing it. "I have to go... the kids..."

"Sure."

Sam stepped back, then opened the front door. "I'm your brother," he said quietly. "So if you need me..." He hesitated. "We don't have to talk about what happened."

"Thank you."

"Also, I don't care who you love as long as you're happy, Gabriel. You know that, right?"

"I know that."

"Let's mend this, okay?"

"I want to."

With a slow nod, he left, closing the door behind him.

I sat there for a while, until my ass was numb, and it was growing darker outside with heavy clouds I could see through the glass in the door. No point in going anywhere now, not when my head felt stuffed with cotton wool. I may as well head over to the office and relieve Devin because I was in no mood to go courting Tiber and trying to get him to see the man I was.

Not when I wasn't sure who that was.

I'd been honest when I told Sam that attraction had escaped from the darkness inside me, but that wasn't enough. Tiber deserved more than someone scarred by the past. Resolute, I headed for the SUV, but somehow, as if my subconscious had taken over, I drove past the office and out of town towards Tiber.

His place, with his animals, and his smile, and the warmth I felt there, made it homey, and I needed that right now.

I parked outside his home, grabbed the bag of human and animal treats, and in quick strides, bypassing Frank the tortoise, who was loitering with intent, I headed up to his door and knocked before I could change my mind. Tiber peered through the window much the same as he had last time, with a suspicious gaze that cleared when he saw it was me. With a few short commands, all barking stopped inside.

I wonder if he has a command to stop me from being attacked by a tortoise?

Do they bite?

Tiber opened the door with a flourish, and I pasted on a smile that I hoped would fool Tiber into thinking I was fine.

"What's wrong?" he asked immediately. So much for my fake-ass expression.

"Nothing."

He focused his unwavering gaze on me. He could see right through me, and maybe that is what I needed tonight, and I let the smile drop, because, the very last thing I wanted to do was smile.

"I brought treats for…"

He tugged me inside and I stopped talking. "I'm serious. What's wrong with you?"

"Nothing," I lied, then sagged as the weight of it all dragged me down. "Everything."

He took the bags from me, placing them on the small table where I saw his keys, then he cradled my face with his hands.

"It's all going to be okay," he murmured.

And caught in his compassionate gaze, I thought maybe it would be.

Chapter Twenty-One

Tiber

I WASN'T sure if there'd been some devastating development in the case, or if it was personal, but the heaviness, *darkness*, in Gabriel came across to me so strongly, he might as well have been wearing a shroud. It hurt me to see it.

"Come in. Sit down." I pulled him down the hall and pushed him onto the couch.

Coffee? No, this called for something calming. "Would you like a glass of wine?"

He looked conflicted. "No thanks. I don't drink."

Something about the way he said it made me think there was a story there. But that could wait. "Peppermint tea?"

He nodded. "Sounds great."

I went into the kitchen and made the tea, but I didn't want to leave Gabriel for long, as irrational as that was. He was in pain, and the fact he didn't have a visible, gaping wound didn't make it any less real.

I wasn't the only one who felt it. When I walked back into the living room with two mugs, Gabriel had been swarmed by my loving, worried pack. Leo was in his lap, Ferdinand pressed against his side on the couch, Gracie and Duke sat at his feet, and Patch was glaring at Leo from the sofa back, wanting the primo lap spot. Even Renfield was curious, his pink, twitching nose poking out from under the couch.

I paused to watch them. Gabriel scratched Leo's back and put his other arm around Ferdinand, bringing his graying basset head in for a kiss. He sighed. He seemed to take comfort from them, and my insides turned to mush.

Ugh. I could not handle the feels.

"Here we are," I said loudly and walked into the room. I handed Gabriel a mug with an apologetic glance. "Okay, guys. You're all being super-duper supportive, but the humans need to talk. Come on." I shooed them all out of the sliding door into the backyard with the exception of Renfield, who had disappeared again, doing his magic rabbit act, and Fudge, who complained at the window, watching his pack outside without him.

"When you're older, maybe you can go out with

your brothers," I told him. I returned to the couch and sat close-ish to Gabriel.

"Do you have other cats, then? More from Fudge's litter?" Gabriel asked.

I shook my head. "*Brothers* is a figure of speech. We're all family, me, the cats, the dogs, the tortoise, and rabbit, even Sid the spider on the back porch who you haven't met yet."

Gabriel looked like he wanted to pull a yuck face but was too polite to.

I smiled. "Sid is just a tiny spider." I held up my fingers a millimeter apart to show how small. "And he doesn't bite."

"If you say so." He smiled at me, the first smile of the night.

We both drank our tea in silence for a while.

"Thanks for this," Gabriel said, motioning with his mug. He put it on the coffee table. "And for inviting me in. I'm really—" His voice got thick, and he stopped talking. He stared down at his lap. "Sorry. It's been a day, that's all."

I was only human. And there was something about Gabriel's vulnerability that shattered my defenses. I *felt* him—not just his despair, but, under that, a solid goodness. As if he hurt *because* he cared. Because he had a heart.

My kryptonite, apparently.

I put my mug down, leaned forward, and wrapped

him in a hug. A distant warning bell sounded in my head, but I ignored it. He needed this. Maybe I did too.

He froze for a beat, then his arms came around me. A flood of warm pleasure coursed through me at their solid warmth, at the firm-yet-gentle way he enfolded me. Damn. Had it been so long since I'd had human touch that it felt so incredible? I closed my eyes and let myself sink into it. I meant to offer some reassuring words, but my throat had closed up, so I just hugged him.

I meant to make it quick, too. But I couldn't make myself pull away. It felt too good.

My hair was down because I'd been about to go to bed. Gabriel buried his face in it, his breath warm on my neck. He sighed. "Tiber."

That distant warning bell was clanging louder now, but it was so very far away and no match for the warmth spreading through me, the quickening of my blood. I gripped Gabriel harder.

His palm moved up to cup the back of my head, as if to hold me closer. His neck was right there. I ran my nose along the skin. He'd showered recently and there was a faint scent of lemon. I let my tongue taste it.

He groaned. I groaned. Then we were kissing.

Chapter Twenty-Two

Gabriel

TIBER KISSED ME AGAIN, and nudged me back to straddle my lap, pressing against me, deepening the kiss with a flare of passion. I didn't know what to do with my hands, so I placed them on his slender frame, rested them on his hips, and then he was in my arms when I locked my hands behind his back. He was stronger than I'd imagined, making it difficult for me to move, holding me in place on the couch until I had no choice but to let him lead the kiss. Maybe he needed that control, and tonight I was ready to let him have anything he wanted.

He broke the kiss, and when I chased for it, he flashed me a smile. "Okay then," he said, and went in for another kiss. As much as I wanted to be a gentleman and stick with what he was comfortable with, he was hard against me, rolling his hips, and it was me who broke the next kiss.

"I need you." I wanted to bury myself in his kisses, and his smiles, and forget everything that haunted me in my sleep—I wanted the sweetness of his gaze resting solely on me, I wanted him with a selfishness that gripped me, and that I'd never felt before. We fit together so perfectly, his slim body locked to mine. I slid my hands down to rest on the swell of his ass, tugging him closer, and he groaned into my mouth, the kiss slowing to us exchanging breaths and nothing more.

For a moment we stilled, and it was the point where we both could back away and maybe just talk instead, but I wanted this, and was hopeful someone so perfect for me wanted to be with me—the light to my dark. Still I waited, because what if he *saw* the darkness in me? What if he could tell what I'd done?

"It's okay," Tiber murmured, as if he'd come to a decision.

Was he telling me I was okay, or he was, or the kiss was? I didn't know, but this time our taste was frantic and needy. I ended up trying to push him back on the sofa, but he stiffened, and I knew this wasn't what he wanted, only when I tried to lean back he stopped me and instead he laced his hands behind my head.

"Can you scoot up so I can get my legs around you?" he asked.

"Yeah, I want that." I shifted forward, and his legs went around my waist so that he was pressed into me.

"You're so perfect," I whispered against his lips, then deepened the kiss again, dropping my hold a little so our cocks were against each other. I wish I hadn't worn jeans, but I'd never been so happy to touch the softness of his joggers or the fact that I could trail the fingers of one hand to the waistband of them, and feel the warm skin there. "Can I?" I asked, and he mumbled into the kiss, as determined as I was not to break our connection. It was awkward and messy, and I swear I even smiled back at his sigh when I finally got my hand on his cock and circled it with my fingers. Just that single touch made my ass tighten, and I wished his hand was on me. I tilted him a little, and he broke the kiss, offering me his throat, his eyes closed.

"Beautiful," I whispered, "I want this, I want you."

I wanted him to fall apart in my arms, to hold him and watch his face when he lost it... so beautiful, strong, and perfect. Everything I hadn't seen in such a long time.

I twisted my fingers around his cock, tightened them, loosened them, and his eyes opened wide.

"Gabriel," he whispered, and it was that single word on his lips as he arched into me and was coming over my hand, a flush on his beautiful face. It was all too much, watching him come was enough to tip me over the edge, but I wanted to be kissing him when I lost it, connected, and tasting him. He gripped my hair and held on tight as I pressed against him. The orgasm was so hard and fast it made me dizzy.

I held him as pleasure rushed through me, kissing my thanks to his lips, and then everything relaxed, and somehow we still sat on the sofa, him sitting across my lap, his face buried in my neck. I breathed the scent of him, citrus and coffee, an intriguing mix I knew would forever remind me of this moment.

"Why were you crying?" he asked me, his voice muffled in my neck.

So many reasons, so much that I'd seen, so much that I'd done.

I wasn't ready to share everything with Tiber; I refused to let the horrors that visited me to ruin this moment.

"I talked to my brother, and it opened things up." That sounded like nonsense even to me, but Tiber appeared to understand as he sat up, then cradled my face again, smoothing the skin over my cheekbones with his thumbs.

Fuck. I wanted to cry again. He understood, he knew, I could trust him.

Tiber could be everything to me.

He smiled, although this time it held sadness. "You're trying to hide the things that make you cry and they end up carving you out and leaving you hollow."

It sounded as if experience colored his words, and

not for the first time I wondered what secret behind his dark eyes made him close himself off.

Maybe it was something I could fix? That was what I did—pushed aside my issues and fixed other people's problems.

"Do you want to talk about your brother?" he asked.

"You'll hate me."

"I wouldn't. I know…" He paused, then pressed a hand to my heart. "I see you inside there."

"It's my fault what happened with Sam. When I left, it was because our father didn't approve of my choices, and it was stifling and hurtful and so I ran to LA, leaving Sam with Dad, and our little brother Ezra. Dad hated who I was, said I'd made choices that went against God, wanted me to change. So I hated him right back, because a father should love his son unconditionally. Only leaving him meant I left my brothers and the family business, and I hurt Sam so badly. I didn't come home and now it's Sam's turn to hate me. Only tonight, I thought maybe we connected and that actually he might forgive me, even if I can't forgive myself."

"You came back, to be a sheriff in our small town. You must have known it would be hard with Sam, but you came back. That's brave."

"I'm not brave."

He huffed and pressed a kiss to the tip of my nose,

then frowned as if he'd just realized what he'd done. "I think you are."

I resented that someone was labelling me as brave when all I'd done is run from everything, but also, there was an innocence in Tiber that gave me hope, and I refused to destroy that by explaining the darker parts of my life.

So I shrugged, because I'm a fucking idiot, and I saw the sadness in Tiber that I wasn't explaining a damn thing.

"It's okay to keep our secrets," he reassured me.

"I doubt you've ever done anything wrong to have secrets."

His expression clouded for a moment, and then he quirked his ready smile. "I was ten minutes late to feed Patch last Thursday; it almost caused an international incident."

I closed my eyes then. He was trying to make me laugh, but after his question and my subsequent decision not to tell him more, there wasn't humor inside me. Instead, there were the regrets that had chased me from Prophet to the city and back again, and something else.

I'd needed to forget tonight; I'd needed to kiss Tiber, and lose myself in something good and perfect, and his kiss had stopped me from thinking at all. Instead, it was all about the touch of his fingers, and the taste of his tongue as it tangled with mine. I forgot everything when he was in my arms.

"We should move," he said after a while and his
voice had changed, become more matter-of-fact.
"Bathroom is down the hall. I'll use the other one. Meet
you back here on the sofa."

It was clear from his expression he'd separated from
the connection we'd had.

When I finally returned to the main room, Tiber had
let the animals back in from outside. The dogs were
excited to see me, even Duke, who wagged his tail and
then sat next to me, pressed against my leg. It was so
good to see the change in the once terrified dog, and I
wondered if Tiber was having the same effect on me.

"I made you this." he handed me a bowl of pasta and
sauce, and a fork. "Eat."

"I brought snacks for us all. The bag is in the hall;
there's stuff for everyone, but I wasn't sure what to
bring Frank and the rabbit…"

"Renfield."

"Yeah, so I got a lettuce because the internet said
tortoises and rabbits both eat lettuce."

"And the chips were your dinner?" he asked, and my
cheeks heated. How did he know that?

"Yeah—"

"Eat the pasta instead, it's healthier, also it's the
closest I had to your favorite mac 'n' cheese."

I took a mouthful, and it was perfect, only then it hit
me. "How did you know my favorite is mac 'n'
cheese?" Had he somehow heard my conversation with

Sam? Surely he couldn't have because he was way over here in his house? Weird.

He paused, his gaze slipping, a flush of heat pinking his cheeks, and then he shrugged. Seems like we both had secrets we wanted to play down. "You seem like a mac 'n' cheese kind of man."

"Oh," was all I had on that. "It's so good just to stop," I said as I ate the pasta, and sunk lower into the sofa. Leo had his head in my lap, and Fudge jumped on my leg to cling to my pants, using them as a ladder to end up on my chest. I yawned as I held the kitten in my hands and petted her.

"When was the last time you slept?" Tiber asked as he handed me a mug of cocoa. I should have mentioned I wanted something to keep me awake, and cocoa may tip me over the edge into being asleep.

"Last night," I yawned again, and Fudge batted at my hand.

"I mean *properly* slept?" Tiber prompted with that tone a parent uses when they weed out a lie.

Ahh, the age-old query about whether I was sleeping; it was my counselor's go to question at the start of every session.

"A while."

Thankfully, Tiber didn't push, and we sat in companionable silence. Minute by minute I felt easier in my head, almost as if getting off with Tiber was magic.

Tiber broke the silence when he cleared his throat. "We probably need to talk."

I waggled my eyebrows. "I'm ready to go again, or at least think about going again." I was teasing, but it didn't make his smile reappear, and my chest tightened.

"I'm not going to regret what happened. Obviously, I'm not immune to you. And maybe we both needed it. But it can't go anywhere."

What? That was *not* what I was expecting. "Okay, but—"

"If I ask that we can just... have a working relationship. Or be friends. Please respect that?"

Disappointment surged in me. I'd been hoping that this might be the start of something, but it seemed I was wrong.

"Of course. I won't force myself on you, Tiber." We sat in silence a moment, "Can you tell me why?" Tiber wouldn't meet my gaze, sitting quietly, staring at his hands. "You don't have to. But I'd really like to understand."

"Someone..." He stopped and, as if he needed the distraction, he fussed over Leo, scratching behind his ears. Was it wrong to feel jealous of a dog?

"Someone hurt you?" I finished the unspoken sentence, and he nodded. "Who do I have to kill?" I tried for a joke, but my anger that anyone would hurt Tiber probably came across as threatening.

He shot me a frown. So much for a stupid possessive joke.

Tiber sighed. "I suppose I owe you some explanation. At least, I want you to see that I'm serious when I say that I don't intend to get into another relationship."

He didn't owe me anything. But I wanted to hear this, so I nodded.

"So... his name was Jeff. I met him while I was in grad school. He seemed so perfect at first. Incredibly good-looking. Charming. Very interested in me. Said I was wonderful, gorgeous, etc." He crossed his arms over his chest. "I fell for it all."

He gave a bitter laugh. "Leo never liked Jeff, but I made excuses for his antipathy. Way to take my own advice, right?"

"What happened?"

At first I thought he wouldn't elaborate, but then he began to talk.

"He was... manipulative. A master at gaslighting. Everything was always my fault. Everything was a debate—and he'd win. He could talk his way around anything. I should dress like this and eat like that. I shouldn't have this friend or watch those movies. Pet consultation was stupid. I could earn a lot more starting a vet clinic. He'd always act like that's what a partner did, *give advice*, and that he had my best interests at heart. And it was gradual, you know? Like at first, I was great. Then, little by little, he picked me apart, and then he'd be all nice if I threatened to leave. It was exhausting."

I'm not like that. I want you as you are.

I want to kill this Jeff guy for hurting someone so sweet and perfect.

"He sounds like a huge asshole," I said instead, in case I scared Tiber away.

Tiber shrugged. "The worst thing is, I'd probably still be stuck with him except for one horrible night when I realized—I finally *saw*—that he was a total sociopath." He scrubbed his face with his hands. "I still have nightmares about that night."

"What happened? Did he hit you?"

I will find him. I will track him down.

"Not me." Tiber squeezed his eyes shut. "I don't know why I'm telling you this. You don't need to hear it, but I just need you to understand why I am the way I am."

"You're perfect—"

"That's what *he* always said, so please… don't."

Shit. Way to fuck up. "I promise I won't…" I didn't know what I was promising.

"Jeff had an older brother named Steve. Steve was all macho guy and I know he hated the fact that Jeff was gay. Only he couldn't really do anything about it. Jeff was so successful and his parents thought he walked on water." He sighed again, and Leo butted his hand.

"Steve *really* hated me. Probably thought I was too femme and too brown and too soft or whatever. He used to corner me and tell me I wasn't good enough for Jeff, that I was ruining his life. Jeff never stepped in. And the whole animal behavior degree? I was still working on my master's at the time. Steve thought it was stupid. Like, he'd tell gruesome hunting stories in front of me just to upset me."

"That's fucked up." I reached for his hand in reassurance, but Leo's head was in the way.

"One night Jeff insisted we go to a concert with Steve and his girlfriend. We were coming back that night, in the dark, on a country road. Steve was driving, and Jeff and I were in the back seat of his truck. We passed a car going the opposite direction and the lady driver was waving an arm out her window frantically. So Steve slows down and rolls down his window to see what she wants."

He drew in a shuddering breath, his eyes going suspiciously glassy. "She tells us there's a mama deer and two fawns on the road up ahead, to be careful. Steve thanks her and rolls up the window. He takes off…."

"I kind of knew by the way he gave me this evil look in the rearview mirror… He sped up, and he hit those two fawns. On purpose. He fucking did it on purpose."

"Oh, my god."

Tiber wiped at his eyes. "It was horrible. I lost it. As

we drove away, I could see the mother deer. She was screaming. And frantic. And I begged Steve to stop the car so I could go back and at least move the fawns off the road. Because I knew she'd stand there trying to get them up, and she'd be hit too. I don't know. I just had to do something. And Steve laughed. He wouldn't go back."

"And Jeff did nothing again?"

"Jeff told me to calm down. He said it was an accident. Like, the next day, he tried to convince me it had just been *accidental* and that I should feel bad for Steve. I mean, every part of that is so fucked up. Somehow it was a turning point, and I packed up my shit when he went out, and left. I haven't spoken to him since."

"Jeff sounds like a complete and utter tool. I'm nothing like that," I said, but the guilt of the things that I'd done when undercover made my assertion more of a lie than he could ever know.

"If it means anything, I don't think you are like him, but sometimes there's darkness in your eyes that… I just can't do it. I don't trust myself anymore. I've always been too sensitive. I let myself be manipulated. I couldn't stand up to him. I was vulnerable. And I know myself well enough to know I will *always* be vulnerable. I can't deal well with people. And I never want to be stuck in something toxic again."

"Did I move too fast?"

He shook his head. "No. Please. I'm happy here with the pack, and I don't need or want anything else. That's all."

"Tiber—"

"You said you wouldn't push." He wrinkled his nose.

I thought I detected disappointment in his expression. Fuck, I was the worst kind of person to force anything on him after what he'd just told me.

My watch vibrated with an alarm. How was it eleven forty-five already? "I have to relieve Devin from his custody watch at the office."

"Okay." He seemed relieved.

I grew desperate. "Can we be friends at least?"

Tiber buried his hand in Leo's fur. "Yeah. We can do that."

We hugged at the door, and for a brief shining moment of hope I thought Tiber might change his mind and kiss me one last time, but he stepped back quickly, and when I left I felt as if my entire world had shifted. It hurt that I'd had Tiber in my arms and might never have that again.

When I was back in my SUV heading into town, a familiar melancholy crept up on me, and when my headlights picked up the glimpses of wildlife on the side of the road, it reminded me of the pain in Tiber's eyes as he told me the story of the fawns, and of Jeff's control over him.

For different reasons, we were two messed-up men, and maybe friends were all we could ever be.

It was probably best we stayed away from each other.

I tried to rationalize my feelings, going in circles until I focused on the fact I'd gone without a meaningful relationship for a long time, and I was okay.

Yes, losing possibly the best thing that might have happened to me sucked.

Hurt.

But I could handle it. I was okay.

Right?

Chapter Twenty-Three

Tiber

I WAS on a client call the next morning. A Shar Pei in Montana was displaying concerning behavior towards the family's toddler. We were just getting to the root of it when my phone buzzed. I had it on silent, but the screen displayed the name.

Sheriff Thompson.

I felt a rush of hot then cold, and I stumbled over my next words. I turned the phone face-down and focused determinedly on Norman, the Shar Pei, for the next thirty minutes.

When the session ended, I checked my phone. There'd been two calls from Gabriel and a text message. I felt a wash of dread. I hoped to God it was something important and not him being claustrophobic and stalkery.

But no. It was about the case.

Hi. Was wondering if Duke would be up for going back to Sentinel Rocks and helping us find where they moved Mike's body from. Let me know.

I rechecked my schedule—no more consultations today—then called him back.

"Hey, Tiber. Thanks for getting back to me."

"Hi. Um… so no luck with that cult guy?"

"Mr. Dorman? No. We took him out to Sentinel Rocks this morning and tromped around, but he couldn't remember exactly where he'd found Mike's body. It would seriously help the case if we could locate the spot."

Phone pressed to my ear, I walked out into the main room. Leo and Ferdinand danced at my feet. Patch meowed for food. Duke stood staring out of the back window, panting. I had the feeling if I put him on a leash and opened the door, he'd drag me to the car. Or maybe down the road again. Duke had unfinished business. I wished I could read his mind to see how much he understood, and what it was he felt he needed so badly to accomplish.

"We can do that," I said to Gabriel. "We can take him over there and see how he reacts. If he gets too stressed, we can shut it down."

"That's fair. Want me to pick you guys up?"

"Yeah. Sure." I swallowed a sudden mouthful of spit as my body did something Pavlovian. *This is just business. Chill.*

"What's a good time? If possible, I'd love to do it today before it gets dark."

"I understand. Give me thirty?"

"I'll be there." Gabriel hung up.

I'd never been in this situation before, where I had to work with a guy I'd just... made out with. And then brushed off like a dweeb. *I just can't do this.*

Ugh. This was why I didn't people.

It was awkward. But I knew, from the tone of Gabriel's voice, that this was important. He would put the case first, and I needed to also.

Maybe it was a good thing. Getting right back on the horse. I did want a working relationship with him. A friendly relationship. He was the sheriff of the goddamn town. And the longer I went without seeing him again, the more awkward it would be, and the more I'd dread it. Until I ended up not going into town at all just so I could dodge him. That was not healthy.

Besides, I reminded myself for the thousandth time, this wasn't about me. This was a murder investigation. And it was about Duke's daddy.

When Gabriel picked us up, he did not seem weird at all. He gave me a tired smile and squatted down to greet Duke. Duke sniffed at him, skittish and wary but getting bolder. He smelled Gabriel's hands, then his ear, then under his armpits. Gabriel took it all with a stoic expression, relaxed. Then Duke dismissed Gabriel and went to his SUV, standing there waiting.

"All right then. Guess he's ready to go," I said.

"Guess so."

Gabriel let us both into the back seat.

The drive was familiar from the first time we'd done it—going around the south end of Lake Prophet, turning onto a gravel logging road, and unlocking the gate.

"So how long did you look around with Mr. Dorman?" I asked when Gabriel got back into the car.

"Over three hours." Gabriel shook his head. "There's a lot of woods out there, and he said it wasn't on a trail and it was dark. We might have walked right past the place and not known it. That's why I hoped Duke might be able to pinpoint the spot."

I stroked Duke's back. "He wants to help."

Gabriel's hazel gaze met mine in the rearview mirror. "Oh yeah? How do you know?"

"Just know." There was no point trying to explain it.

Gabriel nodded. "Well, he's been a big help so far."

The look he gave me in the mirror said he credited me for that. But really, it had all been Duke.

I watched Duke closely as we approached Sentinel Rocks. We were on the ridge road and Gabriel slowed the SUV. He stopped the car. "Okay to go down?" he asked.

Duke's attention was focused out of the window.

"Yeah. Just take it slow."

As if there were any other option. The logging road along the ridge followed the national park perimeter for a mile or so, I thought. Right here, high above Sentinel Rocks, it had a clear view down to the lake. But farther ahead, the ridge became wooded and the road was lost in the trees.

Gabriel turned the SUV downhill and we crawled down like a sand crab, going maybe five miles an hour. The SUV's big tires maneuvered over low-lying boulders and scree. I hung on for dear life. Whatever adrenaline-junkie genes existed in my family tree, they'd skipped a generation in me.

We parked near Sentinel Rocks, and Duke scrabbled at the door, whining anxiously. Gabriel had to open it from the outside. The moment he did, Duke jumped down and bounded for Sentinel Rocks.

I scooted out and Gabriel gave me a questioning look.

"I'm not sure he's gonna lead us anywhere. But we can try," I said.

"That's all I can ask."

As we approached the two standing stones, Duke was sniffing and pawing at the ground between them, searching for Mike's scent. It had been a few days, and rainy, but the smell still seemed to be there. He huffed the ground greedily. Then he rolled onto his back, scooting on the dirt to transfer the scent to his nape.

"Is he okay?" Gabriel asked.

"Yeah. This is typical behavior. Some dogs do that over a deer's scent or a squirrel's. Behaviorists aren't sure if the point is to try to disguise themselves with the scent of their prey for hunting, or if they just love the smell. Or maybe they want to take the scent signature back to their pack."

Gabriel nodded and seemed content to wait. That was good. Duke needed a moment.

I gave him ten. When he'd calmed down and just lay between the stones, head on his paws, I moved closer and squatted down. "Hey, Duke."

He lifted his head to look at me. He was still panting, a sign of stress.

He was expectant, anxious, and so was Gabriel. Expecting me to somehow facilitate this mission. But I'd never trained to use a tracking dog, and Duke had never trained to *be* a tracking dog, so I had no idea how to go about this. But he'd led Mr. Dorman to Mike on that awful night. Maybe he'd do it again.

Though, of course, Mike was no longer there. And Duke knew that.

I centered myself and closed my eyes.

Sometimes I talked in my mind to animals. Sometimes it even seemed to work. After all, no one knew how intuitive they really were. Maybe they could pick up images. Or get the general idea from our energy or minute clues on our faces. They were certainly adept at reading humans when they wanted to.

I pictured Mike lying in the woods. I pictured Duke sniffing around him. I felt Duke's sorrow and panic in that moment, letting it well up inside me.

I'm not sure how long I visualized that, but a loud cawing came from right over my head, disrupting my thoughts. I opened my eyes to look. A large black crow was sitting on top of one of the stones. It ruffled its feathers and cawed again. When I checked back with Duke, he was standing up and studying me.

A bit weird, but okay.

"You're such a good dog," I reassured. "Can you show us where Mike was that night? Mike?"

Duke stared. He didn't understand, but he seemed to want to, badly.

"Show me. Show me Mike."

Duke whined and started sniffing the ground again. He knew the name, and he associated it with the scent. But we already knew Mike had been here, at the stones. Just when I thought it wasn't going to work—crow or no crow—Duke headed for the trees.

"You're amazing," Gabriel said with admiration.

I shook my head. "Don't get too excited. He could be tracking a deer or rabbit. I have no idea. I've never tried this before."

"Should I have brought something of Mike's?"

Gabriel asked and seemed worried he'd messed up. "You know, to give him the scent?"

"No. Mike's scent is already here." But, honestly, I didn't know.

"Well, let's see where he goes."

We took off after Duke. He plowed through the underbrush, so it was rough going for us. Duke bounded over every log, fern, and sinkhole, but I was slower, and Gabriel slower still since he scanned the brush, probably for any signs other people had been this way. It was a challenge keeping up with the dog, but we got the occasional glimpse of creamy fur through the trees.

When we finally caught up to Duke, he was standing next to a tree at the base of a fern-covered hillside. He barked when he saw us and kept barking as we approached. It wasn't a bark I'd heard from him before. It was high and sharp—not excited exactly, but insistent.

Pay attention, the bark said. And maybe *hurry the fuck up.*

As we drew closer, Gabriel put out an arm to stop my progress. "Hold up. Just in case this spot is important. I don't want to trample any evidence."

"Okay. What now?"

Gabriel appeared to consider it. "I'll check it out. Can you get him to come to you?"

I could try. "Duke, come, boy. Come!"

Duke ignored me. He pawed at the dirt near the tree and sniffed. He let out an anxious whine and shuddered.

In dog training, you never repeated a command. If the dog didn't come, you went and got it. Otherwise, they learn that a command can be ignored, and with a command like *come,* that can be dangerous. The dog could be in the path of a car, for instance. But Gabriel had told me not to step over there.

"He's fixated on a scent," I said. "I have no idea if it was Mike, but I think it might be. Duke's too upset for it to be just a squirrel or other prey animal."

Gabriel nodded. "Yeah. I can see that. Can you get him away so I can look?"

"It would be fastest if I walked over there and leashed him."

Gabriel hesitated only a moment. "Okay. Go ahead. Just try to tread lightly."

I did as he asked, stepping gingerly and attached the leash on Duke's harness. It took some tugs and some encouraging words, but I got Duke moved back to a safe distance. He and I both watched Gabriel scout around. He narrowed in on the spot near the tree where Duke had been pawing the ground. He put on a pair of blue plastic gloves and took out a small flashlight to get a better look at things. Even though it was still late afternoon, the forest was dim and cool and filled with shadows.

Duke whined and shifted, anxious but focused on Gabriel.

"It's okay," I told him, squatting down to sling an

arm around him. "You're helping Mike. You're a good boy, Duke. Such a good boy."

Gabriel scooped up some dirt with a tool and put it in a clear evidence bag. He held it up and shone his flashlight on it. He checked to the left, then right, expression thoughtful.

"What is it?" I asked.

"There's a dark stain on the ground here. Pretty sure it's blood. The lab will tell for sure. But something's lain here and was wounded. Or dying."

My heart turned over in my chest. God.

Gabriel scanned the ground. "There's a partial print. A man's tennis shoe, looks like. Possibly Mr. Dorman's. Shit. I need to get forensics out here."

He continued to search, moving aside fern fronds carefully, and shining his light on the ground, the foliage, the trees. He stood, took out his radio, and made a call. He requested forensics and for his deputy to get a print of the shoes Mr. Dorman was wearing the night of the ritual.

When he was done, he put his hands on his hips, frowning.

"Why would Mike be out here?" I asked. We weren't close to a trail. And why would he have met his death here? Or had the body been moved here from yet another location?

"Doesn't make a lot of sense, does it?" Gabriel responded. "Mike wouldn't have been jogging in here."

"No."

At the same moment, we both looked at the hillside. It was a steep slope thick with the ubiquitous Pacific Northwest green ferns. The lush fronds were pristine to the left and right. But down the center, the pattern was disturbed. I saw a clump of smashed and broken leaves a few feet up. And as my gaze continued upwards, I saw another broken clump.

Duke started barking and straining at the leash.

And I saw it as clear as day, the crashing, the falling, the sudden stop.

"Mike fell," I said, feeling numb. "Down that hill."

Gabriel tilted his head to check out the way up, narrowing his eyes and straining to see. "I think the ridge road is up there."

The logging road? Could Mike have been dumped out of a car? An icy finger ran down my spine.

Gabriel looked at Duke. "Let him go."

I nodded and, heart in my throat, unclipped Duke's leash. He immediately headed for Gabriel, dodged him, and started up the hill.

We followed. It was forty-five degrees in spots, covered in dense foliage, and the ground was soggy and slick with lichen. I scrambled, using my hands to steady myself and grabbing anything I could find for leverage. I almost gave up, but I could see Duke ahead of us, working so hard to claw his way up the hillside, and I couldn't let him do this alone.

About halfway up, Gabriel paused and parted some leaves on the right.

"What is it?" I asked.

He picked up something with one gloved finger and held it aloft. It was a step tracker watch with a silver band that had snapped. Gabriel and I gave each other a grave look. He put it in an evidence bag and we kept going.

Chapter Twenty-Four

Gabriel

I DOUBTED we'd get data from the watch itself, the strap broken, the glass face smashed, and water leaking from the side, but maybe from the app it connected to?

The very fact it was out here on the steepest of slopes was a clue. This wasn't a marked path, nor was it a shortcut route hikers had worn away. Yes, a wild animal *could* have dragged some random watch here, but it was difficult to ignore that it was the same as Mike's watch. We continued climbing a little at a time, Tiber slipping back frequently, and muttering in exasperation. Duke was anxious—hell, I didn't have to be a dog whisperer to see that, from the way he would rush ahead then dart back to collect us.

The going was slow, with Duke sometimes sitting

and waiting by a spot, and inevitably when we got there we would find something. A scrap of material, earth gouged out along with undergrowth, vegetation snapped, but no blood—it had been too damp, and too many days for there to be signs of anything as obvious as that.

"Think we're close to the top?" Tiber asked from behind me.

I stopped in my tracks and held out a hand to tug him over a section of rocks. He tripped and tumbled into my arms, and I held him for a while longer than was strictly necessary.

I wanted to make sure he was steady on his feet.

That was my excuse, and I was sticking with it.

He threw me a rueful glance as he eased himself away, Duke right by his side. "I'm a hazard to myself," he deadpanned, but all I could think was how gorgeous he looked in the gloom of the trees, his face pink with exertion, his smile so sweet.

He took my breath away for that brief moment before reality hit.

"You okay to move on?" I asked, probably more gruff than I needed to be.

"All good," he reassured me.

We carried on and reached the bottom of a sheer drop from the road. The path before us climbed near vertically at least eight feet up, and it took me a while to locate a way to get to the top. I scrambled up first, trying not to catch myself on old roots sticking out from the side, and then lay on the road, arms outstretched for Tiber. Duke had gone missing—I assumed he was finding another way up, evidenced by the fact he barked and it seemed distant, and then abruptly he was at my side as Tiber grabbed my hands and I pulled while he slid and scrambled. I had a moment's thought that maybe I should have made him go first, then at least if he fell he'd have something soft to land on, AKA, me.

Finally he was at the top, breathing heavily, lying on his back, staring at the sky, a fine mist dampening his skin, his lips parted as he inhaled lungs full of air, and Duke snuffling at his hand and whining.

"I'm okay," he reassured me, but he was talking to Duke and not to me.

I stood, and extended a hand to help him, but this time I didn't hold onto him, because if I did that too often then I'm sure that contravened my promise not to get up in his space and demand kisses.

I really wanted kisses.

"Where do we start?"

I turned a full three-sixty to check our surroundings. I'd already had a good idea where we'd come out—the old logging road running along the ridgeline. A hundred yards to the left was a turn-out. I went to a crouch, assessing the space from that level before walking the perimeter from the point we'd climbed up, to the turn-out and back. There were deep tracks in the mud there off of the gravel, but rain had filled them, and the recent storms had done their worse and probably destroyed tire marks.

When I reached Tiber and Duke, Tiber was talking to the dog in a reassuring voice, encouraging him with the word, Mike. Duke didn't move from his position at the edge of the drop-off, his nose on his paws, staring down at the trees and vegetation below.

"This is where Mike fell," Tiber said, and stroked Duke's head. "Duke knows that."

I ran through all the evidence we had. "So say he was out running, and he tripped, and tumbled over the side, hit his head badly on the way down, which caused the brain injury, which led to his death." That theory would explain a lot of things apart from the fact that Duke was trembling, and Tiber was pale. "Tiber? Talk to me."

"Whatever happened here made Duke scared, angry, so frustrated and sad. Mike did fall, but he wasn't *right*." Tiber tapped his head. "He was already sick or hurt when he fell."

"That's your theory?"

Tiber glanced at me with sad eyes, then shook his head. "It's what Duke saw."

I wanted to know more. I wanted to understand how Tiber could know what Duke saw. But now wasn't the time to dig into his empathic nature or understand his conviction that he was right. Instead, I walked the perimeter again back to the turn-out, hunching into my coat as the rain grew heavier, and studying the gravel for clues.

When I saw it, lying in the gravel, everything made horrible sense, and this time when I went to a crouch it was to take photos of what I'd found. Then to collect fragments of glass, plastic and metal of a wing mirror, plus the remains of a sticker into an evidence bag.

The image of the Smith's van, with the broken wing mirror and the tiny spider that lived there, sat front and center in my thoughts. What was it the coroner said? That Mike has fragments of glass in his hair? If the fragments in Mike's hair matched the van, then it could prove that they were, at some point, parked here.

"Okay then," I murmured to myself. "Let's head back," I called over, and both Tiber and Duke looked over at me. "I think I might have something. You want to follow it up?"

DUKE DIDN'T WANT to leave the drop-off at first, but after some coaxing he was content to go on the leash and walk alongside us back to the main road and down the less steep hill to where my SUV was parked. Tiber reached out and gripped my hand and we made our way to the car. I put Duke in the back, but Tiber was shaken, and I wanted him close to me. He didn't object when I guided him into the passenger seat.

"Gabriel," was all Tiber said when I got in the car, his expression tight, and it was my turn to cradle his face, twisting awkwardly in my seat to do so.

"I know," I murmured.

"I felt it," he added, and I didn't ask questions, because he was tired and pale and overwhelmed. I fought my instinct to kiss him, instead I released my hold and reached over for the belt, making sure he was secure before buckling up, and then connecting to Hen back at the office.

"Dispatch, get Devin out to Applecross camping area. Tell him to park on the road before, and hang back."

"Copy," Hen acknowledged. "He's on his way."

We headed up to the last place the Smiths had been camping. I stopped for a moment before entering the parking area and waited until Devin pulled in behind me.

"Stay here," I ordered Tiber, and he nodded.

Devin was out of his car, a small Toyota 4x4 that had seen better days, the department budget only running to one official vehicle.

"Sir?" he asked.

"Body cams on from now on, okay?"

"Sir." We both switched on our cams. "I'm going to talk to Mr. Smith, accompanied by Tiber and Duke," I gestured at the sheriff's SUV. "I need you to hang back and wait for me to call if I need you."

"Don't you want me as backup?"

"Two cops turning up might well freak the guy out and turn the situation bad. Stick here, stay alert."

"Yes, sir."

Tiber and I carried on, and next to me he was very quiet, a softly whining Duke in the back.

"What do you think we'll find?" he asked, his hands in fists in his lap.

"I don't know. Stay behind me, don't let go of Duke, and if you sense anything is wrong, you head back down to Devin, okay?

"Okay." He pressed a hand to my knee. "Do you think we should bring Devin with us?"

"Not right now. We don't want a showdown if he thinks I'm coming in heavy. I just want Duke to get a look, and then we leave. Okay? No heroics."

He removed his hand, and I immediately missed his touch.

"I can faithfully promise there will be no heroics from me," he deadpanned.

I wasn't sure they'd even still be camped here, but sure enough, the van was there, two chairs outside, and a cooler, and no sign of Mr. or Mrs. Smith at all. I deliberately parked the SUV far enough from the side of the road that I was blocking them in, but near enough not to give them a heads up we were here for anything but a friendly visit.

"Wait in the car until I locate the suspect," I aimed

the order at Tiber, but it was his control of Duke I was
concerned about, given that Duke was standing on the
seat staring out of the window and growling.

"No," Tiber muttered, and clambered out before I
could stop him.

"At least leave Duke to—"

"No." Tiber was determined, and I waited until
Duke was on his leash, close to Tiber's side, his hackles
up and that growl ever-present. "He knows this van,
he… *sees it*."

I didn't argue, but with Duke growling, and Tiber
agitated, I unclipped my weapon—just in case.

As we drew closer to the van, I saw movement
inside, a twitch of something at a window, and gestured
for Tiber to stay back and out of the way. The man
inside—Mr. Smith—was armed, and I wasn't taking
chances, but pulling a gun straight away was asking for
trouble. My heart in my mouth, I stood to the side of the
door and raised my fist to knock, only the door opened
before I could even do that.

"Sheriff," Lewis acknowledged, his face red,
scratches on his cheek, blood on his shirt, and from
inside a whisper of something, maybe a whimper. He
slammed the door behind him and stepped toward the
trees, leading us from the van. "What the hell do you
want now?"

I rested my hand on my weapon, the snap open, and
his hands were loose at his sides. His pistol was in view,

and I didn't trust him one bit. I had this whole list of questions, but I never even got to number one, because Duke snarled, dragging Tiber to his knees, and then wrenching free of his hold. In a second, Duke launched himself at Lewis.

Tiber scrambled after him calling out a command to stop, Lewis yelled as he fell back into the side of the van, which shook with the impact, and I tried to get in the middle of it as Duke sunk his teeth into Lewis's leg and shook this big man like a rag doll until Lewis slid in a messy heap to the ground.

"It was him!" Tiber announced, attempting to yank Duke away.

Duke barked and growled and snarled, and I've never seen such a vision of hate in an animal.

"Get the fucking dog off me!" Lewis was bleeding from where he'd hit the van, from his leg, and all of his bluster had vanished in anger. "I'll fucking shoot him!" He scrabbled for his weapon, but I pulled my gun first, and pointed it at his chest.

"Stand down Duke," I snapped.

As if he understood me, or maybe Tiber had quietened him, Duke sat back on his heels, shifting from one front paw to the other, still snarling and snapping, but under Tiber's control.

With my gun steady, I made a small gesture. "Take your gun out, one finger, toss it my way."

"It's mine!" Lewis shouted, a hint of his arrogance

back as he saw a leashed Duke and realized I was stopping Duke from finishing what he'd started.

"Take the gun out. One finger. Toss it my way."

"Fuck you!" Lewis cursed, and for a second I imagined a standoff, but he did as I asked him, the gun ending up at my feet. Then he crab-walked back when Duke yanked at the lead and growled. Not such a big guy without the gun then.

I collected the gun, emptied the chamber, and pushed it into my coat, zipping the pocket.

"Why is there blood on your shirt?" I pointed at him, the rain already washing away what was there.

"Fuck you, I know my rights."

A crash from inside the van caught my attention, and Lewis' eyes narrowed. I could almost see his thought process; calculating where my attention would be if I checked the noise—would it be enough to get the gun— would Tiber let go of Duke? I didn't move, but Tiber did, skirting far enough so that Lewis wasn't near them, and then peering into the van's small window.

"His wife, he has her..." He glanced back at me. "She's hurt."

That was enough for me.

"On the ground, on your front," I ordered Lewis, who balked.

"No fucking way, there's—"

"On the ground!"

He finally did as he was told, wriggling like a fish

on a hook as I kneed him in the back and, one-handed, yanked at my handcuffs. I'd done this before, in another time and place, knew all the tricks, and had to rely on the fact that Tiber was there with a snarling Duke, and that Lewis wouldn't try anything.

I read him his rights as I cuffed him to the van, making him sit on the ground with his back to the van's wheel.

"I'm arresting you for the murder of Ranger Michael Bressett—"

"I didn't kill no one!" he shouted at me, and I repeated the Miranda, just in case.

I called Devin up to assist as Tiber opened the door and helped a bruised and bleeding Mrs. Smith out, and as he did so, there was a slyness in Lewis's expression when his wife appeared.

"Hey baby," he cooed as if she wasn't standing there covered in blood. "They can't hold me baby, don't worry."

"No, Brad," she said, shaking. Brad? Not Lewis then.

"Babe, you know I love you."

She turned to me, reaching for my hand, her own hand bloodied, and tears welling in her eyes. "Can you help me?"

"Yes," I said.

Lewis must have sensed the sea change, that maybe he'd gone too far this time, and that his wife had found a strength she didn't know she had. He'd laid his hands on her, and I knew the abuse for what it was and could see the pain in her eyes. So instead Lewis—Brad—turned belligerent. "I didn't touch that asshole ranger! Tell him Zoe!

She stayed silent, and Tiber held her. Duke quietened at her side, whining anxiously.

"Tell him." Brad shouted, straining against the handcuff. He was so big I wouldn't put it past him to wrench the part of the van away that I'd cuffed him to, so I held my gun steady.

"No," Zoe murmured. Then stronger. "No!"

"You fucking tell him, you bitch!"

She winced, then caught my gaze and lifted her chin. Shaky, with tears running down her face, but then with determination she pointed at him. "I won't lie this time!"

Tiber met my gaze. "She needs a doctor," he half whispered.

"I'm okay," she said with determination, but she slumped more on Tiber who held her steady. "I'll tell you everything."

Chapter Twenty-Five

Gabriel

It was two hours before I could interview Zoe Callan.

I only knew her real name when she told the doc, and I didn't have time to ask her anything until I'd dealt with Brad.

Doc decided for me where the interview would be—he said she didn't have any broken bones, but he refused to let us take her to the station where her husband was currently ranting about a lawyer who was due to arrive soon.

We told the recording device our names, she was Zoe Callan from Coeur D'Alene, Idaho, and her husband was Brad Callan.

"You promise he can't touch me again?" She

seemed so disbelieving that someone might want to help her.

"We'll make sure you get to a shelter." I couldn't make too many promises—not when she was a witness. If I promised her the moon then that could be seen as a bribing her to encourage her to create lies about her husband. Though if Doc said there was evidence of consistent abuse, it would help her case.

She took a moment to compose herself. "Where do you want me to start?"

"How about you tell me about the last time you saw Ranger Bressett."

"Uhm, okay. After we left Green Rocks, we parked at another place, over by the creek, for two nights. But then a bunch of other campers came. Like, three separate vehicles, but they were all together. Some family thing. And they were loud. Brad said they were Mormon or something. So he wanted to move."

"What day was this?"

"Wednesday."

Mike had been killed that night.

"What time did you leave there? And where did you go?"

"It was afternoon. We packed up and went driving around looking for a spot. Brad was pissed we had to move, got angry and shit, went on with one of his speeches about true religion and guns and..." she winced as she pressed a hand to her temple, "the usual stuff."

I nodded in encouragement.

"Brad took this gravel road with a sign about official vehicles only. I told him we shouldn't, but he wasn't in a mood to hear it. We came out on this high road. Real nice views. And there was this wider dirt area. Like for turning cars around? And Brad wanted to set up camp there. I didn't think it was a good idea, 'cause I'd seen the signs about how it wasn't open to campers, but he said no one would know we were there. And the views were real special...."

Dread flooded my stomach with heat. I could picture it clear as day, that camper parked up there where no one should be. Yes, the views were spectacular on that ridge road. So much so that it was also an excellent place to go running. If you knew it was there. If you had a job like, say, park ranger.

And I knew what it was to be an officer of the law. I knew how I'd react if I came across someone parked up there. On duty or not. The scene unfolded before me like a slow-motion car crash as she went on....

WEDNESDAY EARLY EVENING. The sun was still warm, and the ridge road was bathed in golden light. Duke kept pace easily next to Mike, his tongue out in a doggy grin, his gaze straight ahead. His legs hadn't gotten the memo that gravity was a thing. Duke could run at Mike's pace forever, probably. For now, they were both in the zone, happy to be together, happy for the rare gorgeous weather.

It was a perfect run, in fact. Until Mike spotted the camper.

The glow of the moment was shattered the instant he saw it parked in the turn-out. Two folding chairs outside, and the unrolled awning, showed they had set up for the duration. They were camping there. And Mike saw red.

Those fuckers. He'd had to chase them away from one spot already. Now they were in an area where there was no camping at all. They weren't even supposed to be on this road.

He didn't think, didn't consider that he wasn't in uniform and didn't have his camera or anything else on him. He headed for the van. Duke was hesitant at his heels, sensing the shift in mood.

Mike pounded loudly on the camper's aluminum door, which rattled under the assault. "Hello? Park ranger. Open up, please."

After a moment, the camper door opened and a blonde woman peeked out. Mike recognized her. She'd looked nervous when he'd seen her at Green Rocks, and she looked nervous now. "What... um... what is it? My husband—"

"Hey!" a man shouted.

Mike turned to see the guy walking around the side of the van. He was carrying an armload of deadfall he'd obviously picked up in the woods. Another violation, of course. Fires were only permitted in designated fire pits.

The guy was wearing a black T-shirt with cut-off sleeves and jeans, and his face was dusty from the woods. Fuck. Mike had forgotten how big this guy was. And how angry.

Mike reached his hand to his side, but his firearm wasn't there. He wore sweat pants and his T-shirt was tucked into his waistband. A flicker of doubt crossed his mind. But he straightened his spine regardless and gave the guy a hard stare. "Hi. It's Mr. Smith, right? I spoke to you down at Green Rocks a few days ago. Mike Bressett, park ranger."

Smith eyed him up and down then stepped past him to dump the load of wood in front of the trailer.

"I don't see a uniform." Smith turned, his expression challenging.

"I'm not on duty at the moment, but—"

"How do I know you're a ranger? Why don't you just fuck off?"

The flicker of anger Mike had felt on spotting the camper was back and hotter this time. "I have no doubt you remember me, Mr. Smith."

"Nope. No idea who you are." Smith looked at his wife who was still peeking out from behind the partially *closed door. "We've never seen this guy. Have we, honey?"*

She hesitated. "No."

Mike gritted his teeth. "It doesn't matter. This road is for official vehicles only. You can't drive on it and you certainly can't camp on it. Please pack up and go—and I won't have to issue you a ticket."

"I don't see any tickets," Smith eyed Mike up and down, his lip curled.

Mike knew all about de-escalation techniques. He'd had the training. But goddamn, it had been his last few days off work before his new job started, and he'd really been enjoying the run. This asshole had to ruin it. And maybe because he wasn't in uniform, his professionalism took a back seat to his irritation.

He took a step closer to Smith, puffing up. "Here's the deal: I'm gonna return to the ranger station. If you're still here when I get back with my vehicle in about thirty minutes, you will be banned from the park permanently."

Smith's face went red. He took a step closer too, so they were nearly nose to nose. Mike got a whiff of him— sweat and weed and musk. "Fuck you. This land doesn't belong to you. It belongs to the people. The American people. And I'm an American. Now walk away while you still can, ranger. Because I am over this bullshit."

Mike stared back at the guy. A moment ticked by. What he saw in the man's eyes was ugly—nasty to the core. He was suddenly aware that he was alone up here and that he'd have no proof of this encounter. He didn't even have his cell phone on him since he preferred to run without it. And Smith was armed.

Mike wasn't afraid. But a tendril of caution reasserted itself.

Best to get backup. Or at least his body camera and a weapon.

Hell, he wasn't even supposed to be on duty yet. This wasn't his problem.

He also became aware that Duke was growling. He looked down at his dog. He'd only heard Duke growl once before, and that was during one of his doggy nightmares. Duke was standing rigid by his side, his hackles raised and his angry gaze on Smith.

"And take your fucking dog with you before I shoot him," Smith said.

That was the wrong thing to say. Something inside Mike snapped. He wanted to punch Smith, badly, but he just managed to rein it in. Instead he poked a finger, hard, into Smith's chest. "Thirty minutes. Be gone, or else. Come on, Duke."

Mike started to turn away. He had every intention of following through with the threat, jogging back to the ranger station, calling it in, getting backup.

He never saw the fist coming. It landed on his temple with so much force he flew backwards. His head struck something—one of the trailer's side mirrors. It gave way with a crack as he dropped to his knees.

The next thing he was conscious of was being on all fours, fingers splayed in the dirt of the ridge road. His ears rang and black spots danced in his vision. A throbbing pain pulsed in his head, radiating out from his temple. It felt like he'd been hit by a truck.

He became aware, distantly, of the sound of barking and snarling, a man's shouts, a woman's cries.

"Don't' hurt him! Brad, don't hurt him! Stop it! Stop!"

A cry of pain. Duke.

Mike swallowed down nausea. He had to get up. That fucker was hurting his dog. He pushed against the ground and rose, but it didn't feel right. It didn't feel like his body. The scene swam before his eyes.

Duke was latched onto Smith's leg—it looked like he had hold of his jeans—and was pulling and snarling. Smith struck at him, punched Duke in the neck. But he was off-balance and the blow was glancing.

"Don't hurt the dog!" Mrs. Smith wailed, tugging on Smith's arm.

"Then get him the fuck off me!" Smith yelled, his voice high and fearful.

"Duke, stop!" Mike ordered. "Come here!"

His voice sounded firm but far away somehow. Still, Duke obeyed. He let go of Smith's pants and backed up, fur all raised like a puffer fish, teeth bared.

"Duke, come!" Mike repeated.

Duke ran to his side and licked his hand. He was shaking, totally freaked out.

Mike tried to focus on Smith, but there were several of him. "Thirty minutes!" Mike said. Did he say it? He thought so.

He walked away. He couldn't show Smith how badly that punch had hurt. He wouldn't give him the satisfaction. It was just one punch, for fuck's sake. But damn, it had been a haymaker. And assaulting a park ranger was definitely going on the charging list, along with animal abuse. But at the moment, Mike just had to get out of there. His knees felt like water.

He walked as steadily as he could. The road swayed like a hammock in front of him.

"We're going, Mister!" The woman called after him. "Please, Brad. Let's just go."

"Yeah. Fuck this shit," Smith complained.

Behind him there was the sound of banging. They were packing up. Mike didn't look back. He didn't want to turn his head. He just put one foot in front of the other.

Duke walked close to him, brushing his side, glancing up at him every few seconds with worry.

"It's okay," Mike told him. He managed to move his hand to pet Duke's head.

Just keep going. Bit dazed is all. Gotta get to the ranger station.

One foot in front of the other.

The camper drove past him, accelerating too fast on the gravel road. A cloud of dust rose in its wake. Then it was gone.

"We'll be okay," Mike told Duke.

It was just a punch. As soon as his head cleared, he'd be fine. Just keep moving.

"I KNEW IT WAS BAD," Zoe sniffed, eyes pleading as she soaked up her tears with a tissue. "I *heard* it. When Brad punched him. There was a sound... I don't know how to describe it. But that ranger.. he went down hard. You know, Brad used to box. And he... I dunno... he was really, really mad."

She blew her nose. Her voice was thick with mucus. "But the guy was fine when we left, I swear! Only Brad was convinced he'd press charges or something, so he told me we needed a story. He was saying that since the guy wasn't in uniform and didn't have a camera or phone or anything, we'd just say we'd never seen him that day. It'd be his word against ours. I had to go along with it. If I hadn't..."

She held out her hands, a bandage on one of them. She began to sob.

I wanted to feel bad for her. And probably I would, later. But at the moment, I had to think of Mike. It was easy, in hindsight, to say he shouldn't have approached Smith at all. But would I have done it any differently?

Fuck, I'd done so many off-the-book things in my past, broken rules, crossed the line, and it was only by the grace of God I wasn't dead. Or it was down to idiot's luck.

Mike hadn't been lucky.

She was wrong about one thing, though. Brad *had* killed Mike. The blow, according to the coroner's report, had caused internal hemorrhaging and that had been lethal. It had just taken a while for death to catch up. From what I'd seen on that road, Mike had made it a hundred yards before he'd fallen down the hillside—unconscious or so dizzy he'd stumbled off the ridge.

I felt sick.

I looked at Devin in the corner. His face was pale. He glanced at the machine, which was still recording, and nodded.

"That's all for now, Mrs. Callan," I said. "You'll be called upon again to give testimony." She nodded. "I should warn you that if, at any point, you decide not to cooperate, we will charge you as an accessory to murder." I felt like an asshole—I'd seen abuse and knew the consequences.

Sometimes closer than I wanted.

She gasped, startled. Then swallowed hard as that sank in. "I won't change my mind, but I told you all of that only you said you'd get me somewhere safe. He'll kill me if… Is that still… can you…"

"Don't worry," I said, fists clenched. "Brad won't be getting out. He's not going anywhere. And Mrs. Callan?"

"Zoe," she said in a quiet voice.

"We'll keep you safe."

Epilogue

Tiber

AFTER DUKE IDENTIFIED the camper van guy as the killer, Gabriel dropped me and Duke off at my place, and then I didn't hear a peep from him for two days. I figured he was busy dealing with Mike's killer, and his poor wife, and probably a ton of paperwork, talking to Mike's family, and whatever else happened when one human being kills another. But I couldn't help feeling as if Duke and I had been dismissed. The sheriff didn't need us anymore.

Was I overly sensitive? Hell yeah. And that was why it was easier all around when I didn't try to people.

Anyway, Duke needed me. He was upset when we got home and hid in the back of his crate. I spent an hour talking to him and reaching in to stroke his back, telling him how good he'd done, how he'd helped get the person who hurt Mike.

I worried that we'd pushed him too hard. But he came out of his crate to sleep in my bed with the rest of the pack that night, and in the morning he ate his breakfast and seemed tired but okay. So I was thankful for that.

His demeanor changed too. From being anxious and staring out of the window, or wanting to get in the car, he became lethargic, heavy in a way that felt resigned and also peaceful. As though his work had been done.

Friday evening I got a text from Gabriel asking if he could stop by and offering to bring take-out. I made myself wait ten minutes before replying to say that would be great.

The days were long in Washington state in June, so we sat out on the back deck in two side-by-side rocking chairs and ate the sandwiches he'd picked up at the cafe in town. I was anxious to hear everything.

"Brad Callan has been booked and he couldn't make bail. He's been transferred to the Clallam County Corrections Facility where he'll be held over for trial. He has a record—two past violent assaults. And Mike was an officer of the law. So I imagine they'll throw away the key."

"Good." I looked at Duke, who was lying in the sun next to Gracie, both of them chewing contentedly on bully sticks Gabriel had brought. Leo and Ferdinand were doing the same down on the back lawn. "What about Mrs. Callan? Is she going to be okay?"

"Yeah. She's not looking at any charges as long as she continues to cooperate."

"I certainly hope not! She shouldn't be blamed for what her asshole husband did. That's not fair. She's a victim too."

Gabriel laid a hand on my arm as if to calm me. And yeah, I was getting a little worked up.

"Her medical records show a history of abuse at Brad's hands. And it helps that Mike was on his feet when they left him. She didn't report a murder because she didn't know there'd been one. In fact, the charges against Brad will be manslaughter, not murder in the first degree or even second. But with his past convictions, I'd be surprised if he sees the outside of a jail cell before his hair turns gray."

Personally, I hoped he stayed there until he needed a pine box. But I didn't want to sound too vengeful, so I kept that to myself. "Are you gonna pursue the charges against that New Age group too?"

"Madame Borschski and Tom Dorman, yes. The rest will be offered immunity if they testify. It'll be an open-and-shut case with all the testimony. The desecration of a corpse charge alone could get them seven years."

I nodded. "So you got your man. Men. And woman."

"*We* got them." Gabriel squeezed my arm.

I wasn't sure what to say to that. I put my head back on the rocker and closed my eyes, enjoyed the warmth of the sun on my face.

Yes, *we* did. It had been kind of fun, too. That was, horrible for Duke, and a terrible tragedy. But it had been keenly satisfying to get the bad guys, to work with Duke to make that happen. Too bad that wasn't a thing—pet detective.

As we sat there enjoying the back deck, Gabriel's hand lingered on my arm. It seemed to grow heavier, warmer. I became overly aware of it—and of the way it made me feel.

It would be so easy to put my hand over his, to link our fingers. It would be easy to invite him to stay, to invite him into my bed, into our lives—the lives of me and my little pack. Too easy.

Easy to start, maybe. But not easy to get out of. Not easy to heal from if things went wrong. Not easy to trust myself now or put myself back together when it was over.

Just ask Zoe Callan.

I shifted in my chair, turning towards him. It made his hand drop from my arm in a way I hoped wasn't obvious. "What about Duke? Did you discuss him with any of Mike's relatives?"

Gabriel grimaced. "Yeah. Unfortunately, his parents are deceased, and he was an only child. I reached an old girlfriend of Mike's from Montana, but she's in an apartment that doesn't allow pets. She asked if I knew of anyone here who would be interested in adopting him. I know you've got a full house, and it's not your responsibility, but I figured I'd check."

I checked Duke, gnawing away so peacefully next to Gracie.

He was such a sweet dog, and he'd loved Mike so much. I couldn't take anything more away from him, not his budding friendship with Gracie or, I hoped, his growing sense of security in this house, this place.

"I can keep him," I said.

Gabriel chewed his lip.

"What?"

"Are you sure? If you can't... I mean, I could take him."

"You?" I was surprised.

He cleared his throat. "Well. Sure. I figured I'd get a dog eventually. Once I got settled. Of course, I work a lot. But it would be nice to have a dog to hike with. Take out on the lake. I can see he's already attached here, though, so it's probably better for him to stay. He wouldn't be alone for long hours."

"He kind of is attached. To Gracie for sure. And vice versa."

"Maybe we could share. I mean... maybe I could take him out hiking now and then. Give you a break. Or —maybe *we* could take him hiking once in a while. If you want." He looked at me hopefully.

I froze, unsure of what to say.

Maybe I should push him away. All the way away.

But I could have friends, couldn't I? There was nothing wrong with that. I could hear my mom yelling at me in my head. *You need to be around some actual humans too, Ti, for the love of God!*

Gabriel and I could be friends.

Leo liked him. Hell, all the animals did. I didn't trust my judgement after Jeff, but couldn't I trust theirs?

"I'd like that," I said. "It would be good to have someone to hike with. Have you ever done Sol-Duc Falls? I've been wanting to get back there."

He smiled a genuinely happy smile. "Not since I was in high school, if you can believe it. I'd love to do it again. Hurricane Ridge is another one I've been meaning to get back to."

"For sure! It's been on my list."

"Cool. What is today?" He paused. "Fuck, I have no idea."

I laughed. "It's Friday. Poor Gabriel. When was the last time you even slept?"

"Sleeping is for wimps." He chuckled. "What about Sunday?"

"Forecast is for heavy rain all weekend."

His face fell. "Crap. I generally don't mind the weather around here, but once in a while…."

"I hear ya. Maybe the weekend after?"

Gabriel settled back in his rocker with a sigh, his

expression lightening. "That's right. We've got plenty of time. After all, we've solved the only murder to hit Prophet in ten years. I'll have nothing but free time for the next ten, right?"

Famous. Last. Words.

THE END

Next in the Lake Prophet Mysteries
_____

Equinox

Three months after the death of Mike Bressett, the
sleepy town of Prophet faces another tragedy—the death
of Billy Odette, a well-liked Makah man who ran trail
rides for the tourists. When Billy is discovered to have
been the victim of a vicious animal attack, dragged right
off a popular trail, angry locals are quick to blame a
wolf pack that's recently moved into the area. But
Sheriff Gabriel Thompson learns that the death isn't as
simple as it seems when decades-long animosities and
secrets come to light. While Tiber and a local wildlife
painter fight to protect the wolves, Gabriel attempts to
unravel the motivations and methods of an uncanny
killer.

Coming soon

What Lies Beneath (Lancaster Falls 1)

In the hottest summer on record, Iron Lake reservoir is emptying, revealing secrets that were intended to stay hidden beneath the water. The tragic story of a missing man is a media sensation, and abruptly the writer and the cop falling in love is just a postscript to horrors neither could have imagined.

Best Selling Horror writer Chris Lassiter struggles for inspiration and he's close to never writing again. His life has become an endless loop of nothing but empty pages, personal appearances, and a marketing machine that is systematically destroying his muse. In a desperate attempt to force Chris to complete unfinished manuscripts his agent buys a remote cabin. All Chris has to do is hide away and write, but he's lost his muse, and not even he can make stories appear from thin air.

Sawyer Wiseman left town for Chicago, chasing the excitement and potential of being a big city cop, rising the ranks, and making his mark. A case gone horribly wrong draws him back to Lancaster Falls. Working for the tiny police department in the town he'd been running from, digging into cold cases and police corruption, he spends his day's healing, and his nights hoping the nightmares of his last case leave him alone.

The **Lancaster Falls** Series

How to Howl at the Moon

Sheriff Lance Beaufort is not going to let trouble into his town, no sir. Tucked away in the California mountains, Mad Creek has secrets to keep, like the fact that half the town consists of 'quickened'—dogs who have gained the ability to become human. Descended on both sides from Border Collies, Lance is as alert a guardian as they come.

Tim Weston is looking for a safe haven. After learning that his boss patented all of Tim's work on vegetable hybrids in his own name, Tim quit his old job. A client offers him use of her cabin in Mad Creek, and Tim sees a chance for a new start. But the shy gardener has a way of fumbling and sounding like a liar around strangers, particularly gorgeous alpha men like Sheriff Beaufort.

Lance's hackles are definitely raised by the lanky young stranger. He's concerned about marijuana growers moving into Mad Creek, and he's not satisfied with the boy's story. Lance decides a bit of undercover work is called for. When Tim hits a beautiful black collie with his car and adopts the dog, its love at first sight for both Tim and Lance's inner dog. Pretending to be a pet is about to get Sheriff Beaufort in very hot water.

Howl at the Moon Series

Also By Eli Easton

For a full list of ebooks and links please scan the code above
or visit eliseaston.com

Also By RJ Scott

For a full list of ebooks and links please scan the code above or visit rjscott.co.uk/rjbooks

Meet Eli Easton

Having been, at various times and under different names, a minister's daughter, a computer programmer, a game designer, the author of paranormal mysteries, a fan fiction writer, and organic farmer, Eli has been a m/m romance author since 2013. She has published over 30 gay romances.

Eli has loved romance since her teens and she particular admires writers who can combine literary merit, genuine humor, melting hotness, and eye-dabbing sweetness into one story.

Website & newsletter - elieaston.com

facebook.com/100008994061782

twitter.com/EliEaston

amazon.com/stores/Eli-Easton/author/B00CJUKM9I

bookbub.com/authors/eli-easton

goodreads.com/7020231.Eli_Easton

Meet RJ Scott

RJ is the author of the over one hundred and sixty published novels and discovered romance in books at a very young age. She realized that if there wasn't romance on the page, she could create it in her head, and is a lifelong writer.

She lives and works out of her home in the beautiful English countryside, spends her spare time reading, watching films, and enjoying time with her family.

The last time she had a week's break from writing she didn't like it one little bit and has yet to meet a box of chocolates she couldn't defeat.

www.rjscott.co.uk | rj@rjscott.co.uk

Newsletter - rjscott.co.uk/rjnews

facebook.com/author.rjscott

twitter.com/Rjscott_author

instagram.com/rjscott_author

amazon.com/author/rj-scott

bookbub.com/authors/rj-scott

goodreads.com/rjscott

pinterest.com/rjscottauthor